ARACHNE'S EXILE

CHRISTOPHER L. BENNETT

eBooks
Pennsville, NJ

PUBLISHED BY
eSpec Books LLC
Danielle McPhail, Publisher
PO Box 242,
Pennsville, New Jersey 08070
www.especbooks.com

ISBN: 978-1-949691-15-3
ISBN (ebook): 978-1-949691-14-6

All persons, places, and events in this book are fictitious and any resemblance to actual persons, places, or events is purely coincidental.

Interior Design: Danielle McPhail
Cover Art and Design: © Mike McPhail, McP Digital Graphics
Cyber-Web Graphic © Mike McPhail, McP Digital Graphics
Copyeditors: Danielle McPhail and Greg Schauer
Reflection nebula around the pulsar © Jurik Peter, www.shutterstock.com

*To the folks at Shore Leave,
for always making me feel welcome.*

CONTENTS

But to the Goddess yield, and humbly meek
A pardon for your bold presumption seek;
The Goddess will forgive. At this the maid,
With passion fir'd, her gliding shuttle stay'd;
And, darting vengeance with an angry look,
To Pallas in disguise thus fiercely spoke.

— Ovid, "The Transformation of Arachne into a Spider"
(translated by Samuel Croxall)

PART ONE

PENAL TRANSPORTATION

PROLOGUE

"DON'T GET TOO CLOSE TO THE EDGE, SITA!"

"I'm fine, Nilly," Sita Bhatiani said absently as she leaned further over the railing, gauging the distance to the water in the canal below. "If I couldn't handle being on edges, I'd never have signed onto *Arachne*, would I?"

R'nilinnath hopped over to Sita, resting her blue-skinned, kangaroo-like body on its thick tail and rotating her chameleonesque eyes downward to lock onto the diminutive xenobiologist. "I'm glad that you've resolved to overcome your fear, my friend. But don't overdo it. Ss'chh is the most alien place you've seen so far."

The young Chirrn was right about that, up to a point. All the migration fleet's previous rest stops in the first few days of the journey from Shilirrlal had been at other Chirrn-built space habitats, variants on the cylindrical design that had come to feel almost familiar to Sita over the past six months—though she would never forget her first sight of one as a torn-open ruin, when the survivors of the Lesshchi habitat had pulled *Arachne*'s crew from their hibernation dreams and forced them to behold the devastation they had carelessly wrought in their haste.

The habitat called Ss'chh, of all things, was a modest-sized megastructure orbiting the giant star Theta Scorpii, over 270 light years from Solsys and nearly as far from Shilirrlal. It resembled a vast, elongated mollusk shell, a conical double helix with the wider end facing the star as it rotated around its long axis. This gave it a continuum of centrifugal gravity levels, from below Lunar at its tapered end to several times Earth's at its fat end. The canal Sita studied ran down its entire spiraling length, the water flowing downhill due to both the slope and the gravity gradient, then refiltered and pumped back up through the central axis.

On disembarking for the night, senior mediator L'chellin had brought her Arachnen charges to a Chirrn-compatible gravity level occupied only by familiar species such as Chirrn and Seekers of the Zenith, and not many of them at that. It made sense that the caravan crew would choose these comfortable environs for their rest break; but not for the first time, Sita had trouble shaking the feeling that the mediators were carefully controlling the Arachnen's access to information about the larger galaxy. The human colonists — well, most of them — had accepted culpability for Lesshchi's destruction, agreeing to assimilate into Chirrn society to repay their debt as contributing members. So why did those responsible for their education shy away from important topics such as galactic history and sociology?

The temptation to strip her kit off, dive in, and let the canal's current carry her down to more exotic levels, populated by who knew what kind of novel alien sophonts, was tempered only by Sita's realization that the strong current would sweep her lightweight body away like a leaf. Being the size of an average twelve-year-old was bollocks sometimes.

At least no one will mistake me for a preadolescent dressed like this, she thought, glancing down at the open-fronted Chirrn-style vest she'd finally started wearing — the two-strap variety, a bit more modest than the usual one-strap design, but bringing out her cleavage more, much to the appreciation of her husband. But she hadn't started wearing it out of vanity.

Ever since the Lesshchi disaster and the subsequent assault she'd suffered from her vengeful captors, Sita had lived in fear of the Chirrn, a fear that had overridden her natural fascination with alien life and kept her secluded in the Arachnen's probationary enclave for months. The Lesshchin refugees' second, more recent assault, resulting in the death of her unborn baby, had only worsened her terror — and her guilt, for she had been one of the women whose inadvertent intrusion on a solemn Lesshchin procreative ritual called a kiss dance had triggered their retaliation. But the Arachnen's administrator Oyama Kazuko, whose miscarriage had not been her first, had been a bastion of strength for Sita and the other bereaved parents — including Kazuko's platonic parenting partner Ravinder Pritam, as well as astrophysicist Justine Nguyen, who had been carrying one of the expedition's six hundred frozen, pre-fertilized embryos. Only Kweli Ndege, the Arachnen's chief physician, remained inconsolable, sequestered in her quarters and uninterested in the galaxy beyond. Kweli's husband, Tarik Bahar, did not have that luxury, for in Cecilia LoCarno's absence he was the acting captain of *Arachne* and had to be strong for the crew. Yet Sita could see how much he longed at every moment to be there for his wife, to give her the strength she could not find in herself.

Sita had spent months in hiding after the first attack, but the support of Kazuko and Justine had helped her find the conviction to seize onto the migration as a new beginning, to move beyond her fears and embrace discovery once again. Though she and Stephen had grown closer in recent days, following months of tension over their differing attitudes toward the Chirrn, Sita now felt more capable of functioning on her own, seeing her husband's strength as a supplement to hers rather than a substitute for it. The Chirrn wardrobe symbolized her acceptance of her new life as part of their community and her willingness to put herself out there once more.

Literally, she thought, scratching under her right breast.

She studied R'nilinnath thoughtfully, considering that she was large enough for Sita to ride on her back—and that the Chirrn had evolved from aquatic ancestors. "Nilly, you're a really good swimmer, right?"

The apprentice mediator gave a snort of distress through the array of small nares atop her snout, ruffling the stiff bristles that surrounded them. "Oh, no, Sita. Don't even conceive the words, let alone spawn them. We're on a schedule, and I don't dare risk delaying things by getting you lost."

"And here I thought you were the adventurous one."

"It's not like there's even much to see out there. It's a very old habitat, not used much anymore. It's mainly just a way station in the wormhole network."

Sita stared. "That just makes me more curious! Why did people stop using it? Where did they all go? Not just here, but all through this space."

In Chirrn terms, the caravan was traversing the Central Void toward the Antispinward Void; in human terms, through the Local Bubble toward Loop I. According to Justine, a wave of star formation and supernovae had swept through the Orion Arm millions of years ago and blown four huge bubbles of low gas density. The Chirrn called these the Four Voids, home territory of the Void Alliance, which included the Chirrn, the pterosaurian Zenith, the bizarre behemoths called the Ryohoch, and at least a couple of species she had yet to meet.

So far, the Voids were living up to their name, with plenty of empty space between the population centers the fleet passed through en route to the sparsely populated sector where the migrants would construct a new habitat, far from Shilirrlal and the surviving Lesshchin—and still farther from Earth and humanity's handful of colony worlds, with which the Arachnen had sworn off any further contact as a condition of their parole.

Nilly fidgeted. "Well…you know. People migrate. Like we're doing. Sometimes they just… drift away from somewhere for a while."

The London native crossed her arms and held the Chirrn's gaze. "Seriously, Nilly, what's got into you lot? Not just you, but the whole caravan. I've seen your body language, not just here but at all our rest stops. You don't have the confidence you had before. You're tentative, restless, like you're searching for something." Sita looked away. "At first, I thought I was just projecting my own state of mind onto you."

"The state of mind you're overcompensating for by leaning too close to the edge?" Nilly reminded her.

Sita sighed. "Right, I get it." She stepped back from the railing, and the two friends began to stroll alongside it at a more comfortable distance. Nilly's "stroll" was much like a kangaroo's slow walk, using her arms and tail as a tripod when moving her long legs forward. It angled her torso downward, keeping her silver-maned head at Sita's eye level.

"It's the migration," the apprentice remarked after a moment. "Not just the physical one, but the transition from their old guilds to this one. They've left behind their old consensus memories and thoughts, taken on new ones. They're still finding out what their new personalities are like."

Sita understood. A migratory species, long-lived and serially hermaphroditic, the Chirrn had always seen identities and allegiances as fluid, evolving things. Their minds existed as much in their habitats' information clouds as in their own skulls, and their personalities were shaped by the memories and processing algorithms they shared with others in their guilds. Moving to a new habitat or career meant altering one's personality, leaving pieces of oneself behind and assimilating new ones.

Her hands moved reflexively to her belly. "Like they've lost a part of themselves," she whispered, "and aren't quite sure who they are anymore."

Nilly's eyes swiveled in surprise. "I hadn't thought of it that way. It's hard to understand what you and the others are going through. So few of us have had babies, let alone lost them. And memories that painful aren't always shared with the consensus." She lowered her brow ridges in thought. "But I guess if a baby is something that's both part of you and outside of you, that's a bit like a consensus memory. I understand that, now that I'm sharing fully in the Migration guild's consensus. I'm like the others — still figuring out who I am now."

Sita's restlessness returned. "But at least you have something to fill the void. That makes it easier."

"I don't know about that," Nilly said. "There are migrants from many guilds and estates. It takes lots of different skills to build a new world. Every estate has people seeking transition to a new life, so we had no trouble finding recruits. But they all come with different habits of thought. They don't leave all of it behind. We're still testing out each other's memories and modes of thinking, seeing how they change us." She snuffled unhappily. "It's hard to put it in human terms."

"You don't seem to have changed that much. Neither have L'chellin or Broadwing."

"Well, Intersocietal is the core of the Migration guild. Nearly half the collegium came along."

"Makes sense — they literally share the same thoughts about the reasons behind the move."

"Not the *same*, exactly. But mediators are generalists to begin with. Our thought patterns are tailored to be malleable and eclectic — well, compared to the Chirrn norm," she admitted with an amused drumming of her toes. "So all that influx of new ideas hasn't changed L'chellin or Broadwing that much."

"And yourself?"

She shook her short mane, a Chirrn smile. "I'm a kid. Everything's new to me. Besides — I'm finally a full guild member! I'm an adult now!"

"Make up your mind. Are you a kid or an adult?"

"Can't I be both?" Nilly asked.

Sita laughed out loud for the first time since the attack. She threw her arms around Nilly's neck and hugged her warmly. "You be whatever you want, love. Just don't ever stop being you."

1

Stephen Jacobs-Wong had spent most of the journey from Shilirrlal on autopilot, putting up the front of leadership and charisma that came effortlessly, but not really letting anything outside his ship and crew engage him even as the wonders of the galaxy passed them by. His thoughts were still preoccupied by the series of tragedies for which he blamed himself—and by the schism between himself and Cecilia LoCarno, *Arachne*'s captain and his dearest friend, over their responsibility for making amends. With the onset of the migration, Stephen and Sita had finally begun to reconnect and heal each other's grief at the loss of their baby, easing the burdens on his spirit. Yet that effort had required keeping his focus inward.

But in time, the sky became too beautiful to ignore. The caravan had entered the Upper Scorpius subgroup of the Scorpius-Centaurus OB Association, a lively star-formation region dominated by bright young stars like Antares and Sigma Scorpii and vast clouds of nebular matter surrounding them. The nebulae were barely visible to the unassisted eye at close range, but those stars were far brighter than they'd ever appeared from Earth, and with a little adjustment of their adaptive optics and a little enhancement from *Arachne*'s viewports, the Arachnen could see the beauty of the yellow-orange and magenta hazes surrounding them, a mix of reflection and emission nebulae. Stephen soon found himself gazing out raptly with the rest of the crew.

Yet once they reached the Antares system—a journey of over 550 light years from Shilirrlal, made in only eight days—the fleet's port of call made the sky around them look positively dull. The habitat, orbiting the blue-dwarf companion star Antares B at some fifteen AUs, was a sphere nearly fifty kilometers in diameter, a garish starburst of incredibly tall fairy-tale castles, impossibly slender spires, and massive, clear-roofed aerodromes, all crafted from gleaming crystals, metals, and metamaterials and festooned with vivid, multicolored lights. It was like a cross between Escher's *Tetrahedral Planetoid*, the skyline of old Shanghai before the floods, and a sea urchin dressed up for Mardi Gras. The interplay of illumination from the piercing blue star nearby, the bloated red-orange Antares A nearly six hundred AUs away, and the dense planetary nebula surrounding them both made the habitat gleam with particular resplendence, and its architecture strove to match the grandeur of its surroundings. Twelve enormous towers jutted from its equator, supporting a scintillating docking ring over a hundred kilometers above the surface and tapering dozens of kilometers further into elegant launch spines, slender threads that gleamed in the multi-directional light. It was a gorgeous vista, albeit a bit garish to Stephen's eyes. But Sita wept at the sight, and they were the first tears he'd been happy to see her shed.

"It's a Star Palace," Arachne's voice announced over the cockpit speakers. The humans reacted to the name with recognition.

Mediator Broadwing blinked his lower two eyes in surprise. "You know of them?"

"Human astronomers have imaged several megastructures of this design around various giant and supergiant stars," the shipmind answered. "A few are internally lit, but most are detectable only by reflected starlight and are believed abandoned. As yet, we have been unable to make contact with the species that constructed them."

"In fact, you have," Broadwing fluted in his elegant calliope voice, produced in resonating cavities within his three iridescent headcrests. "One spreads his wings before you even now." The lean-bodied, silver-hued pterosaurian matched his actions to the words, clicking his three beak mandibles together as he did so.

"The Zenith built the Star Palaces?" Sita asked.

"Yes." Broadwing refolded his wing dactyls and membranes back along his forearms, leaving his shorter dactyls to function as fingers. As always, he moved with a grace that made the zigzag shape of his legs, and the way his wing-arms went up from his shoulders before bending back down, look totally right even to human eyes. His crests sang again, the translation appearing as subtitles in Stephen's retinal HUD. "As Seekers of the Zenith, my people were naturally drawn to space. When we reached the stars, we built aeries around the brightest and most impressive ones so that all would know of our majesty."

"That explains a lot," Stephen said.

For decades, human astronomers, engineers, and xenobiologists had debated how and why the structures were built in this configuration. Given the Zenith's acrophilic nature, it went against their grain to build Chirrn-style habitats where the sky was inward. No doubt, he realized, the Star Palaces used programmable quark matter to generate artificial gravity. If PQM could take on the properties of the exotic matter necessary to make warp cages and wormholes possible, then surely it could also, say, generate gravitons with a greatly increased coupling constant, allowing a relatively small mass to exert the pull of a planet-sized one. The Zenith most likely lived only on the surface of the Star Palace, competing with one another for increased status and the privilege to live higher up in one of its many ornate spires.

"Hold on," Haim Silbermann said. "Isn't Antares A due to go supernova sometime in the next few million—I mean, the next *yanarrenn* or so?"

"Enough time to relocate," Broadwing told the gray-bearded engineer. "For now, this is the most glorious star in the region, so naturally the Zenith must claim this height."

"With your technology, couldn't you prevent the supernova? Lift away enough of the star's hydrogen to reduce the pressure on the core and prolong its life?"

"Why would we want to do that?" R'nilinnath wondered. "Supernovae create heavy elements. They promote evolution on planets. If we stopped supernovae, we'd prevent new species from evolving. Few enough worlds spawn sophonts as it is." Nilly shook her mane, a Chirrn smile. "Now do you see why smart civilizations don't live on planets? It's hard to move a planet out of danger."

Stephen recalled Sita's musings about the Fermi Paradox, the mystery of why evidence of alien activity had been so hard for humanity to detect. What the old Kardashev theories of galactic-scale engineering had overlooked, it seemed, was that the civilizations that survived to the interstellar age were the ones that learned to live in harmony with their environments rather than forcibly reshaping them. Nilly's words drove home that the galaxy had its own ecology of star and planet formation, one that galactic society took care not to disrupt, so that its footprint was nearly invisible except at a fine scale.

The caravan's ships soon docked along the Star Palace's spaceport ring, settling in for a stay of moderate length, and the Arachnen were finally free to leave the ship—escorted by the mediators, of course, and by Arachne's physical avatar, a silver-and-blue smart-matter construct in the form of a four-armed, metallic-skinned woman's torso joined to the abdomen and hind legs of a giant spider.

Stephen noted the avatar pausing by a viewport in the disembarcation lounge, looking out at the starship her core mind occupied. "Something wrong?" he asked.

"It's nothing," the avatar said in Arachne's calm, warm voice. "We should keep moving."

"Arachne, you always take care of us. If you need a moment for yourself—or if you need to talk—it's fine. It's just you and me." He knew he might be anthropomorphizing, but he believed he knew Arachne well enough to recognize her moods.

"Appreciated, Stephen. It's simply that I'm still not used to being in a cage."

He joined her in gazing out at her remade body. Once, she had been a wispy spiderweb of magnetic sail coils with habitat and cargo modules strung along its support lines like dewdrops—the lightest, sleekest starship ever created by humanity, reaching an unprecedented eighty-four percent of lightspeed. Now, her modules were bundled together like logs and crammed within the cylindrical collar of a Chirrn-built warp cage, an intricate lattice of PQM conduits that could unfurl into a sphere to protect the ship within from the stresses of warp or wormhole passage.

"I can see how it would feel confining."

"I miss the quiet. The long, slow contemplation of the universe, the comfortable routine of keeping you all safe as you slept within me. Now..." The arachnocentaur's legs shifted uneasily, and Stephen wondered if it was merely an affectation. "To be honest, traveling by warp cage scares the hell out of me. The universe isn't supposed to work that way!"

He laughed in surprise. "I'm sure you understand the physics far better than I do."

The avatar's beautiful, multi-eyed face turned fully toward him. "That's exactly why it terrifies me," she said with incongruous calm. "I know precisely what extremes of energy density it requires and how closely I skirt the edge of disaster at every moment.

"And that cage doesn't help. It feels like an alien limb grafted onto me, with its own will and habits I'm still struggling to reconcile with my own."

"Have you spoken to Haim or Yonchon about this? Maybe there's... an adjustment that can be made."

"Unnecessary. I appreciate the opportunity to voice my discomfort, but it's not something that needs to be addressed. My priority is keeping you safe."

He clasped the avatar's shoulder, for what it was worth. "Arachne, you deserve consideration too."

All her eyes locked on his. "Stephen, I murdered more than eighty-eight thousand sapient beings to protect you, and yet all of you are paying for my mistake. Captain LoCarno and the other Unrenounced are still caged far more literally than I. Save your consideration for them. I do not deserve it."

The avatar moved on. As Stephen watched it scuttle gracefully toward the others, he reflected how unusual it was for Arachne to admit to needs of her own. He'd recruited her for her relentlessly maternal dedication to the welfare of her charges.

No doubt that was why her thoughts were with the Unrenounced—the nine remaining holdouts who had refused to disavow their planetary ties and assimilate into Chirrn society to raise families in freedom. It frustrated Stephen that Cecilia LoCarno and her fellow "loyalists," as they called themselves, refused to see the truth: that their trial and conviction had been a ritualized ordeal meant to prime the humans for adoption as probationary members, replenishing the community's loss with their own numbers and contributions. To the Chirrn, atonement for criminal acts was merely another transition between identities, casting off past mistakes to remake oneself as something better. Yet the Unrenounced's pride in their heritage and independence would not allow them to yield. Thus, they remained confined, isolated from the renounced Arachnen and subjected to behavioral experiments that they perceived as punishment, but which were actually part of the ritual ordeal to cleanse their sins, a duress that would end as soon as they accepted culpability and embraced transition.

It must frustrate Arachne, Stephen mused, *that some of the very people who recruited her for her protectiveness are now denying her the ability to do her job.*

It struck him then that the shipmind's show of vulnerability just now had been for his benefit, to draw him out of his introversion and remind him of his own responsibility to lead the Arachnen through these challenging times—and to find a way to heal the rift with Cecilia and the Unrenounced.

He smiled. He was the one who didn't deserve Arachne.

"You are about to encounter a number of sapient species you have never seen before," Churrlaya told the loyalists as they reluctantly donned confinement jumpsuits under the scrutiny of several Chirrn guards. The relatively small, green-skinned Chirrn, whose ringlet-styled, powder-blue mane had earned him the nickname "the Frog Footman" from his human captives, had explained that the migration caravan had docked at a habitat belonging to the pterosaur-gargoyle species called Seekers of the Zenith, yet used as an interstellar travel hub by many species. The prisoners were to be transferred to a temporary holding facility in the habitat's docking ring while the Chirrn spacecraft that had been their prison for the past week or more underwent inspection and maintenance. Cecilia LoCarno would have appreciated the change of scenery if not for the tight jumpsuit, which bound her hands in clumsy mitts and would go rigid if she made any abrupt or threatening movements.

"None of these sophonts have wronged you or been wronged by you in any way. However, many will be even more alien to you than the Chirrn or Zenith. How does this make you feel?"

"Anything that's not Chirrn is an improvement," Amrita Dhillon spat. She took Evan Jiang's hand to comfort him; the young planetologist had stiffened with xenophobic terror at Churrlaya's statement. Cecilia was pleased to see a gesture of kindness from the slender mining engineer, a departure from her habitual anger. This ordeal had hit Amrita the hardest, reawakening her traumatic memories of seeing her parents tortured by the oppressive regime of her native Trojan-asteroid habitat. During the journey, Amrita had become involved with her fellow Strider Nik Zacharias. The Cerean doctor had resisted her sexual invitations before, uneasy with her rage, but he'd finally consented in the hope that he could calm her fury—and it seemed he had, if only marginally.

James Oates was about to say something confrontational and stupid, but Diego Narvaez pre-empted him. "I have nothing against the beings here in and of themselves," the tall Guatemalan engineer said. "But if they assist you in holding us hostage, then they *have* wronged us."

Churrlaya turned to Cecilia. "And what is your reaction?"

"I'll be pleased to meet someone new," the captain said.

"Yeah," Kahina Amrouche put in. "We're sick of seeing your face every day."

Cecilia gave the programmer a stern look. *Remember, hold the high ground. Prove we're better.*

"We came out here as explorers," Cecilia went on, as much to her fellow loyalists as to Churrlaya. "Naturally, I'm excited by the prospect of encountering new forms of intelligence. But the circumstances are unfortunate."

"You know how to change that," Churrlaya reminded her.

She didn't take the bait, remaining silent while the Chirrn guards led the nine loyalists out into the docking facilities within the Zenith habitat's freefall orbital ring. Once she got her first look at the variety of sophonts working in the docks, Cecilia felt a thrill of fascination at their sheer alienness and diversity. She was unsurprised to see the same reaction from Nik Zacharias, and from the group's resident ecologist, Ibrahim al-Bakri. The two programmers, Kahina Amrouche and Zhao Changkun, held hands and stifled laughter, their eyes widening in wonder at the technologies around them. But Diego and his clique of hardliners huddled together, giving wary, hostile looks to the beings they passed.

"Have all these species renounced planetary living?" Cecilia had to ask. "Are you all part of some habitats-only club?"

"One can rarely generalize behavior to an entire species," Churrlaya pointed out. "But these sophonts choose to reside in a space habitat, as most do in time."

"Do they all consider planets that odious?"

"On the contrary — they value planets. Planets can spawn new life, and occasionally new sophonts. Which is why they should be left free to do so. A biosphere that has evolved to the point of producing one sapient species has the maximum potential to produce others. Rather than staying on a planet and despoiling it, most choose to leave their planets eventually, so that other sophonts are free to develop."

Cecilia had to admit to herself that she found Churrlaya's words fascinating. Their jailer had been a survivor of the Lesshchi disaster and one of the witnesses against *Arachne*'s crew in the trial—the clear conflict of interest proving to Cecilia that the Chirrn had no interest in justice, only in punishing the humans who refused to renounce their planetary allegiance. Indeed, for months, Churrlaya had exploited his power over the prisoners to devise the most degrading and uncomfortable "sociological experiments" he could within the pretense of ethical research the Chirrn flimsily maintained, and had made little secret of enjoying the power he held over them. Yet in the weeks since the attack on the human mothers, something about Churrlaya had changed. Cecilia had come to recognize that the diminutive green Lesshchin had been trying as hard as she was to rein in his anger. Most likely he'd been attempting to outdo her, to prove that Chirrn were still more civilized than any lowly planet-dweller, despite the obscene act his fellow Lesshchin had committed.

The party moved into a corridor that stretched nearly a kilometer in either direction, Cecilia estimated, before its curvature blocked the line of sight, suggesting that the docking ring's radius was at least a hundred and twenty kilometers. Any Coriolis effect was too mild for her to sense; perhaps this was a stationary hoop about a rotating habitat, but then how did the interface work?

A shimmering point in the distance soon resolved into a flock of Zenith flying to meet them. They were led by a tall, resplendent administrator who spoke to Churrlaya for several moments in a fluting, multitonal language that the Chirrn translators did not interpret for the loyalists. The Zenith then escorted the Chirrn and their human prisoners down the endless corridor toward the holding facility. They passed a number of port personnel of various species—none of them Chirrn, interestingly enough—and most took care to give them a wide berth. "What, they've never seen upright bipeds before?" Cecilia asked. "Or are they simply shocked at these fashion disasters you have us wearing?"

"They are aware of your destruction of Lesshchi," Churrlaya told her. "It frightens them. The concept of death on such a massive scale—caused by sophonts against other sophonts, rather than by natural disaster—is difficult for them to accept."

Cecilia scoffed. "You mean they've never had a war? Never seen terrorism?"

"Such things are rare. Mature civilizations find better ways of solving their problems than arbitrarily killing large numbers of people."

"Like torture and enslavement," Amrita shot back. "So civilized."

Nik Zacharias put a calming hand on her shoulder. "Don't they have history?" the doctor asked. "No doubt they killed each other quite happily back when they were 'immature.' So what gives them the right to judge us?"

"Most of them," Churrlaya told him, "have rarely or never known war in their species' history. It is not the universal norm you assume."

"No war?" Ibrahim al-Bakri asked in fascination. "How do they do it?"

Churrlaya hesitated. "You are not ready to understand."

Amrita *harrumphed* at what she no doubt found a predictable, condescending response. But Cecilia was puzzled. For weeks, Churrlaya had been all too happy to talk about his culture's values and traditions, apparently hoping that the loyalists would be seduced by all that Chirrn civilization had to offer. Why would he be reluctant to share the secret of galactic peace?

Or were the Chirrn even privy to that secret? "And what about you?" she asked him. "L'chellin told us about the ancient war between spacegoing and planet-dwelling Chirrn, the one that drove you out into deep space. How long did it take you to 'understand' what these others knew? Or are you still working on it?"

Churrlaya met her eyes, but she saw the subtle outward twitching of his chameleonlike orbs, as if he were resisting an impulse to look away. Was it a sign of deceit... or of embarrassment? "You have not yet understood the meaning of that tale either. I wish that you could, for its words begat all that has happened here."

"Then I'd sincerely like you to explain it to me, Churrlaya."

Now his gaze held hers firmly. "I believe you, Cecilia. But I am not sure anymore if I am competent to judge its meaning." He maneuvered closer, and as always she envied the Chirrn's deftness in freefall. "Tell me. Do you believe that your wars, your disasters and plagues, your oppressions and tyrannies have made you a better people? That you have drawn strength and wisdom from their lessons?"

She considered it for a time. "I don't think they made us better. I think the strength and wisdom we embraced to defeat them made us better."

"Then if they had never occurred, do you believe you would have found that same strength and wisdom?"

Cecilia studied him, but he gave no hint of the purpose behind his questions. "Honestly? No. We're a lazy people. Make our lives too easy, too free of challenge, and we squander them. Character is a muscle—you need stress to make it strong."

Churrlaya searched her eyes. "Then do you think that strength is worth the terrible cost?"

She chose her words very carefully. "I think… we don't have the luxury of avoiding terrible things. It's not a price we can escape paying; the universe will exact it from us when it sees fit. All we can do is choose whether we let it diminish us or make us stronger."

The Lesshchin moved closer still, lowering his voice to a soft hiss. "And you believe that remaining unrenounced keeps you strong?"

"It does."

His eyes rolled left, directing her attention toward Diego's clique, who stared at the aliens they passed with a mix of emotions: cool contempt from Diego, agitated suspicion from James, terrified revulsion from Evan, burning hatred from Amrita. "All of you?" he asked of her alone.

She had no answer.

They reached the cell, a bare room with opaque walls and minimal amenities beyond basic handholds and perches, and Churrlaya left her there to contemplate their discussion. As their confinement suits relaxed and they began pulling them open to free their hands, Diego sidled over. "Captain… it troubles some of us to see you speaking so intimately with the Frog Footman. I've heard the others complaining that you spend more time with it than with us."

"I'm trying to prove we're not barbarians, Diego. That we're capable of more than hate and bitterness. I understand how you and the others feel, but we must not let them goad us into being as degraded as they think we are."

"I get it, Cecilia. You're trying to domesticate the beast. Just take care it doesn't domesticate you."

"What's that supposed to mean?" She was having difficulty wrestling her arms out of the sleeves; it had been a while since she'd been forced to wear one of these.

Diego had successfully stripped to the waist, so he gently pushed her hands aside and grasped her coverall's wide neckline. "Just that I'm not convinced everyone understands your reasons for ordering us to abandon our escape attempt back at Shilirrlal." His palms caressed her skin as he slid the garment off her shoulders and down her arms. "I understand—you didn't want us to resort to violence. You thought the risk of backlash outweighed the chance of our escape. I respect that—even admire it." He finished freeing her hands from the sleeves and clasped them in his. Their eyes held each other, and she could feel the warmth of his bare chest near her own. "But you need to reassure the others that you haven't lost your way. That your allegiance remains with your own kind." He raised a hand to stroke her short, silver-blonde hair.

After a moment, she moved back, pulling up her jumpsuit and tying the sleeves over her flushed breasts. At another time, she might have eagerly returned his advances. Diego was as much a natural alpha male as Stephen, but with much more of the bad-boy charm that attracted her. They'd had a number of very satisfying dalliances over the months of confinement, as partnerships had shuffled under the impetus of Chirrn mind games and personal temptations. And the prisoners had long since left behind any shred of body modesty out of necessity. But she didn't care for his rather blatant attempt to manipulate her with sex. Cecilia took her pleasures at her own time and for her own reasons. "What did you have in mind, Diego?"

"I studied the layout as we passed. This facility isn't designed to be a prison. And there are many ships here, ships that could take us to Cybele or Earth in weeks, maybe less. This could be our best chance to escape."

"All right," she said after a moment. "It's certainly worth considering." She turned to the rest. "But we mustn't get overambitious. We wouldn't know how to fly one of those ships. And I don't want to leave Arachne and the rest of the crew behind without giving them a chance to join us. Our best bet is to escape into the habitat, find someplace to hole up. Maybe we can lose ourselves in the crowd, find allies to back our cause against the Chirrn."

"Why would any of them help us?" James demanded. The pale-skinned American's time in captivity had only amplified his tendency toward paranoia.

"Did you see their reactions? Sure, they were afraid of us, the big bad Chirrn-slayers. But aside from the Zenith, I didn't see any of them talking to the Chirrn either. I got a feeling that the Chirrn aren't that popular themselves. We've been wondering why they choose to hide in darkened habitats in deep space. Maybe somebody out there doesn't like them."

"Or maybe you're projecting what you want to see onto creatures whose body language you can't read," Diego countered. "The animals out there are as likely to be our predators as our helpers. We can't rely on anything but our fellow humans. And not even most of them. As far as I'm concerned, the traitors have renounced their humanity and are no longer our responsibility."

"Even though they still have souls?" Cecilia challenged.

"That's debatable, since they sold them so cheaply. All it means is that I won't do anything that might cost them their lives. Traitors or not, their lives are still sacred and only God has the right to take them." His eyes roved across the group, ending on Cecilia's. "But God also gave humans dominion over other living things. If we have to kill nonhumans to save ourselves, that is our right, and we must be ready to do so without hesitation."

"Only as a last resort," Cecilia emphasized.

Diego gave a gracious bow. "Of course."

"And traitors or not, we need more humans with us. We don't know if we'll ever get back to Earth. We need a larger breeding base than six men and three women."

"If breeding is even possible," Kahina Amrouche said. "What if whatever the Chirrn did to prevent it is permanent? I mean, I know it's reversible, but if only they know how…"

"It might be better not to procreate," Diego said. "Bring children into a galaxy that isn't theirs?" He shook his head. "No. We need to get back to human civilization, not just for ourselves but so we can warn them of what's out here, help them build defenses against the Chirrn."

Diego spoke with authority, as though he, not Cecilia, were the one in charge. Distressingly, the others seemed to accept this. Cecilia feared that Diego was right—she had lost the loyalists' trust by shutting down their escape attempt back at Shilirrlal.

And she feared there might be no way to win it back without leading her people into a fight they had no chance of winning.

2

As the Arachnen and their mediators entered the spacious elevator carriage that would take them down, they were met by a foursome of diminutive sophonts, less than a meter and a half tall with wide, wing-like ears, large dark eyes, and short muzzles, giving them a cervine appearance. Their build was vaguely centaurian, with a third leg at the rear and a third arm emerging from mid-chest. Their downy fur was mottled in various shades of green and gold, and they were nude aside from matching head adornments and various pouches and belts. "We convey greetings between Antares Star Palace and Migration guild from Shilirrlal," one of the elfin creatures intoned, speaking the Universal dialect of Chirramh in a soft, cooing voice with surprisingly little accent. "We assist with luggage, supplies, queries, and other service upon request."

As the delicate-looking creature continued its spiel, R'nilinnath sidled up to the humans. "Zhalevey," she explained. "Very ancient, found almost everywhere. They thrive on service to others, so everybody likes them."

"So why weren't there any on Shilirrlal?" Tarik Bahar asked, sizing up the adorable sophonts with a wary gaze. Stephen thought the burly, thick-mustached acting captain was being overprotective, but that had always been Tarik's nature, ever since his days as an Istanbul police officer — and more so than ever since he and Kweli had lost their baby.

"Chirrn like to be self-reliant. We won't kick them out if they visit," Nilly went on, using a shared idiom that was far more literal in Chirrn usage, "but they get bored with nobody needing them and go somewhere else."

A Zhalevey with a mostly golden face framed by green floated over to Stephen. "Greetings between Antares B Star Palace and Arachnen in migration. Limitation is acknowledged: Arachnen in transition through probationary status. Physical and network access within Star Palace are conditional upon supervision by Shilirrlaln, designated mentors of Arachnen. Otherwise, Zhalevey shall provide any service desired."

"Thank you," Stephen said. The messenger made the message more palatable. Up close, the Zhalevey's muzzle was a surprisingly flexible fleshy tube with flat grinding surfaces visible within. Their limbs bent smoothly without joints, more like tails, and indeed their whole bodies seemed somewhat mutable: the Zhalevey greeting the humans adopted a more erect posture (even in free fall) and drew in its sock-puppet muzzle somewhat, while the ones tending to the Chirrn angled their bodies forward and even seemed to increase the separation between their eyes. It was like being attended by a gaggle of stuffed animals. "Um, do you have a name?"

"Phlrntsya."

"Phril... Phler..."

"Phlrntsya."

"Phuller..."

"Oh, just go with Fred," Sita interposed.

"As you will," the Zhalevey consented without pause.

Despite their floppy appearance, the Zhalevey handled the party's luggage with ease while escorting them to the carriage's comfortably appointed lounge. The hundred-kilometer descent would take nearly an hour, enough time for their bodies to acclimate to the greater atmospheric density the Zenith favored. The Arachnen's nanorepair systems, with a bit of Chirrn augmentation, had grown respiratory filters that would let them endure the dense air without suffering oxygen toxicity, nitrogen narcosis, or hypercapnia, but it would still take their bodies and filter implants time to adjust to the rising pressure, as well as the increase in gravity as they descended toward the surface.

"Antares B Star Palace is the customs port for the wormhole node that allows direct access to Lode Seven, the neutron star system where we shall obtain the quark matter," L'chellin explained to the Arachnen as they gazed out the lounge windows and watched the scintillating towers of the Star Palace draw gradually nearer. "We must negotiate for access. We may be here for several *narrissh*," the cobalt-skinned, vanilla-maned mediator went on. Stephen still needed to remind himself that a *narrissh* was a Chirrn "day," a bit under fourteen hours.

"Neutron star?" Haim Silbermann echoed. "That's how you get the necessary conditions to make PQM, isn't it?"

"Correct. Or rather… it is made on the surfaces of neutron stars, and we obtain it afterward."

"Made by what?" the chief engineer asked.

"Or whom?" Sita chimed in. "There have been theories about nucleonic life… organisms living millions of times faster than carbon-based life, because the particles are so much closer together, the interactions so much faster." The fascination in her eyes delighted Stephen.

"That is not entirely removed from truth," L'chellin said.

Broadwing focused his three eyes on her. "Do you also have theories about metasapient life?" Arachne's subtitles offered a variety of translations for the term Broadwing used, but "metasapient" was the recommended one.

"There have been experiments to create both cyber and organic consciousnesses more advanced than the human mind," Arachne answered through her avatar. "But beyond certain limited augmentations of speed, memory, and the like, they always result in collapse or insanity. Sapience is a controlled instability, dynamic enough to innovate and adapt, but not so much as to fall into chaos. Make a mind's processes too complex and the internal chaos overwhelms any useful thought or awareness of the outside world."

"A world such as the realms we inhabit, yes," Broadwing replied. "The complexity of our minds is suited for the complexity of the environment in which we evolved. When inputs from the outer world are removed," (<sensory deprivation,> added Arachne's annotation,) "our inner processes overwhelm us and we can suffer mental breakdown. So it follows…" He trailed off.

Sita picked up the thread. "That a more complex mind could be stable… in a more complex environment?"

"Exactly! Higher levels of consciousness can be stable in environments rich and dynamic enough to balance their inner complexity. Many metasapients live near the galactic core within nested Dyson shells of smart matter, powerful enough to simulate or physically create environments of sufficient complexity to sustain them. Some, it is believed, create their own pocket universes with a density and temperature approaching the early moments of our own universe."

"And others," R'nilinnath chimed in brightly, "live on neutron stars."

"Where they make programmable quark matter?" Tarik asked.

"Of course. You don't think *we're* intelligent enough to have created a thing that virtually breaks the laws of physics, do you?"

Broadwing preened the silvery featherfur on his shoulder. "More to the point, manufacturing femtotechnology such as PQM requires temperatures, pressures, and materials only found on neutron star surfaces or in the cores of stars and giant planets. And the computations are so complex that it requires femtotechnology to build it in the first place."

"Now, hold on," Haim said. "At the trial, Captain Rillial said that most civilizations don't travel the stars extensively until they achieve gravity control—meaning warp cages and the like. Which requires PQM. So if you have to go to neutron stars to get PQM, how do new civilizations get out to the stars to begin with?"

L'chellin responded promptly, as though she'd been expecting Haim's question. "Once a species has made contact with PQM-equipped civilizations—whether through slow migration, electromagnetic communication, or other means—there is a system by which the more mature civilization can sponsor the novice one, offering mentoring and guidance into the galactic community and eventual access to the technology and resources thereof. It is a very… gradual process."

"So that's what Phler—Fred meant by calling you our 'designated mentors?'" Stephen asked.

"That is… an adequate understanding for these purposes," L'chellin affirmed, a bit tentatively.

"So where do these metaminds fit in?" Sita asked. "Do you actually buy the stuff from them? What could they possibly want from you?"

"There is no direct exchange," L'chellin explained. "Metasapients are so far above our level of thought that understanding them is impossible, just as your pets could not understand this conversation. Whereas they do not even notice us as individuals—or so we believe. We are below their perceptual threshold. To the extent that they are aware of us, it is in the aggregate."

"So they just *give* you the PQM?"

"Essentially. They launch it into orbit, where we collect it and process it to suit our needs. The raw material is delivered in multiple forms, allowing us to adapt and combine it to any purpose we require."

"But why?"

"We can only guess their motives. Some believe it is simply a waste product of their civilization."

Broadwing shrugged his wings. "But it appears too deliberate to be accidental. Many believe that the metasapients give us PQM so that we will have the means to join them. To travel to places where metaminds can exist—or to create such places—and gain sufficient understanding of the universe that we may learn to reach their level of being."

"After all," L'chellin added, "the more minds that join them, the more complex their environments become. If there is one thing we do know for certain, it is their need for hypercomplex, hyperstimulating environments."

"So why haven't your species made the jump yet?" Sita asked.

"We don't know how," Nilly said. "Metaminds can't survive outside their special environments, and normal minds can't survive in them. So how do you get from one to the other? Before you can make the transition, you need to solve that problem."

L'chellin put a hand on the apprentice's back, quieting her. "Which presupposes you would be looking in the first place," she said. "The Chirrn are comfortable with our own form of existence. Metasapient thought may be more complex, even more advanced, but that does not necessarily make it better. Metasapience is much like death—no one who has made the transition is able to report back about the specifics."

"That's a very Chirrn sort of caution." Sita turned to the other mediator. "But knowing the Zenith, I'd think you'd jump at the chance—pardon the expression—to climb to a higher level."

Broadwing was slow to respond, and Stephen noted L'chellin's gaze fixed sternly on her fellow mediator. "Most Zenith," Broadwing finally answered, "consider it a false ascension. It requires traveling downward to a neutron star surface or to the core of the galaxy, sinking deeper into a gravity well. In fact, it is to descend—to remove oneself from galactic society rather than seeking to rise within it. It is not what the Seekers of the Zenith aspire to." Sita took in his answer with a skeptical moue.

Once they reached the surface and exited into the grand promenade of the Antares B Star Palace, Stephen and the others got a look at what the Zenith *did* aspire to. And it was worth the wait. The promenade was a vast open space hundreds of meters high and wide, extending clear around the planet's equator with no breaks save for the dozen space-elevator shafts that pierced its center. Stretching beyond the tight curve of the habitat to east and west and nearly to the horizon to north and south, it made Times Square or Vestalia Concourse look like an Amish village. Everywhere Stephen looked, vast holo-walls, animated ad-sculptures, ornate light displays, massive fountains, vertiginous overhead bridges, and hovering platforms festooned the space, along with other sights he didn't trust himself to interpret—and that was even without being granted access to the local augreality network. Exotic sounds were everywhere, pervading the space, and he couldn't tell what was music, what was speech, and what was machinery noise.

But the scenery was rivaled by its occupants—sophonts of all shapes and sizes striding, strolling, hopping, flying, scuttling, and slithering through the promenade, as well as riding through the immense space in various trams, aircars, groundcars, and even things that seemed to correspond to bicycles and pedicabs. Numerous drones flitted about overhead, carrying parcels or displaying animated ads or tracking certain members of the crowd. Dozens of species intermingled effortlessly, seemingly untroubled by their differences. The local gravity was about two-thirds of a g, toward the lower limit found on worlds suitable for life on land, for the convenience of a wide range of sophonts.

"Bloody gobsmacking," Sita gasped, her big dark eyes gaping wider than ever at the sights around her. "How come there are so many more species here than in the Central Void?"

"Migration patterns have been shifting," Broadwing told her as the rest of the Shilirrlaln and Arachnen debarked from the elevator car, Zhalevey skittering underfoot to tend to their luggage and gear. "For millennia, populations have been relocating away from the hypergiant variable binary system that dominates the near portion of the spiral arm antispinward of here."

"Eta Carinae," Arachne interpreted. "A star expected to go hypernova in the very near astronomical future. Its preliminary eruptions alone have approached supernova magnitude."

"Those eruptions were controlled discharges engineered to reduce the intensity of the eventual cataclysm," Broadwing said, dropping the cosmic bombshell with a casualness Stephen was beginning to find routine. "Yet even they released radiation and interstellar medium disruptions sufficient to endanger life for many parsecs around. A sizeable volume of surrounding space, larger than the Four Voids, has needed to be evacuated ahead of the final destruction. It has caused a ripple effect of migrations—established populations shifting outward in response to increased crowding in their own territories—and now this diaspora front has expanded far enough to impinge on the Antispinward Void."

"That wouldn't be why you decided to found a new habitat in this part of space, would it?" Sita probed. "To shore up your territorial claims along this border?"

"'Territory' is a planet-dweller's concept," L'chellin interposed before Broadwing could reply. "There is always abundant room in space. What we control includes our own habitats, the space adjacent to them, and the routes between them."

"Then why did those 'established populations' decide they had to move when the refugees came?"

The elder Chirrn replied slowly. "Do not concern yourself, Sita. The migration prompted by the impending hypernova was of extraordinary size and density. At these reaches, the impact is more diffuse and manageable."

Stephen tapped Sita's wrist to get her attention, giving a subtle shake of his head. He'd been tolerant of her efforts to probe beyond what the Arachnen were currently cleared to know, hoping it could help her move past her grief. The return of her natural determination was good to see after her months of fearful isolation. But their initial entry into an environment this alien was not a good time to push limits, even aside from the penalties they could face if they violated their probation. He hoped Sita would figure that out on her own.

Sita ignored his wordless caution. "But if territory matters so little, why are the Voids so empty to begin with?"

"You know the Voids were created by a wave of star formation," L'chellin told her. "Most civilizations choose to migrate away from such hazards."

"But that was millions of years ago, well before the Chirrn emerged. There's been more than enough time to repopulate, even without FTL. So why didn't—"

Her words choked off when Broadwing rose to his full height and unfolded his wing dactyls, letting out a deafening calliope shriek before leaping skyward with a powerful downstroke of his wings. The gust of wind almost knocked her over, but Diana Thorne caught her, holding her steady. Sita gave the statuesque, bronze-haired engineer a quick look of thanks before turning back to follow Broadwing's flight, a grin on her face.

Focusing his adaptive optics, Stephen saw multiple dining facilities suspended from the roof of the promenade, all patronized by numerous Zenith, hundreds in all. Despite the Zenith's dense native atmosphere, it exacted a very high metabolic cost to power both a set of wings and a sapient brain, so essentially all Zenith social activity revolved around meals. As others flew down from the eateries to confront and challenge the new arrival, Stephen recognized that Broadwing's name might be something of a boast; as impressive as he was to human eyes, he seemed scrawny and dull next to his challengers, with not only smaller wings and body, but smaller, less brilliant crests. Zenith headcrests were indicators of status; as they gained in social standing and contentment, their serotonin-analogue levels rose, stiffening the keratinous microfibers in the crests and intensifying their diffraction-grating rainbow effect.

Stephen noticed that Arachne provided no subtitles for their challenge and response cries. "Why isn't it translating?" Sita asked the avatar in frustration.

"It's a different language than the Shilirrlaln Zenith use," the cyber replied. "I haven't evolved a translation matrix yet."

Fred the Zhalevey sidled closer on their three floppy legs. "Zenith translation summary available. They challenge the new arrival's right to be present. He sings of accomplishments as arbiter and mediator, yet they mock him for association with dirtgrubbers and ferals."

The Arachnen stared at the gold-faced Zhalevey, who seemed amiably oblivious to any insult. "Well, it is the closest translation," Nilly pointed out in its defense. "And it's not like you're really dirtgrubbers anymore."

"Some of us never were," pointed out Diana, a proud native of the Vanguard habitat in Sol's asteroid belt.

Sita frowned. "But we are feral?"

L'chellin hushed Nilly and threw the humans an apologetic look. "Do not be concerned," she said. "The point of Zenith challenges is the act itself; the specifics of the taunt are arbitrary. Rest assured that you are as welcome here as we are." Nilly snorted a bit and twitched her tail, making Stephen wonder what amused her so. But the young Chirrn fell silent under another glare from L'chellin.

The elder mediator straightened, taking on the distracted look of a Chirrn receiving a message through the consensus network. "Excuse me," she said after a moment. "R'nilinnath, tend to the Arachnen, please. I shall return shortly."

L'chellin bounded off through the crowded plaza, soon intercepting a trio of sophonts who were being escorted their way by another gaggle of Zhalevey. At first, Stephen assumed they were some new ethnic variant of Chirrn, but he soon realized they were something different—more upright-bodied and pear-shaped, with blunter snouts, stubby downturned tails, and no manes. They hopped like Chirrn, but without the same power or grace. All told, they gave the impression of being the Chirrn's fuddy-duddy grandparents.

L'chellin and the threesome exchanged a greeting that looked like a standard Chirrn challenge-and-recognition ritual. Yet L'chellin seemed at once deferential and wary toward the newcomers. "Who are they?" Sita wondered aloud.

R'nilinnath gave a faint hiss through her teeth. "Shayal. Here to intrude in our affairs, no doubt."

"Are they some kind of… Chirrn offshoot?"

"We evolved on the same planet," Nilly grudgingly admitted. "But we're no closer than you and—what is it called?—a gibbon."

"Ohh, bloody brilliant! Two coexisting sophonts of the same evolutionary line! Did you evolve at the same time, or…?"

Nilly chuffed. "They never let us forget that they were first."

"I take it they migrated into space and left the planet to you," Stephen said, his tone suggesting that the young Chirrn should be more grateful.

"Yes, acknowledged."

"Is that why the Chirrn followed their example?"

Nilly fidgeted. "It isn't just theirs. Most sophonts do it."

L'chellin seemed to be arguing with the lead Shayal, then threw a furtive glance the Arachnen's way and assumed a more deferential pose. After a moment, the other sophont gave a very Chirrn-like gesture of assent. The triad remained behind while L'chellin returned to the party, looking irritated. "Aren't you going to introduce us to your, ah, relatives?" Stephen asked carefully.

"Perhaps later," L'chellin said, her voice controlled. "For now, this atmosphere will fatigue you quickly until you acclimate. We should see you to your guest suite." She began herding them and their Zhalevey escorts away from the Shayal triad.

"Already?" Sita protested. "But—*this!*" She waved her arms, making their setting an argument in itself.

"Your curiosity is commendable, Sita," the elder mediator went on. "But I would advise you all to stay close for now and allow us, or at least the Zhalevey, to mediate any contacts with other sophonts. Humans are smaller and less durable than many Galactic species, and if you get too close to a sophont whose body language you cannot read, there is a risk of accidental injury."

Diana Thorne crossed her arms in irritation. "Some of us are plenty durable," the towering engineer said.

"And overly eager to prove yourselves. Rest assured, Diana, you will find recreations here to challenge your physical prowess, but please wait until we can coordinate with the Star Palace staff to organize activities appropriate to your physiology—and brief them on your medical needs in case of… overzealousness." Diana's dark, gorgeous face flushed redder. The young Vanguardian's eagerness to test her transhuman abilities against Chirrn athletes had landed her under Kweli Ndege's medical care more than once, even before the injuries she'd sustained in the Lesshchin attack. Despite being the Arachnen's most powerful member, she'd spent more time in the hospital than any of them, to her own deep embarrassment.

But it was Sita who leaned in to Stephen and whispered, "Bugger that. Alien Central Station and we don't even get to mingle? Tell you what—you create a distraction and I'll slip away."

"Sita…" He touched her shoulder. "I'm glad you've moved beyond your fears, but this is not the place or time to get reckless."

"Come on, I just want to take a quick butchers."

Sometimes Stephen was tempted to ask Arachne to subtitle Sita's Cockneyisms. But he got the drift. "You've seen how uneasy they are with us. The last thing we want is to risk… another misunderstanding."

A shudder went through her at the reminder, and Stephen hated himself for provoking it. But there was no way he would risk her safety again. He held her closer. "Look… I'm sure the mediators will be happy to help you tap into the local net, and I'll make sure you're on the first supervised tour we can arrange."

Sita gathered herself. "Right. Cheers. Sounds nice and sensible." But she moved away without another word, and he feared he'd raised the wall between them again, just when he needed her to trust him the most.

As the Zhalevey and the mediators escorted the Arachnen out of the grand promenade toward their guest accommodations, a swarm of small drones descended on the group, followed closely by a small mob of xenosophonts of more species than Tarik Bahar could count. Their aggressive approach immediately put Tarik on the defensive. The memory of the Lesshchin attack remained vivid: *Waking to an angry mob of Chirrn bursting into his bedroom. Leaping up to protect Kweli, being struck down by the sweep of an attacker's heavy tail. Coming to with hands and feet tied and ribs broken, dragged out into the public square, forced to watch as Kweli and all the other pregnant women were beaten in the womb. Screaming in fury, nearly breaking his wrists in his desperate struggles to tear free, to run to Kweli's side, to save her and Mehmet even if it killed him. The unbearable guilt of being utterly helpless to stop his unborn child from being murdered. The fear that he would lose Kweli as well. The relief when the Chirrn doctors managed to save her, at least… and the long weeks of despair since, the fear that the warm, joyous, playful, kind woman that he loved was lost to him after all.*

Yet Tarik's attention quickly turned to his wife and the other women in the here-and-now. Kweli, Sita, Kazuko, and the others drew back in fear, huddling together. Fists clenching, Tarik moved forward to shield them. He would let nothing happen to them again.

Diana Thorne joined Tarik, for which he was grateful. The Vanguardian superwoman was the only Arachnen taller and stronger than he was, and Tarik knew her bitterness at failing to protect the babies rivaled his own. Arachne's spider-woman avatar joined the cordon, her Greek-sculpture face morphing into a more threatening arachnid appearance—though some of the beings in the advancing group might well find it more appealing.

L'chellin stepped to the fore as well, though her body language was not confrontational. "Reporters," she explained. "I apologize. I have been fending off their interview requests since we arrived," she went on, tapping her head to clarify. "But it seems Broadwing's departure has emboldened them. I shall persuade them to leave us alone."

Stephen came up alongside her. "Hold on, L'chellin. We've seen how our reputation alarms people out here. This is our chance to get ahead of that narrative. Tell the galaxy our side of the story, make it clear that we have no wish to be a threat."

L'chellin spent a moment communing silently with her Mediation guildmates through the consensus network. "Agreed. A brief statement, with limited questions. I shall interpret between you and the reporters. Your Chirramh is still… idiosyncratic… and we desire no miscommunication."

After a few moments' further discussion, Stephen stepped forward with L'chellin and began to recount the oft-told tale of how he had escaped the poverty and racial oppression of the hurricane-ravaged, strongman-ruled southeastern United States, built a philanthropic-industrialist empire centered in Brazil by the time he was thirty, poured his resources into the advancement of interstellar technology over the next decade and a half, and finally led the *Arachne* expedition to colonize Cybele, the most distant yet most Earthlike world that humans had ever attempted to settle. No doubt he was trying to counter the aliens' perception of the Arachnen as mass murderers from a primitive, savage race.

Tarik had no wish to be reminded of the rest of the story, of *Arachne*'s inadvertent destruction of Lesshchi and all that had followed. Besides, he had more immediate concerns. Moving back toward Kweli and the other women, he saw that the Zhalevey had huddled in close to them, offering protection and comfort. Kweli was on her knees, snuggling two of the plush creatures and weeping softly. Sita, meanwhile, was visibly controlling her fear, craning her head in an attempt to observe the various anatomies on display within the reportorial gaggle. That was quite a reversal. For months after her near-fatal beating by Lesshchi survivors on the humans' first night in captivity, the diminutive xenobiologist had been the most timid member of the group, avoiding contact with aliens as much as possible, while Kweli had actively sought out contact and striven to learn all she could about the biology of the inhabitants of Shilirrlal. Somehow, in the wake of the kiss dance riot and her miscarriage, Sita had managed to regain her courage and was now making up for lost time. Tarik hoped it would not take anything so drastic for Kweli to regain her sense of wonder at alien life.

Tarik placed a hand on Kweli's shoulder, disturbed by how clearly he could feel the bone underneath. She had not been eating well since the attack, and her normally Rubenesque figure had grown significantly leaner. "Are you all right?" he asked.

She looked up and gave him a small, sad smile. "I'm in good hands. See to the others."

Was that her innate selflessness talking, or depression? It frustrated Tarik that he couldn't tell.

Once the galactic press's hunger had been sated, the Zhalevey resumed guiding the group to their guest suite. The pair that Kweli had been snuggling stayed with her even after helping them get settled in their room, seeming perfectly content to serve as live teddy bears indefinitely. Kweli noticed Tarik's unease with their submissiveness and sent them on their way. "Thank you so much, but I'm sure you have duties elsewhere. Yes, certainly, if I need you, I'll let you know."

Tarik cleared his throat. "I know I'm not as plushy as they are, but if you still need someone to hold …"

With another sad smile (the only kind she seemed to have anymore), she came over and embraced him. "Don't worry, Tarik. You're still my favorite teddy bear."

Still, Tarik found himself unable to relax into the embrace. "What's wrong?" Kweli asked after a time, letting him go.

Grimacing, he began to pace. "I thought we were done with reporters when we left Solsys. I always hated dealing with that lot. But these may be even worse. Just pushing themselves on us when we're so vulnerable, so easily frightened…" He snarled and struck his open palm with his fist, making Kweli jump in alarm. "There, you see? They've put you on edge. They just don't care!" He moved toward her—and was startled when she pulled away. "Kweli! It's all right. It's just me."

She was shaking again. " 'Just' you, Tarik? Sometimes I think you forget how large you are. How intimidating."

Tarik was bewildered. "My love… you know I'd never, ever harm you."

"Knowing is one thing. Feeling?" She shook her head, turning away. "I can't handle… ferocity… right now. I think… I think I need to be by myself."

He winced. Keeping his voice as soft as he could, he told her, "All I want to do is to keep you safe. To help you heal. I love you."

"I know," Kweli said. "I love you too. But right now… you can't help me.

"Right now… I'm not sure anything can."

The Shayal may have had a few million years of evolutionary separation from their Chirrn cousins, but Sita could still read their body language well enough to tell that the head of the triad had expected their conversation with L'chellin to continue. As she lingered in the common area of the Arachnen's guest suite, watching through its clear forward wall as the mediators wrapped things up with the Zhalevey in the spacious atrium outside, she could certainly read L'chellin well enough to know that the vanilla-maned mediator intended to fulfill that expectation, however grudgingly. It wasn't long before the Chirrn elder bounded off toward the waiting Shayal nearby. R'nilinnath moved as if to join her, then pulled up short, taking on an abstracted look and finally sagging in disappointment.

Sita slipped out into the atrium and joined Nilly. "Don't tell me — she told you to wait here."

The apprentice watched uneasily as L'chellin moved off with the triad. "She is my senior."

"But you're worried about her. About these Shayal. Dangerous, are they?"

Nilly drummed her toes in amusement. "Those stunted-tailed ancients? I could take all three of them easily. Even you could take at least one."

"Oi, now!" But the young apprentice was still gazing after them in concern. "What is it you're so bothered about, then?"

Nilly's eyes flicked outward and back, a nervous tell. "Nothing important. I just don't like being left out."

"Come on, Nilly, what aren't you telling me? And why?"

R'nilinnath's hands came up to tap her brows, a gesture of distress or fear. She forced them down a moment later, gathering herself. "I'm sorry, Sita. But it is not my place to decide what to reveal to you and when."

Sita took Nilly's four-digited hands in her own smaller ones. "That never stopped you before, love."

"And look what happened!" Nilly pulled her hands away, placing them over her outward-swiveled eyes. "I thought I was helping, encouraging you to sneak out and explore. And I... what I did to you..."

Sita stroked Nilly's silver mane. "Nilly, what happened on Shilirrlal wasn't your fault. You couldn't have known..."

"That is the problem. I *don't* know enough. I don't have the full guild memory assimilated yet. I have the surface stuff, the database, but not the deep experience, either my own or the others'. So I don't know what I can tell you and what I shouldn't. If I say too much, what might happen to you?"

Sita hugged her around her neck. "Oh, Nilly. Believe me, I understand how you feel."

"How can you?"

"Because I've been blaming myself too. We all have. Stephen more than anyone, I think. I can't help feeling—what if I hadn't gone with you to the kiss dance? What if I hadn't laughed around the Lesshchin, provoked them in the first place? But then I see the people around me also blaming themselves, and it hurts to see them being so guilty when they don't deserve to be. And that made me realize… maybe I don't deserve to feel so guilty either."

"You don't! You were the victim!"

Tears came to Sita's eyes. "But I'm not alone, my darling. We were all victims. I was a victim of the Lesshchin… they were victims of the disaster… we've all been shaped by past pain. So maybe none of us are really to blame. What happened to us… the causes of it go back farther and deeper than any of us probably know."

Luckily, Nilly's eye could swivel back, so Sita could meet her gaze without having to stop hugging her. "And that's why I need to know what you aren't telling me, love. I feel that whatever L'chellin doesn't want us to know could answer a lot of questions. About why the Chirrn fear planet-dwellers, why you hide your habitats. Why there was so much bitterness toward us even before the disaster." Sita sighed. "It wouldn't make any of this hurt less… but at least we might understand the why of it. Yes, sometimes knowing too much can get you in trouble, but being kept in ignorance is always worse."

Nilly gave her a fond neck-nuzzle before moving away. "You just want me to help you spy on L'chellin."

"Oh, not at all," Sita assured her. "I want to help *you* spy on L'chellin."

The apprentice pondered for a moment. "In that case, come on."

Consulting the local map in the Star Palace's cloud memory, R'nilinnath was able to lead Sita to a skywalk balcony one level below the edge of a plaza where the senior mediator was deep in conversation with the Shayal trio. The balcony's angle let her catch a glimpse of L'chellin, whose body language toward the smaller Shayal was an odd mix of intimidation and defiance, almost like a teenager toward a parent.

Once she was directly underneath the foursome, Sita could no longer see them, but she could hear them over the echoing chatter of the crowd below. Conveniently, they were all speaking Universal Chirramh, so her translator had little trouble with the Shayal's words, spoken with a vocal timbre resembling a Chirrn's but higher in pitch. "Your perspective is noted, Mediator. But if we could only be allowed to examine the Arachnen—"

"They have endured enough, Commissioner," L'chellin replied. "And they are in the midst of a delicate transition. I will not permit you to disrupt that process."

"I offer assurance that we will take their fragility into account. But it would be valuable to assess the degree to which their lack of mentoring has affected their psychology."

Lack of mentoring? Sita thought. L'chellin had described mentoring as a process of guiding novice starfaring civilizations into the interstellar community. Given that humans had only just begun their starfaring era, how could the Shayal's statement make sense?

"Your words betray you, Velesh," L'chellin went on. "This inquiry is to serve the Coalition, not the Arachnen. You hope your increased status in the Antispinward Void will let you win favor at our expense."

Sita whispered in Nilly's ear. "Coalition?"

"The Nine Clusters Coalition," the apprentice hissed back. "Long story."

"Please," continued the one called Velesh. "This is not about our own political standings. Surely we can all agree that the Lesshchi tragedy demonstrates the dangers of allowing current policies to remain unaltered. If the humans had been properly mentored from the onset—"

"That is for the Void Alliance to decide," L'chellin insisted. "And while your presence may be increasing, the Coalition does not yet have enough influence in the Voids to override the existing consensus."

Their voices faded as they hopped away from the plaza edge. Try as they might, Nilly and Sita could not find an eavesdropping point again. "We should get back before we're missed," the apprentice said.

"What did Velesh mean, 'properly mentored from the onset'?" Sita asked her as they respectively jogged and hopped back to the suite.

Nilly hesitated. "Is that how Arachne translated it? Ill-born words, I'd say. Probably a reference to your brief association with galactic society—saying you haven't learned how to behave properly yet."

"But Velesh seemed to be saying Lesshchi could've been avoided. That implies they were talking about how things stood before the disaster."

The apprentice was visibly uneasy now. "Please, Sita. As I said before… I don't know what it would be proper to reveal to you yet. So please stop asking."

Sita recognized that she would get no more answers from R'nilin-nath. And if she wouldn't talk, none of the other mediators would be any more revealing. As for the Shayal, they seemed to have an agenda of their own—and it looked unlikely that L'chellin would allow her any chance to interact with the newcomers.

But Sita's need for answers still compelled her. Surely someone in the Star Palace's cosmopolitan collection of sophonts would be willing to tell her what the Chirrn would not.

The males who challenged Broadwing in the grand promenade had played their parts well. They had presented a convincing aspect of a challenge with their words and posturing, but had backed down when he boasted of his accomplishments as a Shilirrlaln mediator, allowing him to appear victorious enough that his invitation to a private assignation by a watching female would not appear strange. The female was small and scraggly, her crests not appreciably large or bright; her name, Sunflash, was as much an aspirational boast as his own. But perhaps Broadwing had not yet earned better.

"Meridian is present?" he asked Sunflash once they were alone in a private mating gallery, a low-status one whose dome was barely high enough to allow a couple to remain aloft, let alone maneuver effectively. It did little to put him in the mood for more than conversation.

"As always. It is your part that is open to question. Can you deliver upon your promise?"

He uploaded the plans and specifications for the new habitat to her augreality channel, calling her attention to the types and quantities of programmable quark matter the caravan would order at Lode Seven. "It should be more than suitable," he said.

Sunflash shook her crests confidently, and for the first time he started to find her attractive. "Suitable to elevate us, and to knock down the Chirrn a tier or two at the same time. Excellent." She studied him. "And the humans? Will they play their part?"

Broadwing hesitated. "They must be handled delicately. But they are beginning to question the gaps in what they have been told. I believe that as long as I give them the wingroom they need, they will arrive where we wish them on their own."

"How much farther must they fly? They are already the greatest criminals in the Voids, short of the Chirrn themselves."

"Not in their own minds. They seek to prove themselves righteous."

That pleased Sunflash even more. "So much the better, once they learn of our grievances."

Still, her approval did not translate into a sexual advance. After an uncomfortable silence, Broadwing asked, "Do you wish me to disrobe?"

She ducked her head. "I am too lowly to mate with you. Your purpose lifts you to a far higher tier."

Broadwing thrilled at the prospect. *Meridian?* Still, his time among the Chirrn had taught him humility. "I have not yet earned that place."

Sunflash lowered herself further in deference to him. "You have brought us hope of liberation after twelve thousand years. For that alone, we sing your name."

Her praise fulfilled him—but a doubt still lingered. "And the humans… will they share in our liberation?"

"They will serve it," she replied. "Beyond that, does it matter?"

3

After nearly a day in the Star Palace, Sita felt more like a prisoner than she had during the trial. It was frustrating to be surrounded by so many exciting new species, yet constrained from moving about freely. So when Broadwing informed the Arachnen that the Palace's medical staff had requested the opportunity to familiarize themselves with a representative sample of humans in case of emergency, Sita jumped to volunteer. Now that Arachne was hooked into the local translation network, the opportunity for some private conversation with the Star Palace staff was too promising to pass up.

When Broadwing escorted her to the medical center and she laid eyes on the physician who would examine her, Sita had second thoughts. Doctor Rauhoc was a large, intimidating creature built like a walking seesaw, his long, spindle-shaped body cantilevered atop a pair of runner's legs a meter and a half long, with two arms and a heavy, spiky-plated head in front and two arm-like rear limbs ending in bony clubs. *Sod it all, why aren't there more small, cute aliens out here?* she thought, fighting down a surge of panic.

Broadwing assured her that Rauhoc's people, the Gaurim, possessed exceptional expertise in the life sciences — largely due, he had grudgingly conceded, to their preference for living on planets and carefully tending their ecosystems. A chat with someone from more of a planetary background might bring a perspective she wouldn't get from the habitat-based community.

Some things were universal, it seemed, since there was a fair wait for the doctor after the brief initial greeting. Sita didn't particularly mind, though. Not only did it give her a chance to wrestle her cowardice back into submission, but it let her observe the clinic staff and their reactions. Most of the Zenith staffers watched her uneasily, and Sita realized with some amusement that they found her, the smallest and least physically threatening human within a hundred and seventy parsecs, as intimidating as she found them. She caught whispers including the word "feral," the same slur she'd been hearing since those first hours after the disaster. Even the Zhalevey receptionist seemed to echo their mood, following its species' instinct to conform to the herd.

Finally, one of the smaller, less impressively crested Zenith females escorted her to an exam room. "You may feel less weighted down here," she said; Sita took it as an idiom for "more comfortable."

"Cheers," she replied. "But is this really for my benefit, or so a 'feral' won't scare off your other patients?"

The orderly ducked her head deferentially. "I apologize for their discomfort toward you. They know of the destruction of the Chirrn habitat."

Sita winced. "Believe me, I haven't forgotten — ah, what was your name?"

"I am Sunflash."

"Good to know you. I take it you don't share the others' discomfort?"

The orderly twisted her head furtively, then leaned closer. "I spy the truth: The Chirrn brought the destruction upon themselves."

Sita recalled Commissioner Velesh's charge to L'chellin. "Because of their mentoring policies?"

Sunflash made a rude noise. "Chirrn have no grasp of mentoring. Whichever way they carry it, disaster results."

Dr. Rauhoc had entered as the orderly spoke, and the Zenith quailed as the massive Gaurim loomed before her. "Attend to your work in silence or I will send you back down where you belong!" Sunflash almost literally flew from the room.

The doctor said nothing more about the altercation, getting straight to business. According to Broadwing, Gaurim worshipped evolution as the work of the divine (or something roughly analogous) and rejoiced in exploring its permutations. Which in this case meant that Rauhoc couldn't get Sita naked on the scanner table fast enough. It was alarming at first, like being pawed by an ankylosaur on stilts, and Sita prayed she wouldn't ruin her investigation with a panic attack. But the doctor's thick, bone-spurred hands proved to have surprisingly delicate manipulative tips, their wide surfaces able to flex and grip with precision like a snail's foot. Her scientific fascination with his anatomy, rivaling his toward hers, soon overcame her fear. Even his clinical, unsympathetic manner toward her recent traumas was oddly reassuring, allowing her to step back and look at them as medical curiosities.

As the examination proceeded, she directed the conversation back toward Sunflash. "Why were you so cross with her?"

"Her words were irreverent toward the loss of life. I require more sensitivity of my staff."

Sita took a gamble. "So you don't agree that the Chirrn have mentored us improperly?"

Rauhoc was slow to respond. "I have no dispute with the Chirrn's current policy on mentoring. Tell me, Doctor Bhatiani: Are your developed mammary glands a residual effect of your recently interrupted gestation? Do you expect the visible protrusions to subside soon?"

"Bloody hell, I hope not. How would I keep strapless gowns up?" She cleared her throat. "So, ah, why do you think the orderly thought otherwise? Do the Zenith have a different approach to mentoring?"

The doctor gave a foghorn grunt. "I do not think she believes as most Zenith would, or she would reside on a higher level. But these are questions for your own mentors."

Sita feigned a knowing laugh. "Mentors. Always think they know best, don't they?"

Rauhoc looked up at her face. "An odd view."

"What makes you say that?"

"I am no expert in ancient history," he demurred, revealing more than he realized. "But we are taught that our mentors, the Mathadn, intervened no more than we wished of them. We lived within the symbiosis of motherworld Vohaun. When we sought knowledge from the Mathadn, it was knowledge of how other sophonts had nurtured and served their own motherworlds, so that we could best serve ours. When the motherworld suffered quakes or eruptions, the mentors offered healing and protection, which many of us accepted; but more orthodox Gaurim were allowed to die as they chose."

Sita blinked. "Um. But clearly you didn't stay that way forever."

"In time, there were those who sought the luxuries of higher technology, damaging the biosphere. It divided us, bringing us to violence that none wished for but none could see a way to avoid. The Mathadn showed us how others had dealt with similar matters, and helped us discover ways to fulfill our needs without threat to the motherworld. The technologists improved their tools until they meshed as smoothly with nature as our own bodies do. Thus, we could join the community of the stars without abandoning who we are. The Mathadn helped us find worlds we could responsibly settle—worlds with compatible biology and no sapience, so we could add ourselves to the tapestry of their evolution and give their biospheres the gift of higher cognition."

So mentoring was far more than just the sponsorship into space that L'chellin had implied. "Sounds like being mentored from the start did you a lot of good."

"Is that what you heard?" the doctor asked. "I meant to convey that we prefer as little intervention with natural development as possible. The Mathadn respected that wish, except when we asked otherwise. And as I said, I have no dispute with the Chirrn's approach. Now: Those arcs of hair above your eyes are impressively mobile. Did they evolve for long-range signaling…?"

Rauhoc would say no more about mentoring, saying he found Sita's anatomy a far more fascinating subject (oh, if she had a research grant for every time she'd heard that line). While it had been a very revealing interview (in more ways than one), it still left her hungry for more.

Fortunately, she was so far below Broadwing's sightline that she was easily overlooked. After the exam, she managed to slip away from the Zenith mediator and track down their main Zhalevey helper, the golden-faced one she'd nicknamed Fred (who had turned out to be female—so be it). Sita had quickly grown to appreciate the Zhalevey's pliant nature. They instinctively identified with others, making their worldviews and priorities as flexible as their bodies. Which was very handy for someone interested in prying where she wasn't supposed to.

Nonetheless, her initial query about mentoring met with resistance from the diminutive, dewy-eyed triped. "As your status is probationary, the administration recommends you transmit that request through your mentors. Would you like to summon Mediator L'chellin?"

"No, no," Sita hastened to reply. "Listen, Fred, the problem is that there are things our 'mentors' aren't telling us."

"Such approaches are at mentor discretion."

Sita sighed. "Look. Your job is to help me fulfill my needs, right?"

"Zhalevey shall provide any feasible service."

"Well, *my* job is to learn all I can about other species. I have a responsibility to my crewmates to help them understand other life forms and any dangers they might pose." She reached out and stroked Fred's downy head. Zhalevey were very tactile, so it seemed like the right approach. Besides, it felt nice. "You can understand that, right? How important it is that we Arachnen have the knowledge we need to make good choices? You want to help us do that, don't you?"

"To provide service, yes. But countervailing needs must be balanced."

Sita was at a loss. How could she manipulate someone who had virtually no sense of self-interest? Particularly one so cute that she felt guilty trying to trick her?

She decided to try another tack. "What I need is to get access to that Velesh bloke," she muttered, half to herself.

"Commissioner Velesh's appointment schedule accessed. Do you favor a time?"

She chuckled. "I appreciate it, love… but I'd like to keep this off the books, okay? Unofficial, you know."

"Accessing Commissioner Velesh's itinerary. An opportunity for unscheduled contact is available in twelve *narredj*. Recommend employment of Zhalevey to distract Mediator L'chellin's attention."

Sita stared. "You'd do that for me?"

"Countervailing needs must be balanced. As Shilirrlaln wish, do not discuss uncleared subjects with Arachnen. As Sita Bhatiani wishes, enable her to reach uncleared information. Zhalevey shall provide any feasible services as desired."

Sita gave her a big hug. "Ohh, I think I want to keep you!"

"No!" Stephen insisted, sitting up in bed. Sita had waited until they were snuggled together after that night's lovemaking to tell him what she'd done, no doubt thinking that he'd be at his most receptive then. But his afterglow faded quickly at her words. "This is going too far, Sita. You're not just bending the rules, you're defying them outright."

"With good reason," his wife stressed, stroking his chest. "The Chirrn have been keeping information from us at every turn."

"Even Nilly had to earn membership in her guild before she was granted full access to their private memories, their mysteries. We *will* learn the answers once we're ready—as long as we don't blow it by pushing the boundaries too far. Remember, we could still face exclusion if we violate our parole." He clasped her shoulders. "I don't want to see anything happen to you, darling."

She sighed. "I know, and I love you for it. But I'm not a porcelain doll, Stephen. I'm a scientist, and I'm following evidence too important to ignore. Too important to all of us."

Sita recapped her conversation with Dr. Rauhoc. "Stephen, this means mentoring isn't just for spacegoing societies. It's supposed to start much earlier, to guide a nascent civilization away from disaster and needless suffering."

Stephen hesitated, reluctant to face what she was implying. "It did for the Rauhoc. We don't know if that's typical."

"That's why we have to find out!" She clasped his hands. "Stephen… Earth is in Void Alliance space. They've been out here all along, since before our civilization began."

"And they've avoided interaction with planetary civilizations."

"Yeah—but what did we miss because of that? What *would* our history have been like if we'd been in contact all this time? Don't you want to know?"

In fact, Stephen burned to know. The insinuation that the Chirrn's policies had deprived humanity of guidance it had been entitled to was deeply disturbing. But he found it hard to reconcile that idea with the patience and kindness the Shilirrlaln had extended to the Arachnen.

He got out of bed and began to pace, the dense air cooling his bare skin. "I'm not sure I trust the source. From what you told me before, it sounds like these Shayal have some kind of political rivalry going on with the Alliance—and I know how badly the truth fares in such conflicts."

"Granted," Sita said, sitting up in the bed. "And that Zenith orderly, Sunflash… it sounded like she has her own grudges against the Chirrn. Believe me, love, I know better than to take any single source of information at face value." She spoke urgently. "But that includes the Chirrn! Even with the most benevolent of motives, they have their own bias, their own preconceptions, and that filters what they reveal to us. We need an alternative source of data."

"And what about your own bias?" Stephen insisted.

"What bias?"

"The same one we all share—guilt. The burden of responsibility for all this tragedy. I'm afraid you're doing the same thing Cecilia did: looking for scapegoats, for anyone else you can shift the blame to."

"I'm looking for answers! Finding someone to blame never works, because everyone's reacting to their own prior causes. The Lesshchin blame us, we blame them, we blame ourselves… all this blamed bloody blaming, it's just lashing out, not understanding. I've found no answers there, Stephen. Now I'm just trying to get some perspective. We need to know how the Galactics see us, and why, and why we've been excluded from their community. We need to know how we fit into the picture so we can avoid more misunderstandings, more conflicts."

"And that's what the Chirrn are teaching us."

"Piecemeal! Filtered through their own assumptions. We need more than that."

"Rushing in recklessly is what got us into this mess to begin with!"

Sita stared at him. "You brought me along to do a job," she insisted. "To learn about alien life. To find the answers you need to help this crew survive in a hostile environment." She reached up and clasped his hands. "So trust me to do that job—and be with me when I do."

As he gazed down into her eyes, he felt ashamed for doubting her. Had he grown so accustomed to seeing her as a fragile victim needing his protection that he'd lost sight of the keen wit and initiative that had earned her a place on *Arachne*—and in his heart?

He pulled Sita into his arms and held her close for a long time. "You're right," he finally said. "I have been afraid of the answers. But that's all the more reason I have to face them, whatever they are."

She pulled him back down to the bed and gave him a long, gentle kiss. "Wrong, you silly git. It's why *we* have to face them. Together."

After an estimated two days in freefall confinement, Cecilia Lo-Carno and Nik Zacharias had convinced Churrlaya to grant them an exercise period. Their confinement suits were able to create dynamic resistance for their muscles, and to vibrate in the low-frequency cat's-purr range that helped stimulate muscle and bone healing in Terrestrial life forms, but the doctor had argued that both would work better if the captives had a better opportunity to *use* their muscles—and that a change of scenery would do them good as well.

Churrlaya had readily agreed, even fabricating some rough exercise wear for the group's comfort. His cooperation drove home something Cecilia had begun to realize in the wake of their conversation the other day. In the weeks since she and Churrlaya had stopped sniping at each other, they'd actually found themselves starting to *listen* to each other—to what Cecilia suspected was their mutual surprise. The ensuing discussions had been intriguing and enlightening, and she'd grown to look forward to them. Diego may have seen that as disloyalty to her own kind, but Cecilia felt it was quite the opposite. After all, if she could persuade a Lesshchin to understand her point of view, perhaps it could even lead the Chirrn to change their minds about the humans' imprisonment. *Just what Stephen would do,* she thought, *if he ever came to his senses.*

For now, Cecilia simply welcomed the chance to stretch her legs. The free-fall exercise room to which they were escorted held strange-looking equipment that their Chirrn and Zenith guards had to explain how to use, and that could only be reconfigured so far to fit human proportions and strength. But on the plus side, the room had an extraordinary view. It was the first time they'd been able to look out a window since they'd left Shilirrlal, and Cecilia found herself glued to the port. They were in a scaled-down Clarke ring connected by a series of space elevators to an artificial worldlet like something out of an Escher woodcut, festooned with colored lights like the aftermath of a Christmas decoration competition run amok. "We're at a Star Palace," she realized.

"But where?" Diego Narvaez asked.

"Antares, I'd say," Cecilia replied after studying the bright stars outside. "We've detected Star Palaces there, and the system configuration looks right. That would put us… a hundred seventy parsecs from home."

"How do we ever get home from here?" Evan Jiang whined.

"We should be trying to reach Cybele," Nik countered.

"Not this again," Diego fired back. "We have an obligation to report to Solsys about the aliens and the threat they pose."

The doctor sighed. "I know, I know. But I came out here hoping to build a new world."

"We all did," put in Ibrahim al-Bakri. The ecologist had felt utterly useless during his months in these technological prisons.

"They'd never have let us reach Cybele," James Oates insisted. "For all we know, they've invaded Earth already."

Hoping to deflect another of James's conspiratorial rants, Cecilia spoke up. "On the subject of building worlds, how in the hell can this Star Palace possibly work?" She pointed out the viewport. "Look at the angular motion in the starscape. The rotation period can't be more than ninety minutes. If it's canceling the Palace's gravity, given the apparent altitude of this ring, then its mass has to be greater than that of Davida," she said, referring to one of the larger Outer Belt asteroids. "But it's packed into such a small volume that it would have to consist partly of degenerate matter. How could that be?"

"It's been suggested that antimatter explosions could compress matter to a degenerate state," Diego mentioned idly, "so it could be coated in a layer of diamond to prevent its re-expansion. It would be incredibly difficult to pull off, though. And if the diamond shell ruptured, the whole thing would blow apart in the blink of an eye."

Amrita cackled, stroking Nik's shoulders. "Wonder if we could find a way to trigger that here. Kill all the monsters in one big bang." Evan and James joined in her laughter.

Nik squirmed under her grip, visibly disgusted, but he strove for calm. "What would that accomplish?" he asked his lover in a gentle tone.

But it was easier for Nik to soothe Amrita's hatred when Diego wasn't around to feed it. "A diversion," the taller man said. "A strike to ensure we'd be free from pursuit. Drastic, and unlikely to be achievable, but we should consider every option, no matter how remote." Diego's gaze bored into Nik's eyes. "Or how disturbing to the squeamish."

"Don't be so soft," Amrita advised. "It'd be over before they knew it, so no suffering." She chuckled. "More's the pity."

Nik pushed away from the windows, but Amrita followed. "Oh, lighten up, will you?"

The doctor caught a handhold and whirled on her. "There's nothing 'light' about the kind of jokes you all keep making. You of all people should know better."

"Me of all people? What's that supposed to mean?"

"You know!" Taking a breath to calm himself, he stroked Amrita's cheek, her rough-cut hair. "You know what it's like to suffer from other people's cruelty. I don't believe you'd really be so glad to see others suffer."

Amrita slapped him. "You bastard. You self-absorbed Sheaver with your cushy, entitled upbringing. You can't understand the evil of monsters like them. How much they relish causing suffering—how much they deserve to be shown what it really feels like."

"Okay, the Chirrn, that's one thing. But not all these aliens are Chirrn."

"They're helping them, that's enough. They're the enemy."

He sighed. "Maybe. But you don't have to enjoy it so much."

"You have no idea what I need."

"And I don't think I want to know! Look... this isn't working. From now on, we should just—"

"Fine," Amrita snarled before he could even finish putting the breakup into words. "I don't like weak men anyway."

Once Amrita had let Diego escort her away, Cecilia made her way over to the doctor. "I'm sorry," Nik told her once they could speak confidentially. "I thought I could help her heal, but she's too far gone. I'm afraid Diego's just making her and the others worse."

"Hey," Cecilia said. "Don't lose faith. We need to stand together in this."

"Why? Sometimes I have to wonder. I'm a Strider. My grandparents helped build the Ceres Sheaf. What am I doing in prison for loyalty to Earth, of all places?"

She met his eyes firmly. "Your loyalty is to your crew, Doctor. And to your oath. You're the only doctor we have."

"The Chirrn take excellent care of us."

"They can never understand what we need." She held his gaze. "Nik, don't waver on me now."

After a moment, the lanky Cerean sighed. "I'm sorry, Captain—I'm just frustrated. But I'm not going anywhere. Giving in to the Chirrn— it would mean giving up my independence, my identity as a human and a Strider. I mean, living in interstellar space, a nomadic existence between the stars—that would be a challenge worthy of the Striders. But only if we achieved it by our own choice, our own initiative. Not on anyone else's terms."

Cecilia smiled, heartened by his words. "That's the spirit, Nik. That's what we're fighting for in a nutshell."

The doctor threw a worried look toward Diego, Amrita, and their clique. "Do they know that?"

As Cecilia watched Diego and the other loyalists laughing and joking about killing soulless aliens *en masse*, she couldn't help hearing Churrlaya's words in her mind. Were they really making themselves stronger, better people through their defiance?

By clinging so fiercely to Earth, were they reinforcing their humanity—or losing it?

Sita and Stephen found Velesh's triad in an upper-level skybox of the Star Palace's sports arena, a high, tiered cylindrical space with perches and platforms at various levels and only hard, uncushioned ground at the bottom. About a dozen big, powerful Zenith males were competing in the air, striving to gain control of the higher, narrower levels at the others' expense. There were no teams; every individual Zenith fought everyone else, or at best formed temporary alliances until the time came to turn on one another. From the frantic way the falling athletes struggled to catch themselves on perches or platforms before reaching the bottom, and from the crowd's intense reactions to their success or failure, it was clear that touching the ground meant summary disqualification even if one avoided injury. It was a compelling spectacle, and Sita had to force herself to stay focused on their purpose.

The altitude of the Shayal's skybox suggested they were afforded high status by the Antarean Zenith. Yet Velesh watched the turbulent proceedings with thinly veiled distaste. Sita got the sense that the commissioner only attended to be polite.

"Quite the spectacle, isn't it?" Stephen said to draw the Shayal's attention.

The triad turned as one to take him in, then exchanged startled looks. Up close, Sita could see their differences from the Chirrn more clearly. Their maneless necks were longer and narrower, with additional bristles down the throat. Their brow ridges flared out and back to cup the ear slits, and wispy hairs grew underneath them. Their legs were stockier yet straighter than a Chirrn's, and their shorter feet did not end in prehensile digits. They would not be as comfortable in free fall as the Chirrn had engineered themselves to be. Velesh had pale blue-gray skin with subtle stripes down the back of the neck; his mates were greener to differing degrees.

Stephen introduced himself and Sita, and Velesh paused briefly before replying. "Welcome. Are your… guardians aware of your presence here?"

"Don't worry, we have an escort." Stephen gestured to Fred the Zhalevey, who stood nearby waiting patiently and adorably for instructions. Stephen's departure from their authorized area had been harder to mask than Sita's, even with L'chellin preoccupied with negotiations for access to Lode Seven, but Fred and her colleagues had orchestrated their distraction quite gracefully.

Sita patted the little triped on the head. "Couldn't be in safer hands. She's got three!"

"And we are supposed to be learning about Galactic civilization," Stephen added. "This seemed like an… informative place to be."

Velesh chose to interpret that as a reference to the sport/ritual combat they overlooked. "Yes. It can teach you much about the Zenith. This is no mere recreation; they battle for the favor of the Star Palace's alpha and her junior females. The higher the placement of the male in the final outcome, the higher the status of the females he becomes qualified to court. They gain additional prestige in the overall community from their athletic victory, of course, and in some Zenith subcultures that is an end in itself; but even there, the ultimate aspiration is to join the harem of a high-ranking female, even if the selection process is more informal." His knobby lips drew together. "In either case, however, the sport is a controlled manifestation of what was once a violent, often lethal competition. The Zenith have… matured much from what they were. But it is valuable to understand where they came from."

Velesh was clearly a natural lecturer, bordering on the pedantic. That could be useful. "It's been fascinating to learn all the variations on sexuality that have evolved on other worlds," Sita said, clasping Stephen's hand coquettishly. "The planet of origin you share with the Chirrn produced some surprising ones, if you don't mind my saying."

"Not an atypical reaction."

"Yet theirs is so different from yours. Would it be inappropriate to ask…"

"Not at all," Velesh told her. "Curiosity is an essential survival trait in the young. And an underappreciated one among elders, unfortunately. And there is much that you need to learn.

"The Chirrn's alternating sexuality is the natural pattern within our shared taxonomic class, a way of maximizing the birth rate in the harsh seas in which our forebears evolved. There are others of my genus—the one that left the ancestral world first—who retain that flexibility of gender. But we Shayal had ourselves modified with invariant sexuality, the better to relate to the majority of the galaxy's sophonts. My partners are male and female; I am a hermaphrodite, though I employ a masculine pronoun by Shayal convention, for I am committed to a non-procreative role. We traditionally bond in triads with one of each sex."

"Did you mod yourselves that way so you'd be better mentors?" Sita asked.

"That is one of its benefits." Velesh's chameleon eyes, smaller than a Chirrn's, focused more closely on her. "What have the Shilirrlaln told you about mentoring?"

"Well, for one thing," Sita went on, "that you were their mentors." It wasn't a lie, exactly; L'chellin had "told" Sita that through her body language toward the Shayal.

"Long ago, yes," Velesh confirmed.

"They were lucky," Stephen said with care, "to have someone to offer them guidance from the start. After all, you were already there when they evolved."

"Not exactly," the Shayal commissioner told him. "Our ancestors migrated into space before the Chirrn developed full sapience, so that we would not impede their development."

"But if the purpose is to guide them…"

"Guidance is usually only required at the onset of civilization, or a similar transformative event that alters a species' environment or way of life more abruptly than evolution can compensate for. Normally a species' behaviors are suited for its needs by the evolutionary process, but at times of rapid change, evolved behaviors and drives can become maladaptive and potentially harmful."

Stephen nodded. "Like, say, a hunter-gatherer species that develops herding and farming, comes to depend on them instead of hunting. The natural aggressive drives that once served them well lose their healthy outlet, and can be redirected into war, violent crime, oppression, even genocide." Sita met his eyes, noting the tension beneath his cool, scholarly delivery.

Velesh only acknowledged the surface, however. "Indeed. Or a people with strong herd instincts may have difficulty with the concept of political dissent, leaving them vulnerable to poor decisions by their leaders." He gestured toward Fred. "Or to abuse by others. The Zhalevey are so ancient that their mentoring history is largely legend, but they credit their mentors for teaching them to insist on limits to how far they would tolerate being exploited."

Pretty broad limits, Sita thought, before saying aloud: "Right, so what makes some lot of aliens more qualified to know the right way for them to behave?"

"There is no one 'right' way, even within a single species," Velesh corrected kindly, as Sita had intended. The perfect way to get information out of pedants was to get something wrong in their earshot. "The right way for a culture to live is something they must discover for themselves. Mentors simply give them the tools to make that investigation — help them learn how to ask the right questions and develop healthy, productive methods for arriving at their own answers."

Sita could tell her husband was genuinely intrigued. "Like scaffolding," Stephen said. "It's how a lot of humans teach our children. Just giving them the answers — or what we think are the answers — won't help them learn to make decisions for themselves. So instead of teaching them what to think, we teach them *how* to think critically, how to find their own solutions, how to distinguish good arguments from bad."

"Exactly," Velesh replied. "Mentoring is usually overseen by members of long-established, peaceful, and respected civilizations who have demonstrated the necessary maturity, patience, and delicacy. Primary mentors are usually selected based on similarity; for instance, an herbivorous species will be mentored by herbivores or omnivores. But secondary mentors are usually selected to offer a balancing perspective. Ideally, the mix is tailored to the unique psychological profile of each nascent civilization." He lifted his head proudly. "This is why the Nine Clusters Coalition has mentored so many civilizations successfully. We are one of the largest, most diverse civilizational clusters in this octant of the middle Disk."

"I'm so happy for you," Sita said. "But even so, it sounds like a hell of a risk. Sort of thing that could go pear-shaped — no offense — if you weren't careful."

"Truth abounds in this," Velesh said, gesturing emphatically. Arachne must have been smoothing over Sita's idioms in translation, which was probably for the best. "There have been…" He paused, then resumed more carefully. "Mistakes have occurred in the past. Different mentoring communities have… disagreed at times over the ideal application of the Mentoring Protocols. But those Protocols are the end result of *yanarrayth* of experimentation, error, and refinement. Besides — there is risk in raising a child. But would you abandon a child to grow up alone in the wilderness for fear of doing it harm? Before the Protocols evolved, many civilizations grew up traumatized, imbalanced, irrational. The galaxy was devastated by wars, conquests, and memetic plagues that exterminated whole civilizations."

Stephen stepped forward urgently, startling Velesh—and Sita. The Shayal's mates moved in closer, like bodyguards. "But obviously exceptions can be made. *We* weren't mentored. Nobody helped guide us away from our worst mistakes. We *were* abandoned in the wilderness. Never mind the thousands of years of human suffering, the wars, the oppression, the crushing poverty. If humanity had just been in contact with the larger galaxy, the Lesshchi disaster would never have occurred. All the tragedies we've inflicted and endured could've been avoided." There was an intensity in his voice that Sita had never heard before.

"I am sorry," Velesh said, bowing in a Chirrnlike gesture of sympathy and placation. "What your people have suffered, in the past and now, is unconscionable. Unfortunately… the Coalition has never held jurisdiction over the Four Voids. I cannot answer your questions about mentoring policies—or lack thereof—within this region."

"'Cannot answer,'" Sita echoed, moving to stand by Stephen. "Because you don't know? Or for some other reason?"

"Again, I apologize. But I am bound by the Protocols, and now that the Shilirrlaln have… however belatedly… taken on the role of the Arachnen's mentors, I must defer to their judgment. I can speak to you about galactic history as a general subject, but when it comes to your own mentoring, I fear I am proscribed from intervening."

Sita frowned. "But I thought the whole reason you were here was to intervene. To push for a change in the Void Alliance's policies."

"That is a matter to be decided between the Coalition and the Alliance. As much as I would like to assist you, my options are constrained until that debate is resolved."

Something happened in the arena that triggered a shrieking roar from the Zenith spectators, and Velesh turned his gaze back outward. "Excuse me," he said. "Events are moving toward a point of decision."

Once it became clear that the conversation was over, Stephen led Sita out of the skybox. "Yes," he murmured to her. "I'm beginning to think they are."

When Stephen and Sita filled in the senior personnel about what they'd learned of the Mentoring Protocols—with Sita characterizing them as "a happy medium between the Civilizing Mission and the

Prime Directive" — the reactions ranged from shock to confusion to anger. Tarik Bahar in particular reacted with anguish and suspicion. "Why didn't the Chirrn tell us any of this?" *Arachne*'s acting captain still struggled to maintain an even keel in the wake of his family tragedy, even more than Stephen and Sita did, for Kweli's pregnancy had been significantly further along. Only his need to be strong for his inconsolable wife, and his unbreakable sense of duty to the rest of the Arachnen, had held him together.

"Hard to say," Sita answered gently. "But there seems to be some bad blood between them and their mentors."

"What if these Shayal botched their mentoring of the Chirrn?" Oyama Kazuko asked. The elegant Martian administrator paced the common room in thought. "Remember the history L'chellin told us? The great war between their planetary and spaceborne civilizations? That doesn't seem like something that should happen under these Protocols."

"Obviously, the Protocols don't always work," Stephen told her, "or humanity wouldn't have been… *overlooked*. For thousands of years… through conquests and holocausts, famines and plagues, slavery and tyranny…" *Children gunned down in the streets…* "Nobody once came to our aid."

"We managed well enough despite that," Kazuko said. "Cecilia would say it made us stronger."

Stephen shot to his feet. "You don't need to go through hell to be strong!" Kazuko grew very still, studying him with wary calm. He looked down, controlling his anger, remembering what kind of man he chose to be. "And it leaves you with… deep weaknesses too," he went on. "We know how trauma damages the mind, how the abused become abusers. We know it can happen on the level of whole societies — entire cultures traumatized by conquest or fanaticism or natural disaster, left with only violence and despair. We know from our own educators, our own common sense, that the young need freedom without being abandoned." He took solace in the thought of his mother. So many of his peers in Florida had been orphans or victims of abuse. Stephen had grown up barely knowing his father Harry, a man swallowed up by a prison system designed to harden young black offenders into career inmates as a slave labor force for the state. But Theresa Wong had been a pillar of strength and patience, a teacher and activist who had given Stephen and his siblings the love, support, and education they had needed to find their way to that better path when so many had been lost. Without her, he would never have made it to the stars.

Yet she had died in pain, grieving the younger son who had been killed for trying to steal medicine to save her—both of them victims of a culture-wide pathology that humanity had suffered from for millennia. A pathology that, perhaps, they might have been spared.

"Yes," Sita said, "animals that endure trauma can be more violent, more abusive than those raised under more positive circumstances. Particularly in social species, losing parents or nurturers can produce a generation lacking healthy social skills, predisposed to pathological, destructive behavior—like the street gangs of your childhood, Stephen, or the elephant bands in India that lashed out against the humans who devastated their communities back before the sapient rights reforms.

"But—but aggression is still an innate behavior in most species. Even without pathology to amplify it, it's still present, able to be brought to bear at a moment's notice. All it takes is a single unanticipated disaster to turn… even the most civilized and orderly of sophonts into murdering savages." Stephen could see that the memory still haunted her. He took her hand, and she smiled up at him briefly and gathered herself. "So we can't make assumptions about what might have gone wrong with the Chirrn, or whether these vaunted Protocols even work. I know you want to believe it's possible to overcome suffering and injustice with enough effort, intellect, and resources, but—"

"I hear what you're saying," he said. "But these Protocols, they make sense. It's logical that advanced civilizations would find a better solution than either cultural imperialism or total abandonment. That over a *yanarrayth*, a hundred million years or more, they'd refine contact into a science far more sophisticated than anything we ever managed."

Yet it was impossible for Stephen to contemplate that promise without running up against the overriding, agonizing question it created: *Why was humanity cheated of that?*

Why were Mama and Benjamin cheated of their lives?

4

ON THE ARACHNEN'S THIRD DAY IN THE STAR PALACE, KWELI NDEGE decided it was time to stop mourning.

It had not been an easy resolution to reach. The sympatholytic treatments after the Lesshchin attack had eased the emotional trauma of the incident itself, but they couldn't prevent Kweli from being aware, during every waking moment, of the emptiness in her belly, the gaping hole in the middle of her being. They couldn't change the fact that she spent every day surrounded by reminders of her loss. Antidepressants could only do so much, and neither she nor Tarik would accept any more radical treatment, anything that would excise her memory of their unborn son or her ability to grieve for him. Her memory of him was all she had left.

She knew it had been hard on Tarik, caring for her through her grief when he bore so much of his own. The time he spent with her was just a reminder of his loss, and though she loved him dearly for standing unwaveringly by her side, she felt guilty imposing that burden upon him.

But the more time Kweli spent amid the beauty of the Antares B Star Palace and its wonderfully diverse denizens, the more she knew that here was a place where she could find solace. And so she allowed Tarik to convince her to join him and several others on a tour of the habitat's attractions, chaperoned by Mediator Broadwing. Tarik's tearful smile when she agreed to come out with him brought her great contentment.

Now they stood together on a viewing deck high above the Star Palace's surface, where the gravity was noticeably lower. Calling it just a deck was an injustice; it was a whole park, a broad, domed-in area over a hundred meters in radius, with six residential towers serving as support legs and a seventh piercing the center and rising dozens of stories above the dome. Exotic flora approximating trees filled much of its volume, with broad paths separating clusters of different types of vegetation—from different planets? Kweli assumed there must be biochemical compatibility issues involved, but surely interstellar civilization had had millennia or more to work them out.

The view beyond the dome was just as spectacular. Both Antares stars were immersed in the sloughed-off remains of the dying supergiant's atmosphere, a dense planetary nebula that glowed yellow-orange, lit up by the central star like a Japanese lantern. But half the sky was filled with a brighter blue-magenta glow—reflected light from the B star blending with fluorescence from the surrounding nebulosity excited by its radiation, so Tarik explained while she pretended to understand. Even as Kweli watched, the brilliant blue pinpoint of Antares B ascended slowly behind the fairy-castle skyline, causing fingers of ruddy shadow to caress the upthrust contours of the cityscape below. Refractive or photoreactive layers in many of the towers caught the light and redirected it, amplified it, subverted it to enhance the towers' own resplendence. Astronomers back in Solsys had observed the shimmering radiance of the occupied Star Palaces without ever knowing the reasons for it. Now, Kweli understood the displays as manifestations of Zenith psychology, their overpowering need to outcompete each other in altitude and glory. It brought her immense satisfaction to finally have the answer to one of exobiology's greatest mysteries.

She derived further pleasure from observing the other guests who had come to enjoy the flora and watch the sunrise. The range of body types in evidence surprised her, with few conforming to an upright bipedal plan; yet Kweli noted recurring anatomical features among what appeared at first glance to be different species. When she quizzed one of the ubiquitous Zhalevey helpers, the solicitous triped confirmed that, like the Chirrn and Shayal, those species had spawned from a common planet of origin—or in some cases, a single species had diverged into an entire genus as it spread across the galaxy over millions of years. Kweli delighted in the discovery. She knew she would never have the opportunity to study all these variations of life, to learn about their evolutionary histories and interrelations; but here and now it was enough to experience the raw sense of wonder, knowing others would do the work in the future.

After watching Zenith dive through openings in the broad central tower and spiral down to other levels far below, Kweli convinced Tarik to take her gliding. The Zenith-designed habitat had so many wide, high interior spaces that there was abundant room for it, whether with one's own wings or with artificial substitutes, and regular gliding tours were offered for visitors. A few known species were close enough to a hominid shape that the Zhalevey were able to call up a pair of gliders suitable for human use. The safety straps were a bit loose even on Kweli's well-rounded frame, but she assured Tarik that all she had to do was hold on. He was so happy to see her serene and active that he let himself stop fussing over her just this once.

The dense atmosphere meant the wings were smaller than an Earthly hang glider, which made it easier to maneuver and swoop through the grand, vaulted spaces of the Star Palace. They dove through immense, cathedral-roofed canyons, rode updrafts from enormous ventilation grates, and soared past wide shafts boring deep into the habitat, where the intense gravitational pull of the PQM drew down the air and drove the Star Palace's circulatory patterns. They even found themselves caught up in a light shower, for the interior spaces were vast enough for weather to form. Kweli laughed with Tarik as the cool water spattered their faces, as she breathed in the refreshing fragrance of the rain. This was the way to experience this wondrous place: the way its builders had intended, soaring on high through the air. Kweli felt her burdens lift away.

It was time.

She waited until Tarik was distracted before curving away, angling her course back toward the bore shaft. By the time she heard him screaming her name, the downdraft had already caught her, sucking her down to the lower levels where the gravity grew exponentially stronger the nearer she came to the PQM layer. The glider made alert sounds and tried to angle her back to safety. But all she had to do was slip out of the loose straps… and stop holding on.

She was weightless. And at last she was free.

Kweli Ndege's medical expertise had let her choose her method of suicide all too well. The Star Palace's finest surgeons, working with the migration fleet's Doctor Mh'lellish and consulting with Joana Caravalho

National Suicide Prevention Lifeline
Help is available. Speak with a counselor today: 1-800-273-8255

on the finer points of human anatomy, worked for hours to recover what they could—but the gravity at the base of the ventilation shaft had been high enough that her brain and body were beyond repair. Kweli had made certain there was no coming back.

Doctor Rauhoc delivered the news. Tarik had resisted letting the massive, bone-plated alien anywhere near his wife, but L'chellin had assured him that for a Gaurim surgeon to be available on a Star Palace's staff was a rare and fortuitous circumstance, and if Rauhoc could not save Kweli, then no one could. Yet now Tarik raged at Rauhoc, at L'chellin and Broadwing, at whoever he could find. "How could you have let this happen? All your technology—how could that shaft not have been safeguarded against jumpers?" Stephen held him back from going at them physically, though the only reason he wasn't screaming at them himself was that Tarik was doing it for him.

"There was no sign that Kweli was in distress," Broadwing explained, his body language subdued. "Her equipment was functioning properly, and her actions were calm and deliberate. There was nothing to suggest to any monitoring systems or individuals that anything was amiss until it was too late to act."

Joana sighed heavily. "In humans, suicide is often preceded by serenity, calm, even apparent happiness. Relief that the pain will finally end soon, a sense that all one's burdens have lifted."

Tarik had fallen quiet, sagging in Stephen's grip. "She was so… content. So resolved. She drank in all the sights and experiences so eagerly… I thought she was finally healing. But she just… she wanted one last perfect day before…" He couldn't finish.

Rauhoc stepped forward, his gentle manner belying his frightening appearance. "The administration wishes me to convey its deepest condolences," he rumbled. "We do all we can to make Zenith facilities safe for non-flying species, but the precautions are designed against accident, not… self-destruction. Such a degree of untreated mental illness is exceedingly rare."

"It *was* being treated," Joana protested. "We've done everything we could to help the mothers through this. But there was only so much we could do under… the circumstances."

"The circumstances!" Tarik cried. "You mean being trapped here, no choice in our fate, no way to free ourselves from the Chirrn! We're still prisoners as much as ever," he shouted at L'chellin. "Kweli never had a chance!"

Stephen led Tarik over to the far wall and held him for a moment until he settled down. Tarik clung to him and murmured to himself in Turkish, which Arachne subtitled: *"Whoever curbs his anger while being able to execute it, Allah will fill his heart with certainty of faith."* Finally he said, "I'm sorry. I'm the one who should've seen the signs." He turned away, muttering, "It was my job to protect her," and pushed through the doors into the waiting area. Stephen went after him, but by the time he got through the doors, Tarik had already rushed past the others who bided outside, their condolences too much for him to bear.

No, Stephen thought as he gazed after his friend. *It was my job.* He had been responsible for every member of this expedition since he had first recruited them. He had convinced them to put their lives in his hands, and all that had resulted was turmoil and tragedy. He thought he had prepared them for the risks of an unprecedented journey, but he'd been a fool to think he had the slightest idea what that would mean. He had named the expedition's vessel all too aptly. Like Ovid's Arachne, he was being punished for his hubris. The difference was that he had brought down punishment on thousands of others in the process. How many more members of his crew would suffer for his arrogance?

Cecilia had been uneasy when Churrlaya had escorted her to a private room to meet with Stephen. Although a part of her still missed her old friend, she feared that the Stephen she knew was lost. Sitting through another sales pitch to abandon her allegiance and self-reliance, to spend the rest of her life as a prisoner or a dependent refugee at best, would only be a painful reminder of how deep the rift between them had grown.

She was therefore taken aback when she saw the grief on Stephen's face, the way he seemed weighted down even in the microgravity of the docking ring. "What happened?" she demanded.

He wasted no time on preliminaries; at least he still respected her contempt for such things. Yet as he told her, slowly and plainly, how Kweli Ndege had taken her own life, Cecilia almost wished he had cushioned the blow somehow. But nothing really could have. A member of her crew was dead. There was no worse news a captain could ever hear.

And she feared that Kweli would only be the first.

She threw a glance toward Churrlaya, the only convenient target for the burst of rage and hatred she felt toward the Chirrn. Yet he gazed at her with silent sympathy. He had spoken to her so often of his grief and loss that she knew intimately how those emotions looked on a Chirrn, and what she saw now was a reflection of her own pain.

No, he was not the one who deserved her anger this time. "How much longer?" she demanded of Stephen. "How much more do you have to lose before you realize that submission to the Chirrn is toxic for us?"

He clung to a handhold to steady himself. "You don't need to remind me of what I've lost, Cecilia. But it all goes back to the same loss. The same tragedy. All these sorrows are ripples from Lesshchi." He glanced at Churrlaya, but he could not hold the Lesshchin's gaze. "We won't be free of them until we find a way to heal the wounds and move on. We can't do that unless we do it together, Cecilia. All of us."

"I knew it. I knew you would do this! Even this, you have to turn into a speech!"

"You're the one who can't let go of your agenda! I came here to tell you about Kweli because you were her friend, her captain. Because you deserve to know, to grieve with the rest of us. And the first thing you do is start up the argument again. Can't you ever let your guard down, Cecilia? Even now?"

She could feel her face flushing; it came more easily without gravity to hold the blood down. In truth, she feared how Diego and the others would react to this news. After their exercise period the day before, Diego, Amrita, James, and Evan had continued to entertain themselves by brainstorming ways to destroy the Star Palace to cover their escape. Seeing the Chirrn as the enemy was one thing, but their enthusiasm at the prospect of killing countless other, innocent aliens disturbed Cecilia sufficiently that she'd finally spoken up to discourage their malevolent fantasies—which had gained nothing but their resentment. She doubted very much that they could find a way to realize their plans, but she feared for the morale and unity of the loyalists as their captivity continued with no sign of hope.

She sighed. "I just don't understand why you're not with me now, of all times. When you—" She hesitated to land what might be a low blow. But when they had been friends, he had always valued her candor. If she had any hope of regaining that friendship, she couldn't pull her punches now. "When you lost Benjamin and your mother, you moved heaven and earth to get your sisters out of the Gulf Coast. How can you be so complacent a prisoner after what you've lost now?"

Stephen's answer was tightly controlled. "I lost them because of people who refused to take responsibility for the harm their actions caused. I will not let myself become one of those people. God knows, now more than ever I have reason to want to blame the Chirrn for everything we've suffered. More reason than you know." He stopped himself, throwing a furtive glance toward Churrlaya, and Cecilia wondered what he couldn't say in front of a Chirrn. "But that would be the same kind of unthinking bigotry that trapped my family in poverty. The Shilirrlaln saved many lives in the attack, including Sita's, even if they couldn't save all the babies. And they have forgiven me for a hideous crime for which I can never forgive myself. They're just people, like us—trying to lead the best lives they can, trying to cope with the pain and the tragic mistakes of the past. And sometimes they fail. Just as we do."

He blinked, wiping moisture from his eyes, then absently rolled the beads of moisture between his fingers. "We all failed Kweli. Nobody gets to be self-righteous about that. She needed us, but we had our own grief, our own burdens weighing on us… Oh, God, Cecilia, it's just too much. All the lives lost… it's too much for any of us to bear. And that's why we need each other, why we should all be together."

Stephen reached out to her. "I miss you, my friend. I need you. I try—I try to be the strong, stalwart leader, to give them all courage, but I can't do it like you. I can't do it *without* you. I'm… I'm…I can't…"

It was the last thing Cecilia had expected. But in a way, it was something she'd been longing for. She hated to see him in such pain—but it brought deep comfort to know she still cared for him so much.

In all the years they'd been friends, she'd never initiated a hug. It had always amused him that even though she was the proud Italian, he was the physically demonstrative one. Now, she pushed off the wall and came to him, embraced him. He clung to her desperately and cried for a very long time. She stroked his hair, occasionally saying nonsense like "Hey" and "It's" and "Um" and "You'll" and never finding a second word that meant anything. Somehow he took comfort in it anyway, thanking her with wordless, shuddering breaths.

Finally, when it ended, he put his thanks into words. "I've needed that for a long time. A chance to just… turn off the leader face and cry on someone's shoulder."

"Can't you do that with Sita?"

"Sita… It's been hard for her, to share me with everyone else. I haven't made it easy. Losing our baby… that made it harder for both of us. Honestly, she came through it better than I did. Found her own footing. Talked some sense into me just the other day, in fact. I think we're starting to find each other at last, and it's all thanks to her. But… well, other matters have arisen, and we haven't really had a chance to build on it."

Cecilia pursed her lips. "I admit, I'm surprised. Didn't think there was that much substance to her. She got… broken pretty badly more than once."

"She's not as fragile as she looks. I don't think I got that myself until the past few days." He smirked at her. "Anyway, I thought you were a 'That which does not kill us makes us stronger' kind of person."

"Yeah, but only if we have the conviction to use it that way." She sighed. "Which is why I can't stop resisting the Chirrn. That's the only way I can be true to the ideals *you* taught me. Stephen, you're *still* trapped by others' bigotry. I don't understand why you can't see that."

He closed his eyes in regret—then glanced at Churrlaya again. "No, I'm afraid you *don't* understand. There's so much I wish I could tell you… but all I can do is trust you to figure it out for yourself."

"You sound like them. You're complicit in their secrets! Stephen, what aren't you—"

He put his fingers on her lips, and she amazed herself by allowing it. "Don't worry about it now. You're right, we've had this argument enough. It's gotten us nowhere." He clasped her hands. "This… this did me more good than anything has in a long time. I hope, maybe, it'll do you good too, once you have time to reflect on it." He released one of her hands so he could cup her cheek. "It was so good to have this again, dear friend. I love you, Cecilia. We all do."

He clearly didn't expect her to say she loved him too. But once he'd left and Churrlaya had led her from the room, she began to regret that she hadn't.

On the way back to confinement, Cecilia dreaded telling the others, fearing how Diego's clique would use this to fuel their rage. Even Churrlaya provided no distraction. Weeks ago, she would have expected a lecture about how humans devalued their own lives as well as others, or how the ultimate blame lay with the humans for destroying Lesshchi. Now, she was not sure what to expect. "You've been awfully quiet," she finally said.

The Chirrn brooded… and then surprised her. "I fear I have no right to speak. To lose a loved one, with none of their self or memory preserved… even to say I understand would feel accusatory."

In its way, his refusal to damn her for his loss merely left room for her to damn herself. Yet somehow, in the wake of it, Churrlaya's resumed silence felt oddly supportive, as if they had finally achieved some mutual understanding.

Once they arrived at the cell, she lingered outside, doubting that her own people would give her so much space to grieve. How had she grown so far apart from her crew? Was it Stockholm syndrome? Some deft psychological manipulation by Churrlaya?

Or was it instead that her crew was growing apart from her? If so… how could she break this news to them without worsening the rift?

The shock of Kweli's suicide had overridden the Arachnen's concerns over the Mentoring Protocols at first, but with time to reflect, their grief only intensified their larger questions and doubts. Tarik was quick to suggest confronting the Chirrn about the insinuations from Velesh and the orderly Sunflash that they were somehow at fault for humanity's lack of mentoring.

But Stephen wasn't ready to rush to judgment. As much as it agonized him to discover that all the horrors humanity had endured—all his own family had endured—could have been prevented, he wouldn't lash out at the first available target and risk scuttling all the work the Arachnen had done to earn redemption. As he'd told Cecilia, a part of him still wanted to blame all the Chirrn for what some had done to his baby, his wife, his friends. But that was his own traumas driving him, the kind of unhealthy impulse he'd spent a lifetime training himself to resist. He felt he'd gotten a lot of that pain out of his system thanks to Cecilia's kindness.

So he convinced the others to keep the matter to themselves for now, until he could find out more and decide on a course of action. He thanked his lucky stars that Tarik's loyalty and his faith were dug so deep in his bones, for those were the only things that could hold his anguished rage in check.

Afterward, he set those concerns aside in favor of a more pressing responsibility. He made his way to the viewing deck where, according to Tarik, Kweli had begun her last day — the place where she had finally found herself at peace. As much as he regretted, even resented the choice she'd made — suicide was so selfish in its way, causing pain to so many others simply to end one's own — he couldn't blame her for the damage her circumstances had done, and he owed it to her to remember the effervescent, nurturing spirit she had been. So he stood there, where she had stood in her last hour of contentment, and remembered her.

After a time, he realized that Broadwing now crouched next to him, keeping his rainbow-crested head level with Stephen's in a gesture of respect. He met the Zenith's three eyes."Broadwing."

"Stephen." The pattern of calliope tones Broadwing used, as Stephen understood it, was a proper-name inflection of the Zenith for "matriarch's crests," the closest equivalent to his given name's literal meaning of "crown." Probably better than using his full name, which effectively translated as "Crown of the Usurper King" — a fact he tried not to think about much.

"You contemplate loss?" Broadwing asked.

"Yes."

"As we all have done too often in these times."

"Yes."

"When loss comes, we seek answers. We look for some cause we can confront and transcend."

Stephen looked at him, hesitant to reply. "That's a common response. But I think it's better to simply face the loss. To remember what was lost… try to keep it alive inside you." He remembered Sita's words from three days before. "Looking for someone to blame is just a way to avoid facing your pain."

Broadwing lowered his neck fractionally — the barest gesture of submission to concede the point. "This is always your way, Stephen. To look to the heights you can climb to rather than the depths that would drag you down into them."

He nodded, wondering at the similarity of the gesture. "I believe in hope. At least… I try to. It can be hard sometimes… but that's when you need hope the most. I learned that back on Earth, when I lost my brother and my mother. I was tempted to lash out at the establishment that had let them die, but that would've just gotten me killed too and left my family worse off. Instead, I focused on hope. I found ways to improve our situation, gain allies, and finally get myself and my sisters out of there. Hope did more good... well, for those of us who survived."

Broadwing raised his head a bit. "There may yet be hope for the lost as well."

Stephen stared. "What do you mean?"

"It is a faint cloud — some call it a mirage. But many see reason buoying it up. They suggest that the metasapient civilizations, ever hungry for input and complexity, have pervaded the galaxy with sensors at a level of attotechnology too fine for us to detect. That they can track and record the motion of every particle, its electromagnetic emissions, the ripples it creates in the Higgs field... perhaps information we cannot conceive. And the patterns of life, of thought, must be complex enough to hold their interest. So it may be that they record and track the patterns of every mind."

"I thought L'chellin said they were only aware of us in the aggregate, not as individuals."

"That does not matter. If they crave complexity so much, depend on it for their sanity and stimulation, they would let no patterns go to waste. If a mind were lost to death, they would lose input, and they would not tolerate that."

Stephen furrowed his brow, controlling his reactions. "So... you're suggesting that they'd duplicate the patterns of thought they recorded?"

"Perhaps more than duplicate. If their sensors are so pervasive, so subtle, they may be able to capture those patterns directly, preserve them when a physical body dies. Much as a Chirrn network preserves the portion of a mind that extends into it, and an echo of the patterns anchored within the flesh mind. But perhaps more fully, for the metaminds would tolerate no loss of data or activity."

"Are you saying you believe that the..." He didn't know if "souls" would translate. "The consciousness of everyone who died — everyone who's ever died — has been preserved and uploaded into some kind of virtual afterlife?"

"This is nothing so crude as planetary superstition, Stephen. We know for a fact that the metaminds' environments hold enough computing complexity to model entire universes. They could easily sustain those minds in their original patterns, or allow them to expand into metasapience themselves. Given their need for complexity, if they can do it, it is a virtual certainty that they would."

Stephen was at once touched and saddened. Broadwing's proposal was compellingly plausible… but the same could be said about many human religious beliefs. Metasapients may have been tangibly real, but their motives could only be speculated about. However solidly reasoned the argument, it was based in postulates rather than data and thus was as much an article of faith as anything Tarik or Sita or Haim believed in. Although he respected those beliefs and the comfort and inspiration they brought, he knew from hard experience that religion was only as good as the intentions of its believers. He had always preferred to put his faith in what sapient beings could achieve through their own determination and effort. It wasn't enough for him to sit back and hope that higher powers would solve his problems. After all, they never had before.

But he was puzzled as well. "I thought you told me that Zenith saw metasapience as a false ascension. If you think people's… consciousnesses are being captured and preserved in their environments, wouldn't you see that as damnation rather than salvation?"

The mediator reared back, clacking his mandibles, then regained his control. "I said *most* Zenith felt that way."

"Ahh. You never said you were one of them."

That sharp-crested skull trembled; his talons dug into the ground cover. "At least, most Zenith profess to feel that way, for admitting otherwise is… dangerous."

"Why? Why Zenith specifically?"

Broadwing looked around. "I have said more than is wise in this environment. But I can guide you to one who will explain. Not only this, but other mysteries you seek to unravel."

Stephen blinked. It had been a Zenith whose seemingly offhand comments had fired Sita's curiosity about mentoring… and even given her small size, she had found it unexpectedly easy to slip free from Broadwing's supervision and gather the information that had led her to the Protocols.

Seeing his reaction, Broadwing stiffly affected a human nod, a confirmation if ever there was one. The symbolism was clear in Zenith terms as well: by lowering his eyes below Stephen's, he was subordinating himself to the human's choices—placing his trust in Stephen to protect his secrets.

"All right," Stephen said. "Where do we go next?"

Stephen was startled when Sita resisted accompanying him to Broadwing's meeting. "You were the one saying we needed to do this together. You were the one who started this!"

"Not *this!*" she protested. "I only wanted to find the truth. Now I find that Broadwing's got some hidden agenda. Stephen, all your life you've striven for honesty, integrity. Now you're sneaking about and attending secret meetings? Doesn't that trouble you?"

"All of this troubles me. But we need answers. At least we should hear what Broadwing's connections have to say. And I could really use you with me."

Sita pondered for a few moments, then sighed. "Right, then. I suppose if you trusted me enough to go along with me, it's only fair I do my bit in return." He'd hoped for more enthusiasm, but it would do.

Tarik had wished to attend as well, craving answers, but Stephen had feared this rendezvous would feed his suspicions and undermine his efforts to rein in his anger. He had convinced Tarik that the others needed his presence and protection. With luck, that could help the acting captain rebuild his confidence in the wake of his imagined failure to protect Kweli.

So for now it was only Stephen and Sita, along with Arachne's avatar as guard and translator, who joined Broadwing in descending to the lower levels of the Star Palace. The Zenith mediator had worked with Arachne to modify their old prisoner confinement suit design from the trial into strength-boosting servo suits to cope with the higher gravity at these depths. Still, Stephen could feel the weight in his own viscera, a sense of being relentlessly pulled down.

The architecture didn't help. Most Zenith may have shunned these levels, leaving them to their own lowest-ranking members and to other, high-gravity or nocturnal species; but even these depths were designed with the Zenith's inherent craving for altitude in mind. The space was vast and echoing, a forest of skyscraper-thick columns that branched outward into a fractal array of flying buttresses and arches supporting the great vaulted ceiling overhead, the floor of the bright and gleaming world up above. The domed vaults contained openings resembling clerestory windows, channeling light and air from above. Stretching between the immense, window-studded columns at various levels were wide, arched skywalks nearly as wide as city blocks, with walkways on either side and dwellings or businesses along the middle. Everything was designed to make the Zenith feel high above the ground, even while well beneath it.

The residents here provided their own light, in bright colors as garish and raucous as those on the grand promenades and boulevards above; but here in the near-literal underground, it had more of the seedy flavor of old Las Vegas or the Niihama habitat in the Belt than the clean, commercial pageantry of the upper levels. The chatter of alien voices and music was more intense and frenetic. Strange scents and vapors filled the air. Sophonts could be seen doing things to each other that might be violent or erotic or both. And that was just in the streets. The hints of sight, sound, and scent from the doorways they passed suggested that what went on outdoors was just a taste of what could be found within.

The group passed a street fight between a Gaurim and a member of a sibling species, browner and more elongated with more pronounced spikes along the head and flanks. They used the clubs on their twin rear limbs to swing at each other's horn-plated heads and flanks. It reminded Stephen of animal mating competitions, but their audience included no other members of their species; from the look of things, the crowd was betting on the fight. When the other fighter's longer limbs snuck past the Gaurim's defenses, clubbing it in the knee with a forceful crack, the audience roared with bloodlust as it tumbled to the ground. "Ruddy hell," Sita said. "Don't tell Diana about this place, or we'll never get her to leave."

Arachne moved her spider-woman avatar between her party and the fight spectators, keeping several wary eyes on the rowdy group. "I gathered that mentoring was supposed to raise mature, healthy civilizations."

"Even a healthy society needs its release valves, I suppose," Sita replied. "And mentoring is supposed to give civilizations the freedom to do things their own way."

"Indeed," chimed Broadwing, who walked in his crouched stance, the gravity high even for him. "All you see are here voluntarily, with full knowledge of any risks they take. And the Star Palace's safeguards are as present here as everywhere else. Recall, most Galactics are not easy to kill. Those who are… generally choose to be, and their choice is respected." He gave a small shudder.

"But not always welcomed," Stephen commiserated.

"Yes. I have seen too much death of late. That is why I endorsed this migration following the Lesshchin assault on your childbearers. I knew it would most likely be directed toward the Antispinward Void. You were correct before, Sita, about the impact of the migrational shift resulting from the Eta Carinae hypernova. Civilizations which had left the Chirrn alone for millennia, due to their preoccupation with the diaspora, are beginning to exert pressure once again."

"Such as the Shayal?" Sita asked.

"Yes. They are major players in the Nine Clusters Coalition, and they have a… turbulent history with the Chirrn. I knew the Chirrn would want to increase their hold on the Void by establishing a new habitat here. That meant obtaining a PQM supply from Lode Seven, and that meant passing through Antares. And here was where I could find one whose wing I crouched beneath in my youth — one I thought I had left behind, until Lesshchi renewed my need for hope to soar beyond this life. One I believe can help you as well — if nothing more, by giving you the truths the Chirrn have kept hidden."

Broadwing's words made Stephen wary. Was he just taking them to see some kind of fringe spiritual leader, offering them the solace of metasapient heaven?

The Zenith led the party up an arched walkway, one of six that converged to support a large hexagonal pavilion festooned with great, down-angled windows. The two Zenith who met them at the pavilion's entrance were also crouched, but they were females; their triple headcrests were larger than Broadwing's, their tripartite beaks more hooked and pointed, and the halter-type harnesses they wore over their chests and keels were more utilitarian than his, less skimpy and ornate. Once he had made proper obeisance gestures and sounds — an even more elaborate ritual than those Stephen had observed among other Zenith — the females led the group inside, where several more females awaited, including one Sita clearly recognized. "Sunflash," the biologist greeted her. "Imagine finding you here."

The orderly gave a bow conveying polite contrition seasoned with defiance. "I played my part as instructed. That is all."

"Is it, now? Instructed by whom, then?"

But the answer quickly became obvious as Sunflash and the other females turned to make obeisance to a new arrival. This female was even more impressive to behold, her crests the most vivid in the room, her bearing the most confident. She was attended by a large group of males clad only in jewelry, no doubt her harem. From what Stephen had learned of Zenith society, the other females must be her apprentices, adolescents who served the matriarch until they could earn sufficient status to claim a few males from the harem and strike out on their own. The size of her retinue suggested high status. Yet most of the Zenith in the room were unimpressive to look at—their crests comparatively small and drab-hued, their featherfur dull and scruffy, their wings diminutive, their limbs short, their coordination lacking. Even their jewels were less resplendent than those worn by the Zenith up above. These were the sort of Zenith who would only be found at these depths—the lowest in status, the social outcasts, the geeks.

Indeed, as Stephen looked closer at the matriarch, he saw that the glamorous impression she conveyed was largely by contrast with the disreputable group around her. But it was more than that. The matriarch was perhaps not conventionally beautiful by Zenith standards as Stephen understood them. She was small, stocky, her featherfur indifferently shiny, her beak and talons not extraordinarily sharp. Her movements were stiff, suggesting she was a fair way along in an aging process not halted or reversed by regular medical care. She was as much an outcast as the rest. Yet her confidence and poise were clear in the way she held her head high, and her rainbow crests, the most vivid in the room, were a clear indicator of her superior status. The way the males looked at her and tended to her—particularly the way Broadwing's eyes widened and his tail stiffened at the sight of her (and the innuendo there was somewhat accurate, given Zenith anatomy)—reinforced the impression of power and allure… which, to Zenith, were much the same thing.

Yet the matriarch did not engage in the expected posturing as she moved forward to greet her visitors. She maintained a crouch level with Stephen's height rather than looming over him, implicitly greeting him as an equal. She gave a calliope chime as she shook her head in a Zenith greeting gesture. "Stephen Jacobs-Wong," came the translation, "I am Meridian. Welcome to the community of the galaxy."

Stephen did his best to repeat the gesture. "Thank you, Meridian. I am honored by your welcome."

"It is overdue."

Once Stephen had introduced the others, Meridian sang back the translation of Sita's full name, or as close as Arachne could approximate it. "Harvest Goddess of the Morning Light. A resplendent name, well-suited for one of such a gifted species at the dawn of its greatness. And yet you have been unfairly shunned by those above. Come—rest and dine with us so we may remedy that." These Zenith were like their counterparts above in one respect: they conducted all their business over food. Just walking in this gravity must have had a metabolic cost not unlike flying.

"I appreciate the sentiment," Stephen replied. "But their fear of us is understandable, given the tragedy we were responsible for."

"Lesshchi only reinforced their existing fears of feral sophonts," Meridian replied. "And the Chirrn have done nothing to change this."

A slightly smaller Zenith female, her crests nearly as resplendent, awaited them at the table. "My second, Apastron," the matriarch said in introduction.

"You are most welcome," Apastron said. "Broadwing informed us of your dietary requirements. You may be assured the meal is suitable for human consumption." Arachne's avatar gave the table a quick once-over and silently verified this with an eyetext.

"You mentioned feral sophonts," Sita interposed once they'd sat down to eat. "You mean unmentored?"

"Yes," Meridian replied. "To most Galactics, those who are not mentored are considered wild and dangerous."

Stephen frowned. "But what does that have to do with the Chirrn?"

"The connection is intimate. The Chirrn were mentors once." Meridian paused. "Our mentors."

Well, Stephen thought once his initial surprise died down. *Parental issues. Don't expect the most objective assessment here.*

Meridian peered at Stephen. "Tell me what the Chirrn have told you about their history. Did they speak of a war?"

"Yes," Stephen said. "A great war between their early space colonists and their home planet. Eventually, they migrated into the galaxy to put an end to it."

"That is a lie." The matriarch reared her head back with a sharp shake to highlight her crest colors. "The planet was not theirs, but ours. They came to our nestworld in the early days of our civilization, assigned as our mentors. We were their first subject race."

"Subject?" Stephen asked, continuing cautiously: "I understood the mentoring relationship to be more subtle."

"They did not so understand it," Meridian said with meaning. "You have lived with the Chirrn. You know how they judge and reject those who do not meet their standards of propriety."

He traded an uneasy look with his wife. "I know they have a culture with complex rules for social inclusion and exclusion."

A harsh chord emerged from Meridian's crests. "The Seekers of the Zenith did not meet their standards for inclusion. They judged our hierarchies rigid and unfair. They found our competition for hunting grounds barbaric, for as migrants by nature they could not grasp the value of territory. And they disapproved of how we approached the matters between male and female; as both and neither at once, they did not understand how fundamental our reproductive identity was to us.

"So they attempted to indoctrinate us in the 'correct' way of living—the Chirrn way," the matriarch continued. "We found their teachings absurd and resisted the indoctrination… often violently."

"But surely the Chirrn weren't mentoring you alone? From what we've learned, mentoring missions are usually multispecies."

"That reform was instituted in the wake of the events I relate to you now," Meridian told him. "At the time, the rules had grown lax, or the Chirrn would never have been given such license."

After making a permission-seeking gesture and getting Meridian's nod, Apastron said, "The civilizations responsible for administering the Protocols in this octant—including the Shayal and their Coalition—were preoccupied with supernova evacuation efforts. Not only was Eta Carinae already demanding their attention, but another supernova loomed ten times nearer, requiring further effort to shield or relocate the sophonts nearby." Arachne added a text annotation: *<Most likely the supernova some 12,000 years ago that created the Vela Supernova Remnant.>*

Meridian went on. "Enough attention remained that the Chirrn's methods were questioned and protested among the stars. Yet the Chirrn were determined to succeed at their first mentoring, so they offered us an incentive to follow their ways. Recognizing our drive to seek greater heights in all things, they told us of the earlier civilizations that had ascended to metasapience. They presented it as the pinnacle of evolution, the ultimate height to which the most advanced and powerful species rose." Meridian's chimes took on overtones that Stephen recognized as disapproving yet sardonic. "They implied that if we adopted their ways, we would thereby reach the 'mature' level of galactic civilization and ultimately earn metasapience as a reward."

Sita snorted. "Play nice and eat your veg and you can grow up to be God someday."

"I take it your ancestors cooperated?" Stephen asked.

"Naturally," Apastron replied. "We are the Seekers of the Zenith. What higher zenith could there be than metasapience?"

"And yet something went wrong, didn't it?"

"You tried it and failed," Arachne deduced. "I have seen the results of such failures in our own star system. Cybers rendered mad by their own inner chaos, trapped forever inside cognitive feedback loops, or simply burned out."

"It has to be more than that," Sita said, "or we wouldn't have to meet in secret to even talk about it."

"Yes." Meridian gestured around at their lowly surroundings. "You see where we must perch in the galactic hierarchy if we dare express interest in climbing to the same heights that all others are permitted to pursue." Her mandibles clacked together sharply. "This is the legacy of the Chirrn.

"Our yearning for metasapience was a natural goal, but the Chirrn perverted it by convincing us we must change our nature to pursue it. We became obedient and assimilated as they wished. They rewarded us by assisting our technological advancement, chaperoning us into greater contact with the galactic community over the generations that followed. As soon as we could, we sought out all available research into metasapience. Once we were established in the galaxy, with the connections to gain the PQM and other resources we needed, a group of us attempted to ascend."

The matriarch-in-exile lowered her head, her entire retinue and Broadwing following suit. "But their attempt was premature," she continued. "The Chirrn had pushed our people to advance too quickly, to be too eager for a height we had not yet earned—or had earned in the wrong way, for the wrong reasons. Whether as a fault of our ancestors' haste or a punishment for their hubris, the experiment went disastrously wrong."

Meridian turned to Arachne. "The results were far worse than the madness you describe. What they achieved was semi-stable. They were mad, yes, unable to bear the emptiness of the universe as they now perceived it. But they were still functional. They craved stimulation, the input they could gain by linking other minds to theirs. They adapted the nanotechnology that had heightened their minds so that it became infectious, and they began to spread it as far as they could reach. No Zenith population was safe from the madness, and some strains of the contagion mutated to infect other species as well."

"Holy shite," Sita breathed.

"My God," said Stephen.

Meridian blinked. "'Deity of waste'? Perhaps a fitting description. The infection spread widely, for its basis was a science so advanced and subtle that even the Galactics had few defenses against it. The madness spread across worlds, both planets and megastructures. The result was chaos, collapse, and savage violence. Rather than try to cure them, the Chirrn and other sane ones fought back, swiftly relearning the ways of war that had long since been mentored out of them.

"But the half-ascended ones relished the violence, for it filled their craving for intensity. They responded in kind and in far greater magnitude. The chaos tore through the Four Voids for generations."

"Was there nothing the Galactics could do to contain them?" Stephen asked.

"Indeed there was. The Ryohoch, in their ancient wisdom, developed a weapon that could neutralize PQM and render it useless." She hesitated. "Apastron?"

"Yes, my matriarch," the second said. "The neutralizer is based in quantum entanglement. All PQM from a common source can eventually be neutralized over any distance. The half-ascended, both Zenith and those they had infected, could be stranded on their habitats and ships, left to die out or tear each other apart in their madness. Yet the effect only propagated at the speed of light, of course, so groups of half-ascended were able to escape and continue the war in other regions. Eventually, they had to stop moving, or were surrounded, so in time the neutralizing waves overtook the last of them."

"But by then," Meridian resumed, "the civilizations of the Four Voids — those that survived — had fled to safer regions. By the time the last of the half-ascended were hunted down, the Voids lived up to their name. Galactic civilization was mostly gone from here, and few remained beyond the feral natives of worlds such as your own."

Stephen remained silent for a long moment. "Meridian," he said at last, "that is a tragedy on a scale I can't imagine. And yes, the Chirrn of that time made a disastrous mistake. But surely they more than paid for it in the cataclysm that followed." And yet his eyes strayed to Sita, and the memory of a mob of Lesshchin beating her in her barely swollen belly sprang unbidden to his mind. Her own eyes were unreadable.

Meridian moved closer, sidling up next to him and brushing shoulders. "We were not the only ones wronged by their mistake. Hear carefully, Stephen Jacobs-Wong: The Chirrn would not admit their error, their abuse. To save face, they blamed the chaos on the primitiveness of the Zenith mind. They decided that any race still confined to a planet was too immature to be trusted with the power of metasapience—or even the power of Galactic civilization. They argued that young civilizations needed to be quarantined on their nestworlds until they could mature to a 'safe' level on their own; until then, the risk of exposing them to knowledge of metasapience was too great.

"And so they began to campaign against the Mentoring Protocols." Her words struck Stephen like a blow.

The matriarch paced slowly around the Arachnen trio, keeping her right and middle eyes fixed on them at all times. "Normally, they would have had no chance at overturning such an ancient system. However, the war had made many afraid and sympathetic to their propaganda. And the most active enforcers of the Protocols were preoccupied elsewhere.

"The Chirrn were able to win allies among those few who remained in the Voids. The Gaurim, who disdain interference with the evolutionary process they worship. The Zhalevey, doting elders who can see no wrong in anything their juniors do. The Ryohoch, whose reasons make sense only to themselves. Even the surviving Seekers of the Zenith bowed to the Chirrn party line, as a show of penance to redeem their lost status. Together, they were able to force through a suspension of the Protocols throughout the Four Voids."

Stephen stared open-mouthed. Even in this gravity, he felt like he was floating away, his anchor disintegrating beneath him. "Including the Central Void… and Earth."

"Yes. And other worlds whose sophonts were on the verge of civilization, or already in its early stages. At least two worlds had their mentors removed."

"So… suspension of the Protocols… that means no contact of any kind with pre-spaceflight worlds?"

"That was how the Chirrn defined it. Complete exclusion."

His hands shook. "This… is why Earth was left alone? Why we were never visited by aliens, never even… saw any sign of them until we built space telescopes?"

"Correct. The Chirrn ensured that all local activity — what little remained after the cataclysm and the exodus from the Voids — was hidden."

"Oh, my God," Stephen breathed. "That's why Lesshchi was dark. Why we never saw it coming." He squeezed his eyes shut in pain. "They were hiding. From *us.*"

"Stephen," Sita said, tightly gripping his hand. He could feel the pain in her as well, but she was in scientist mode, clinging just as firmly to her own objectivity. "Lady Meridian, with all due respect… I trust you can prove these allegations?"

Meridian blinked at her with only her lower two eyes; the third stared relentlessly. "Stephen Jacobs-Wong, is this your question as well?"

Stephen gathered himself. "She… Sita's right. What you've asked us to believe… it's a lot to take in. No disrespect intended, but we could use more information to go on." He was striving to convince himself, but the words were half-hearted.

The matriarch lifted her head for a moment, then came back to Stephen's eye level. "A fair request. Broadwing can give your cyber the means to circumvent the Chirrn's blocks on your network access. There is much propaganda and distortion there about the Zenith and our history. But even there you will find confirmation of the Chirrn's role in the suspension of the Mentoring Protocols."

"And why go to all this bother to clue us in?" Sita pressed. "What interest do you have in us?"

Meridian replied, but her triple gaze held Stephen's. "We are kindred spirits, and your plight sings to me. We have both had our freedom and our natural aspirations stifled by the Chirrn's self-absorbed condescension. We have both suffered from their crimes — and we have both inflicted unintended blows upon them as a consequence of their poor choices.

"But there is hope now that we may soar above that. You do not know how much the galaxy now speaks of the human race and the fall of Lesshchi. For twelve thousand years, the Chirrn's will has dominated the Four Voids. Now, a blow has been struck against their power and their policies. It creates new questions in many minds. It weakens the

Chirrn's claims of infallibility and righteousness. And it creates an opportunity for us, the victims of Chirrn arrogance, to stand up and begin the process of change. You can be a great symbol in that struggle.

"Together, Stephen Jacobs-Wong, we can free both our peoples from the Chirrn."

With Broadwing's help, it took little time for Arachne to confirm Meridian's account in the Star Palace's historical records. Earth was even mentioned (not under that name, of course) in a list of worlds with known sophont species that had been left "feral" as a result of the decision. Remote observation with gravity-focus telescopes, and the occasional Chirrn-supervised research flyby, had documented the turbulent, violent development of human and other feral civilizations, feeding ongoing debates in the galactic community. The mentoring races argued it was proof of the cruelty of the Void Alliance's policy, while the Chirrn cited it in support of their argument that juvenile, planet-bound civilizations were intrinsically too erratic to be mentored without an unacceptable risk of destabilizing them even further—not to mention the risk of exposing them to the knowledge of metasapience and triggering another cataclysm.

When Stephen insisted on a meeting with L'chellin in the Chirrn's suite, the senior mediator seemed unsurprised. Still, she and R'nilinnath (alongside Broadwing, who still played the role of a loyal mediator) perched quietly on their tails opposite Stephen, waiting for him to speak.

"When were you going to tell us about the Mentoring Protocols?"

L'chellin sighed slowly. "Velesh. Has he spoken to you?"

"We spoke to him. And others."

"In violation of your authorized limits. You should be penalized, but... you have endured so much already." Widening her stance, she tapped her tail on the ground in chastisement. "Still, you need to understand that there are reasons for our rules, Stephen. You have been exposed to knowledge you do not yet have the context to judge wisely."

"I don't know why you thought you could keep it from us for long. It wasn't that hard to piece together the truth about something so basic to all the beings here."

"I suppose not," L'chellin conceded. "But we had to try. We knew how you would react when you found—"

"The truth?" Stephen gazed into L'chellin's eyes, trying to read something inside those hollow orbs. "That for over ten thousand years, you watched us suffer and did nothing?

"It would've been one thing if you hadn't known we existed yet. But you were watching. The whole time. All the great disasters and atrocities of human history. You saw them happen and you did... nothing. More—you actively *prevented* anyone else from helping."

"That is not accurate," L'chellin said. "First, we were not monitoring you constantly or at close range. Most observation was by gravity-focus telescopy conducted from star systems parsecs away. Our real-time information was intermittent, a flyby every few of your generations. But such flybys were suspended once you invented sufficiently powerful telescopes," she added.

"Second, those civilizations that administer the Protocols have long been occupied with other concerns. The hypernova of Eta Carinae and the nearer supernova required massive relocation operations. Moving thousands of planetary populations, helping them to adjust, requires *yanarrach* of time and an application of resources on a multicivilizational scale. So there *were* no others clamoring to come to your aid."

"Then it should've been you," Stephen shot back. "You were left as the dominant power in this region, and you chose to abandon us to our own worst hells instead of—"

"Dominating you? Judging you?" L'chellin's voice carried a sharpness he hadn't heard since she had been male, and not quite even then. "If you know our history with the Protocols, you know of the Zenith cataclysm."

"We read about it." That was all he would tell them about his source of information. "We know you lied to us about your history, your great war with those who stayed on your home planet."

"I told you of planet-dwellers who resisted our influence and swarmed into space, spreading chaos and war for generations, de-populating our native planet in the process. I... allowed you to draw the erroneous conclusion that their birth planet was our own, for you were not yet ready to hear the complicated truth."

"The truth being that you got burned by your protégés, so you decided planet-dwellers were too savage to be allowed into civilized society."

"No." L'chellin's voice was still sharp, yet undeniably sad. "We decided that we could not be trusted to be good mentors. We badly botched the mentoring of the Zenith. Many of us have been reluctant to admit that, and we have embraced a facile prejudice against the planetbound as a protective cover. But I have carefully studied the great debates that led to the suspension of the Protocols in the Four Voids, for I knew the time would come when I would need to justify them to you." She calmed herself, softened her tone before she continued. "Perhaps I did spawn bastard words when I told you of that ancient war, for I told you that we were benevolent and wise and were met with venality and treachery. At the time, I had not come to know you. I had no reason to sympathize with the planetbound, so I did not question the myths we have embraced for our own comfort.

"The truth I now know is less flattering to the Chirrn. We judged the Zenith harshly." That drew a surprised blink from Broadwing. "It is too much in our basic nature to want to exclude or normalize those behaviors that diverge too much from our standards," L'chellin went on. "We tried to change the Zenith on a fundamental level, to engineer their territoriality and rigid gender roles out of their societies altogether. It was a gross abuse of the Mentoring Protocols, an abuse of the Zenith themselves.

"More, we abused the promise of metasapience, took the most sensitive and challenging decision any civilization can ever make and reduced it to a crude reward for obedience. Rather than allowing them to seek their own understanding of metasapience as a complicated option fraught with challenges and uncertainties, we taught them it was the single ultimate aspiration of every species, a goal they should strive toward with all possible haste. And so we damaged their society, turned them into a scourge that devastated worlds and ended hundreds of billions of lives.

"Indeed, it was chiefly due to chance that the chaos did not engulf your Earth. The mad Zenith arose in the Spinward Void, not far from our native world, and their conquests branched toward the centers of civilization in Outward and Antispinward, mostly bypassing the Central Void in between. Eventually, the pincer closed in on Central, but the Ryohoch developed the means to defeat the scourge before the battle lines converged on your home region. Yet by then, the starfaring inhabitants of the Central Void had mostly fled."

L'chellin rose and took a step toward Stephen. "We could not risk such a catastrophe happening again. We began to realize—not as an

attempt to avoid blame, but in hopes of preventing a reoccurrence—
that the mentoring system itself was overly enamored of metasapience
as a civilizational aspiration. We have told you that the metaminds
provide us with PQM, and that we believe their motive is to encourage
us to join them and increase their complexity. They crave new input
and perceive sophonts as raw material—and they are at the pinnacle of
the galaxy's technological ecosystem.

"Moreover, in the past few *yanarruvh*, the rate at which sophont
species have transitioned to metasapience has been accelerating. At the
time of the Zenith Cataclysm, the population density of baseline-
sapient civilizations in this octant had fallen to its lowest level since
the Mentoring Protocols were first introduced. Looking back on that
history, the Chirrn concluded that the metaminds had been influencing
the mentoring process, eroding the safeguards that prevented mentors
from pushing civilizations to advance too quickly."

"And you say you're not trying to avoid blame."

"On the contrary. We too were pushed too quickly by the Shayal,
encouraged to take our own protégés before we were ready. We are *still*
not ready. We are only wise enough to recognize our own limitations—
and thus to slow down and reorient our priorities toward the right of
each civilization to develop at its own pace, rather than being harried
forward in service to the metaminds' agenda.

"Yes, my friend, we left you to develop in isolation. We did nothing
to help you through your traumas and tragedies, and for that I am truly
sorry. But if we had intervened, an alien people with little understanding of your inner nature and the wrong temperament to mentor you
wisely, we could have caused you—and the galaxy—far worse harm
than anything you suffered yourselves."

"Even if it wasn't you, it could've been someone else."

"Who? The Zenith have no interest in mentoring, and would be
too inclined to keep their protégés beneath them. The Ryohoch are
too alien to understand your needs. The Gaurim mostly lead a nat-
uralistic existence and would have been ill-suited to guide you through
technological adolescence. The Zhalevey are herbivores, not equipped
to help you regulate your predatory drives. Any suitable mentor races
were occupied elsewhere in the galaxy. Leaving you alone," L'chellin
finished, "was the best thing we could do for you."

"No." Stephen shook his head, pacing before the mediators. "That's
too pat an answer. If you have protocols for refining the behavior of

other races, you could refine your own as well. Teach yourselves to be better mentors.

"Very few teachers, or, or parents, are ideal starting out. They make mistakes. But they can learn. They can learn from their students, their children, even as their charges learn from them. They can reach out and commit to building a relationship, and the two of them can come together and both become more than they were." He blinked away tears. "When I… when I had to take care of my baby brother, see that he got an education and stayed out of trouble while Mama struggled to keep us fed, I was terrible at first. I neglected him. I yelled at him. I played tricks on him. I treated him like my personal servant. But when he ran away and we almost lost him, I realized how much I'd been hurting him. And, and I made myself change. I taught myself — let him teach me — how to be a better mentor. And we became the best friends you ever did see. And when he… when we lost him, when he was bleeding out on the pavement, I stayed with him and I held his hand and he found the strength to tell me it was okay, because his big brother was with him and he wasn't af-afraid."

Stephen needed a moment to gather his breath. "And that's what makes a mentor, L'chellin. Not being perfect, but *not giving up*. Not abandoning people just because you're afraid you might screw up." Still pacing, feeling more torn up and out of control than he'd felt since Benjamin died, he shook his head and directed a bitter laugh at the ceiling. "You know, you, Rillial and the rest, you talked, at the trial, all about responsibility. About, about our responsibility for the harm we did to Lesshchi even though we didn't know. And I *agreed* with you! I thought, I thought you were within your rights to insist on responsibility.

"But you… you had a responsibility far greater — a responsibility to entire *worlds* — and you just, you just fucking ran away from it! You ran and you hid and you let me — you let us go through *that!* Through the Gulf States Collapse and the Orbit War and the Holocaust and the Great Leap Forward, through the slave trade and the Trail of Tears and the Inquisition… all because you were too goddamn *cowardly* to take responsibility and try to make a difference."

L'chellin crouched wordlessly, keeping her eyes focused on Stephen even though they sporadically twitched outward, instinctively trying to look away. Broadwing stood half-erect, head defiantly tilted. A trembling R'nilinnath hid her eyes with her hands, making the dog-whine sound of Chirrn weeping through her nares. But Stephen was un-moved. "But you know the thing about responsibility? You can't duck it. Try to and it comes around to bite you in the tail. You fled from your responsibility to help us, so that makes you responsible for every horror, every hell you could've prevented. It makes you responsible for our ignorance of your existence, our need to rely on relativistic ships." At L'chellin's startled reaction, he went on. "That's right, L'chellin. The destruction of Lesshchi—all this time I've been blaming myself, but it was you. It was *you!* It was your own damn fault and you've been persecuting us for it ever since!"

He couldn't even bring himself to say the rest. *It's your fault Kweli died. Your fault my baby died.* But he didn't need to.

After a long silence, L'chellin spoke again. "You have borne many words of merit here. We should all take them into our minds as guests and allow them nourishment and attention. These are moral questions that have been under debate for many, many lifetimes. We will not find their decisive answer this *narrissh.*" She moved closer to Stephen, low-ering her muzzle in deference. "All I can say is that we acknowledge and respect your pain, and with your words taken into our minds, we share it. There is much for us all to regret in this.

"But the decisions that led to these events were made long ago, at a level well above our own. I ask that you consider this, and I hope that once your anger subsides, you will remember that we have shared much of value. And that one of the things we share is a responsibility to make the best of what the past has given us, as flawed as that may be, and try to build a better future together. I know that is something you truly believe in, Stephen. Thanks to you, I believe in it more now than I ever did in the past.

"We cannot bring back what we have lost, my friend. All we can do is speak the future into being."

Stephen was very quiet for long moments thereafter, his eyes held shut. Finally, L'chellin sighed and said, "We will talk later. The meeting is adjourned." She and the other mediators rose, but then L'chellin paused. "Understand, though, that any further violation of your probation will have to be met with penalties. Your… erratic behavior can only be excused up to a point by your tragic circumstances. From now on, it is incumbent upon you to behave in a way that will redress the existing imbalance."

Stephen looked up at her through hooded eyes. "Don't worry, L'chellin. I intend to."

He let them leave, saying nothing more. There was no point in further dialogue. Everything the Chirrn had ever said to him had been a lie built on a lie. All of human history had been a lie, a cruel hoax perpetrated on an unsuspecting species through the treachery of the Chirrn. They had used a disaster as an excuse to abandon his world, just as the governors and corporate executives had done to his home state.

And Stephen hated them with every fiber of his being.

5

"You are a hypocrite," L'chellin barked at Velesh as they met in the latter's private chambers. "You profess to honor the letter of the Mentoring Protocols, yet you deliberately violate them to undermine our handling of the Arachnen."

"And you reject the Protocols, yet hide behind them when you find it convenient," the Shayal countered coolly. "Let it be clarified: I spoke only of the general history of mentoring. Their information on the Zenith Cataclysm must have come from another source. Perhaps the Zhalevey; Doctor Bhatiani seemed adept at persuading them."

L'chellin forced calm upon herself, not wishing to seem like the child here. She refused to be cowed by the eerily silent scrutiny of his mates, who hovered nearby as always. She had her entire guild with her in consensus, after all. "Protest all you like, but you have made no secret of your agenda to exploit the death of Lesshchi as fodder for a renewed push to restore the Protocols."

"Surely that disaster compels a reexamination of the Void Alliance's stance on the Protocols," Velesh replied. "And surely the humans are entitled to a voice in the discussion. Not only are they direct parties to the events in question, but they are a starfaring power now."

"They have made some tentative ventures into local space through conventional means. They are not yet PQM-enabled."

"A condition you are about to change."

L'chellin felt her eyes jerk outward in surprise. She snorted. "You would exploit a technicality. The Arachnen have renounced their ties to human civilization. They are of the Chirrn now."

The triad gave her that look of patient condescension that was enshrined in Chirrn mythology and literature as the trademark of the Shayal. "Their very success at adjusting to that identity demonstrates that their species is ready for broader contact," Velesh expounded. "It would be difficult for you to continue to argue, even to your allies, that humanity needs to remain isolated for its own 'protection.'"

L'chellin thumped her toes skeptically. "So you would embrace them as equal partners in galactic life? All humans, not just the Arachnen?"

The hairs on Velesh's brow ridges twitched subtly, betraying his fears. "The conditions for ending their isolation have arguably been met, but the cost of their isolation remains. Naturally, some remedial mentoring would be required. Advisors can be assigned to assess their readiness for peaceful coexistence and, if it is found lacking, to guide them the rest of the way."

"And what standards would you use for defining readiness?" L'chellin demanded. "The humans' isolation has made them exceptional. How can you judge which behaviors are dangerous and which are merely unique?"

"As always, the Chirrn caricature the mentoring process. All civilizations are free to develop uniquely."

"Within the parameters of the Protocols. No matter how broad they try to be, there are still biases and expectations that would make it difficult for a mentored people to fairly assess an unmentored one."

"Consider, Mediator. Further encounters with humans are inevitable as they spread into space. What other crises might arise if they continue to expand in ignorance of the rest of us? Is open contact not worthwhile as a defense against accident and misunderstanding?"

The very reasonableness of Velesh's words put L'chellin on edge. If the Alliance conceded that much, it would be the first pinprick in a hull rupture, a fingerhold the Shayal could use to push deeper into Alliance affairs until the Protocols were restored—and who knew what other policies had been abandoned. Perhaps if the Coalition had chosen different emissaries, she would not have been so resistant. Sending Shayal was a rather blatant psychological ploy—an unsubtle reminder that without their mentors, the Chirrn might have torn themselves apart, their instincts toward exclusion driving them to bigotry and warfare.

But the humans overcame their bigotry and warfare to reach the stars without outside help, she reminded herself. *Perhaps we could have done the same, and been stronger for it.*

"You speak so conscientiously of the cost of abandonment," she told Velesh. "When you make your case to the Alliance, will you acknowledge your own role in that abandonment? It was the Coalition and your fellow mentors who turned your attention away from the Voids."

"You know we had obligations elsewhere," Velesh replied, still unflappable. "Your ancestors begged us for the chance to take over our mentoring responsibilities here."

"And you let them, knowing they were unready."

"We trusted the Chirrn. The Chirrn disappointed us." Velesh stepped closer. "And rather than admit the blame for the chaos that followed, you turned on us, prohibited us from doing anything to heal the damage."

"What would you have done? How would you have convinced the Coalition or the Mathadn or any of the others to allocate the necessary resources to this empty, ravaged backwater when so many other crises demanded their attention in more populous sectors? How could your mentoring be anything other than one-eyed, and how would that be any better than the situation that triggered the Zenith Cataclysm?"

Velesh studied her. "You sincerely believe you are protecting them."

"Yes. From you, and from ourselves." She tensed her legs and tail just enough to be intimidating, subtly reminding the Shayal emissary that the Chirrn were stronger, leaner, and far more dangerous on a physical level. "Do not cross tails with us," she warned, aware of the implications of the metaphor. That silly stump hanging down from Velesh's rear couldn't swat an insect. "We are not juveniles anymore. We will protect our interests. And we — I — will not allow you to exploit the Arachnen, our own young, to advance your politics."

The Shayal gazed at her sadly. "You truly love them. It is a pity you cannot see how badly you harm their species with your good intentions."

"I could say the same of you. Except that your only love is for your own self-righteousness. You know nothing of the Arachnen."

Velesh puffed out his long, flabby neck, unfazed as ever. "That is what I am here to change."

Ever since the meeting with Meridian, Stephen had been closed off again. The thaw in relations that Sita had enjoyed with him since the start of the migration was over. But this time, rather than being emotionally dulled and introverted, Stephen had smoldered with a suppressed anger that Sita had never seen in him before. She had hoped his confrontation with L'chellin would bring him reassurance, or even that the mediator would have disproven Meridian's claims. But Stephen had returned with his anger no longer suppressed. "I was a fool," he told Sita. "I should've listened to Cecilia all along. The Chirrn have been lying to us from the beginning."

He wasted no time asking Broadwing to arrange a second meeting with Meridian to discuss her proposal for liberation. With L'chellin now alerted, there was more risk in sneaking down to the undercity; but Broadwing still had his fellow mediators' trust, as well as Meridian's assistance. Her Zhalevey sympathizers were able to arrange for the loss of certain data in the caravan's entrance application to Lode Seven, requiring L'chellin to spend hours negotiating the bureaucratic maze to correct the error—an exercise that Sita was convinced the mediator secretly enjoyed. And Nilly was having so much fun showing the Arachnen around the Star Palace's many entertainments that it was easy for Broadwing to spirit a group of them away.

This time, Stephen brought Tarik, who shared his newfound desire for escape, and Diana Thorne, who'd insisted that her Vanguardian abilities would be an asset in whatever plan the Zenith had to offer. Their fervor made Sita even more determined to tag along and try to keep them honest. Arachne's avatar joined them as well, but Sita wasn't convinced of the cyber's objectivity. The protection of her human charges was Arachne's overriding priority, a drive that had led her to break the rules back in Sol System—and though she had been right to do so then, Sita couldn't assume that would always be the case.

Not that Sita couldn't empathize with the Zenith, who simply sought the freedom to explore metasapience. It didn't seem fair that their whole species was still being judged by the actions of one group twelve millennia ago, any more than it was fair that *Arachne*'s crew and the Lesshchin had suffered as an eventual consequence of those actions. Given Stephen's history, she couldn't blame him for empathizing with the Zenith. But in his long years of activism back home, Stephen had always advocated finding a way to end the cycle of wrongs rather than adding still more to the list. She trusted that her husband still wanted the same now... but she was not convinced about Meridian.

So she grilled Broadwing about his alpha as he escorted the five Arachnen down to the undercity again. "I belonged to Meridian's dissident movement in my youth," Broadwing told her as the others listened in. "To my shame, I never lived up to the ambition of my name and could not advance far in the society of my native Star Palace. Meridian showed me that I was judging myself by the wrong standards. True, after the Chirrn's mistakes that provoked the cataclysm, we were free to resume our proper gender relations and our natural competitiveness, so long as we renounced any pursuit of metasapience. Yet we were still feared for what our kind had done, so we strove to assimilate and prove ourselves good citizens, obedient to the will of the masses and desiring no disruption. And so we lost sight of much of what we had been."

"So what did Meridian offer you instead?" Sita asked.

"Her kindness and acceptance were enough," he said. "She saw beneath my surface and showed me what I could achieve with faith in myself. And she offered me the hope that we could transcend the limits imposed on us for so long and rise to metasapience at last. It is a taboo notion, one I feared at first, but Meridian convinced me of the folly of that taboo. We are not the people we were, no longer manipulated into rushing forward prematurely. We have had twelve millennia to learn from our mistakes, to study a galaxy's worth of research, and to pursue the knowledge at our own responsible pace."

"Yet the other civilizations don't agree," Stephen said. "So Meridian's group has to live down here, as outcasts."

"And we have often been forced to act as such. I myself was captured for a petty crime against Shilirrlal, though I managed to conceal my ties to Meridian. Like you, I was required to atone by becoming a contributing member of the habitat I had wronged." He greeted the guards at the entrance to Meridian's pavilion and led the Arachnen inside. "Away from Meridian's guidance, I was vulnerable to their indoctrination. I cast aside my ambitions as youthful folly and dedicated myself to becoming a proper, well-behaved Shilirrlaln. For more than four *narrayth* I have lived that way."

"Until Lesshchi reawakened your faith," Tarik said. "And you decided to bring us to your fellow believers. But why?"

"Because you offer hope." It was Meridian, approaching with her head held high. The main chamber of the pavilion was emptier than before, with only Apastron and two other female aides accompanying the matriarch. But Meridian took care to position herself in a shaft of light so her shimmering crests would stand out.

Stephen went on to introduce the others: "Tarik Bahar, one of our administrators; and Diana Thorne, one of our top engineers."

The dissident leader greeted them in turn. "Morning Star of Spring," she said to the former. "A name worthy of a Zenith if ever there was one. And Divine Huntress of the Thorn! I have a cousin of a similar name."

Diana gave a cool smile in return. "Small universe. I once had an aircar by your name."

Meridian blinked. "In any case, they are fitting epithets for two so tall and strong. You are both most welcome."

The matriarch escorted the group to the inevitable dining table Apastron had again prepared. Once they had seated themselves and sampled the food, Meridian got to business. "For far too long—longer than the duration of your civilization, and for most of the duration of ours—the Chirrn have held the neck of the Four Voids in their talons. They have forced you and other young civilizations to go unmentored, to suffer war and chaos. They have forbidden the Zenith to pursue metasapience. Those who protested had insufficient voice to outsing the chorus of the Chirrn and their supporters.

"But now, the brave ascent of humans to the stars may have changed that."

"How?" Stephen asked.

"By what you did. Lesshchi's death was a tragedy, of course. Yet it revealed to all watchers that the Chirrn's doctrines are flawed. Their own insistence on holding feral civilizations down has cost them dearly. It is an opening we could use to push for an alteration of policy."

Stephen pondered. "I assume you want to employ us as more than just symbols, or Broadwing wouldn't have needed to advocate for this migration."

"You see sharply, Stephen Jacobs-Wong. There is a way we can help each other."

Meridian straightened—not quite to her full vertical stance, given the gravity, but high enough to dominate the table more than she had already. "We Zenith alone cannot change the minds of those with the power to affect policy in the Voids—indeed, we would only alienate them, for the scars of our ancestors' mistakes are still too clear here. We need to leave the Four Voids and travel among more open-minded societies to plead our case and gain allies of influence. Moreover, if we wish to pursue our research into metasapience, we will need the technology to make it possible — and we will need the ability to travel to the galactic core or to the neutron star of our choice. We cannot achieve those things with the single, limited-range warp cage we possess."

"You need PQM," Arachne said.

"Yes. As do you, if you wish to regain your independence from the Chirrn. Your vessel is now equipped with a warp cage, but it is one the Chirrn control and can neutralize. To get away from them, you would need a separate supply of PQM. We both need a fresh, unregistered supply that is immune to their neutralizers.

"But we can only attain it now, with your help. Miss this chance and there will be no other."

"Why is that?" Stephen asked.

Meridian prompted Apastron to answer. The second seemed more savvy on technical matters. "Any run of PQM processed at the same time shares quantum correlation throughout," the smaller female said. "A small sample quantity of every run is set aside as a security precaution. Should a PQM supply be stolen and used against the Void powers, the reference sample will be entangled with the neutralizer mechanism, allowing the entire stock to be nullified."

"This," Meridian added, "is why all our past attempts to… appropriate PQM for our own use have ultimately been defeated. If you are to regain your freedom, and if we are to seek the true zenith, we must obtain a supply of PQM that the Chirrn cannot neutralize."

"A large supply," said Apastron, "tailored for multiple uses: starships, wormholes, gravity generators, defensive fields."

"Enough to serve the needs of a small nation," the matriarch went on. "The PQM supply that your migration party will obtain at Lode Seven should fit those needs, if it can be stolen from the factory before it falls into the Chirrn's hands."

Stephen stared at the beautiful gargoyles. "You want *us* to steal it."

"Only you are in a position to do so. You have earned the trust of the Chirrn. You will participate in the construction of the new habitat, so you have a justification for requesting access to the PQM factory as part of your preparation. Of my people, only Broadwing has such access, and he could not do it alone.

"The rest, we have the means to assist you with. Broadwing will be with you, and we have sympathizers among the Zhalevey there." She gave a Zenith laugh, like a toy train whistle. "All have sympathizers among the Zhalevey. But they lack the physical robustness, the guile, and the aggression to accomplish the theft of the PQM and the liberation of your people. Without the access and abilities only you will have, we are without hope. We cannot do this without each other."

The humans exchanged stunned looks, at a loss for words. But Sita's scientific mind kept churning and analyzing despite her shock. "That's not all you want from us, though, is it?" she realized. "This opportunity you see isn't just about the habitat and the PQM — it's about us. A group of people motivated enough to help you with the heist — and unconnected enough to give you plausible deniability. We get the blame for the heist and you clear off with the goods while everybody's chasing after us."

"That… that's right," Stephen said, though it surprised Sita how slow he'd been to catch on. He was usually such a savvy negotiator. "Lady Meridian, both our groups are feared enough already. What will it do to our reputations in the galaxy if we begin our efforts with a… a heist of that magnitude? What might they do to our home system as punishment?"

"Both our reputations are already scarred, Stephen Jacobs-Wong — ours far worse than yours. A theft such as this will not shock the galaxy. PQM is rare and valuable, but replaceable. Its theft will do no great harm to anyone — but it will badly embarrass the Void Alliance, and it will marginally slow the Chirrn's efforts to reinforce their strength in the Antispinward Void.

"Yes, Sita Bhatiani — we do intend to let the attention fall on you, for you would be less harmed by it than we. We could perhaps accomplish this ourselves, but not without being identified and hunted relentlessly by a galaxy terrified of a new Zenith Cataclysm. We would be unable to pursue our research for long, or with the patience needed to avoid such a mishap. If you are blamed — ferals merely seeking escape from their captors, and lacking the knowledge to do great harm with what they have stolen — the consequences will be far less to you as well as to us.

"Indeed, many will admire the boldness of such a humiliation of the Chirrn. There are those in the Four Voids and beyond who dislike their restrictions on mentoring, but who lack the political power to stand against them. Shaming the Chirrn would weaken them and strengthen their opposition.

"As for your world, the Chirrn have left it alone for twelve millennia. They would not alter that policy now, even if you brought your people knowledge of galactic civilization. They are too accustomed to disdaining and avoiding feral, planet-dwelling sophonts."

Meridian leaned closer, bringing her eyes level with Stephen's. "If you still doubt, consider how much the Chirrn have stolen from both our peoples already. Are we not owed some recompense?"

"Yes," Stephen said without hesitation. "They owe us more than they can ever repay." Sita threw him a disturbed look.

"Then repayment from us will have to suffice. The quantity of PQM required to support a Chirrn habitat is considerable. Once our needs are met, there will more than enough left for you to take back to your nestworld, along with a few Zhalevey advisors we would provide. Humanity could be an interstellar power within a generation and nevermore be at the Chirrn's mercy."

Nobody said a word for some moments after that. Meridian rose. "You need time to consider my proposition. Our facilities are at your disposal."

Apastron showed the Arachnen into a side chamber whose panoramic, down-angled windows gave a spectacular view of the forest of columns and archways outside. The humans gravitated to the windows and spent a long moment just staring, trying to clear their minds. Sita watched Stephen closely, trying to get a read on him, but she was beginning to wonder if she'd ever known him well enough for that.

"Are we really considering this?" Arachne finally asked.

Diana turned to the silvery arachnocentaur, all four of whose arms were crossed over her sculpted chest. "You mean helping the Zenith pull off the heist of the millennium?" The Amazonian engineer laughed. "God, I like the sound of that."

"You do?"

"Sure! What an adventure! If nothing else were at stake, I'd be sorely tempted just to see if I could pull it off."

"But there *is* much more at stake," Stephen said. "Freedom, for all of *Arachne*'s crew. With the Zenith's help, we can get Cecilia and the others free — get *all* of us out of Chirrn custody together."

"The Zenith are admitted criminals and outcasts," Arachne pointed out. "Can we trust that they will adhere to their end of the bargain and not take the PQM by force once we possess it?"

"Arachne, I've been dealing with thieves and liars my whole life, either in the Gulf or in business," Stephen said. "I know how to protect myself when making deals with them. We'll be handling the goods ourselves, which gives us the advantage. We can set the terms of the handoff to ensure we don't lose it."

The thought of Stephen Jacobs-Wong contemplating a crime made Sita's head spin. "But what about the Shilirrlaln?" she asked. "What about our friends and neighbors?"

Tarik scoffed. "The only Shilirrlaln we've really been allowed to get to know are the mediators—who've been lying to us, manipulating us from the beginning."

"They're doing the right thing as they see it."

"But they've deliberately concealed their greatest secret, knowing how we would react. They've been blaming us all along for what they *knew* was ultimately their fault!"

Stephen clasped Sita's shoulders. "I can't blame you for your reluctance, darling. Whatever they've done as a culture, you don't want to hurt them as individuals. Neither do I. But really, what will it cost them if we pull this off? They'll be down forty-seven colonists plus Arachne, but they'll still have the rest of the Migration guild to start off the new habitat. They'll lose a PQM reserve, but they can surely order another. They'll be angry that the proper balance has been violated, yes, but they'll soon be too busy building a new world to dwell on it. Who knows? By the time the Chirrn are done building the habitat, the heist may have become part of its founding legends, a hardship they could take pride in surmounting. It might even bind them more strongly as a community."

"Rubbish! Will you listen to yourself? How can you rationalize this so easily? What about Nilly? She takes such pride in being an apprentice mediator. She won't just feel we've betrayed her if we do this—she'd feel she failed in her first adult responsibility. It'd break her heart."

"You know the kid has a rebellious streak," Diana said. "She always gets a kick out of hearing about human crime and depravity. Seeing it happen for real, committed by humans she actually knows, might be the thrill of her lifetime!"

"Or it might burst her illusions and leave her sad and bitter." Sita turned to her husband. "Is this really our only option? What about the Shayal? I think Velesh wants to help us. He certainly did all he could to let you know about mentoring."

"The Shayal didn't come to our aid when we needed it any more than the Chirrn did."

"They were busy elsewhere."

"Just like UNECS was 'busy elsewhere' while Florida decayed into a war zone. It's no excuse. The Shayal are powerful, privileged. They'll never see us as more than a charity case. Meridian's people know what it's like to be on the other end of the stick."

"Even so, can we really trust them? Will we really be the equal partners they claim? It's in their nature to jockey for superior status, you know."

"I trust Broadwing."

"He's a Zenith male, Stephen, and if Meridian is his matriarch, then she practically owns him. He's not going to defy her. And she's basically admitted to using us as scapegoats!"

"We need their help, Sita. Of course we'll be careful, but they have the ideas and the organization we need to get away from the Chirrn's control."

Sita stood and faced him. "So long as we steal for them! It's not enough for you that we're already convicted criminals? You want to make a career out of it? What happens after the theft? Do we spend the rest of our lives on the run? Hiding from the, the Galactic Police? Staging raids on unsuspecting planets and habs to get by?"

Diana chuckled. "Honestly, that sounds like fun."

"I'm not having a laugh!"

"I know that, Sita. But just think of the benefits if we pull this off!" the statuesque Vanguardian went on. "Our own PQM supply, the ability to explore the galaxy and see countless new worlds… it makes the adventure of settling Cybele seem downright ordinary. I think I'd risk just about anything for that."

Sita looked around at the others in dismay. "You're all determined to do this, aren't you?"

Stephen's breath caught. "I won't force anyone else to partici-pate… but I will do whatever I must to free the Arach—the crew of *Arachne*."

Tarik cleared his throat. "I try to lead a righteous life. I'm not a criminal." He sighed. "But I am sworn to protect this crew, and I'd be a poor Muslim if I betrayed an oath—or if I failed to do jihad when my community is threatened. I'm with you, Stephen," Tarik said. "For Kweli. For our children."

"My responsibility has always been to my crew," Arachne said when Sita turned to her avatar. "I will not cooperate if I feel the danger of the heist outweighs the benefit to the crew, but so long as the plan is sound, I will serve as always."

"You've all gone bloody mad!" Sita cried. "Off your nuts, the lot of you!"

"Sita." Stephen took her arm and guided her off to the side. The others—even Arachne, it seemed—fidgeted and looked away. "I don't understand what's happening here," Stephen said softly when they were out of earshot. "You were the one who convinced me to start asking questions about the Chirrn."

"I wanted to find answers, didn't I? I wanted peace! Not just for myself, but I wanted to know what we were getting into, why the galaxy was so afraid of us. I wanted to know how we could avoid further conflict. Further tragedy." She winced, feeling the emptiness in her womb more strongly than she had in weeks.

"Hey." He reached for her, starting to pull her into a hug, but she stiffened. He settled for a light touch on her shoulders. "There's no reason this should lead to further violence. It's just property theft."

"'Just.'" She stepped away, shaking her head. "Damn it, Stephen. I don't know who you are anymore. The great man I fell in love with would never contemplate such a thing!"

"I learned to do what I had to growing up. You know that."

"Sure, nicking a loaf of bread or some fruit! Not robbing bloody Fort Knox! This isn't you, Stephen!"

"Don't assume you know me so well. If I'd… if I'd helped Benjamin steal that medicine, maybe he and Mama would both still be alive."

"More likely you'd be dead along with them. You know that!"

"This is different. The Chirrn state is not innately brutal or murderous." A part of her reflexively bristled, but she knew he was right; the brutality she had suffered was from a traumatized few. "Unjust, yes, but in subtler, more insidious ways. That's what makes them such a threat. It's not just the fanatics and bigots waving assault rifles around that you have to worry about. It's the quiet little everyday injustices of society as a whole, the rationalizations they make to themselves to justify doing nothing to make things better. They're the ones who create the climate of neglect that allows the militants and the haters to gain a foothold. Someone has to stand up and make them realize that change is needed."

He clasped her shoulders more firmly. "Sita, I'm doing the same thing I've always done. Protecting my people. My family. I used to think

I could do that without compromising my principles, and look what it cost us!" He laid a hand on her belly. "What it cost you. Sita, I'm doing this for our child."

She pushed his arm away. "Doing what? Using her as an, an excuse to lash out? To give up on being who you've always striven to be? How does that honor her memory?"

He winced, but refused to back down. "And what about all the other children, the ones still waiting to be born? Is it right to raise them in Chirrn bondage? It would be a greater compromise if I condemned them to that just to maintain my own spotless reputation."

"The means inform the ends, Stephen. I thought you understood that."

He shook his head. "I understand all too well. You're making excuses, Sita. You're afraid and you're not thinking clearly."

Of all the ways he could have reacted to her words, none could have hurt her as deeply as condescension. After that, there was no going back. "Oh, I'm thinking more clearly than I have in a while. Thank Krishna for that, since one of us has to." She pulled off her wedding ring. "Go on, then. You do what you bloody like, I can't stop you. But don't ask me to help or approve, and don't use me — *or my baby* — as your excuse!" Tossing the ring at him, she began to storm for the exit.

He intercepted her. "You know I can't let you leave alone."

"What? Afraid I'll rat you out to the Chirrn?" She knew it was unfair, but she said it anyway.

He winced. "I can't be sure of your safety out there. And if the Zenith see that one of us is against this… well, it's best not to give them cause for concern," he finished uneasily. "Please, Sita."

She knew it was pointless to argue further. The others' minds were made up. Besides, he had a point. Her drive for answers had made her fearless, but the answers had only brought more pain. And she'd known she had the protection of the Arachnen — and the mediators — to fall back on. Now, she felt more alone than she ever had in her life. And the prospect of being alone among dangerous, unknowable aliens filled her with renewed dread.

So she had no choice but to remain as Stephen returned to the others. She kept her distance, not wanting to force them to deal with this private pain any more than they had to. "Let's go give our co-conspirators the good news," Stephen said to them, his voice icy cold.

Tarik spoke tentatively. "Are you sure, Stephen?"

"Yes," Stephen replied. "We've been treated like criminals long enough. It's time to act the part."

Sita followed them out quietly, wondering how she'd ever believed a hibernation dream could be a legitimate basis for a marriage.

Broadwing trembled in anticipation as Meridian sensually stretched her wings before him. They perched on the edge of the pavilion roof, their garments and jewelry discarded behind them. Broadwing hoped he could perform well in this gravity; the dense air should compensate, but he was nervous and afraid of being clumsy. He had never shared a mating flight with a female of Meridian's elevation.

She turned her head backward to peer at him. Her long, sharp, elegant crests shimmered with the movement, blurring out in his upper-eye vision to crown her head in a rainbow aura. "Relax," came the deep, soothing chimes from those same beautiful crests. "You have earned this. You saw an unprecedented opportunity and you had the will to stoop upon it and harry it into our clutches. And so you have given us the chance to climb free of our oppression at last—and perhaps to finally achieve the greatest heights of all." She raised her tail invitingly, giving him a tantalizing glimpse of her distending vulva. "A male of such vision and ambition can serve me well. Should the Arachnen succeed, you could earn the right not only to mate with me… but to be my primary mate."

Broadwing almost lost his balance at that. He flapped his wings to recover his stance, and Meridian chimed affectionate laughter. "Don't worry. I'm sure you have the strength to keep up with me."

He tried not to show his embarrassment. "In truth, mistress, that is not all that troubles me. You are right, this opportunity had to be seized. But… what I needed to do to make it possible… it had consequences I never sought. Suffering caused to those who did not deserve it, who were victims as much as we. Now we again use them to serve our ends. What more might they suffer in the process?"

Meridian turned and loomed above him; her pose and chimes were still seductive, but the display of her superiority was unambiguous. "We are Seekers of the Zenith, Broadwing. Never forget that. It is our destiny to rise above all others." Her point made, she lowered her stance a bit. "Your judiciousness toward your inferiors is commendable. Power needs to be wielded with a soft grip, so that your subordinates will be content to accept their station. But do not forget how your priorities are stacked."

He admired the elegant, outthrust curve of her keel and the powerful wing muscles it anchored. "No, mistress. You are highest in my mind, always."

"Good." Meridian turned back to the edge and waggled her tail coquettishly. "Then catch me if you can."

She was resplendent as she soared, and he launched himself after her, for once not self-conscious of his own appearance, for it was only fitting that he pale next to his matriarch. Still, the sight of her heated his blood and drove his wings harder as he chased her down. His doubts, his regrets—his guilt—lay forgotten below, discarded like his clothing. As much as he yearned for metasapience and freedom from death, becoming Meridian's possession was his greatest aspiration in life. In truth, he had his doubts that the Zenith could ever crack the metasapience problem. In three *yanarrach*, Meridian's faction was not the first to make the attempt, and no others had come even as close as those who had triggered the Cataclysm. But even if he could never achieve that dream, being owned again by the love of his life was a dream fulfilled in itself.

So if that meant more of his Arachnen charges had to suffer or die… well, that was the price of victory.

Part Two

High Crimes

6

CHURRLAYA WAS RELIEVED WHEN THE MIGRATION FLEET FINALLY RECEIVED clearance for Lode Seven, yet he was concerned as well. The last time the Unrenounced had been transferred to a ship, at the onset of the migration, they had used their feral cunning to mount a violent escape attempt, taking Churrlaya and Stephen captive before the two had convinced Cecilia to stand down. Here at the Star Palace, Churrlaya had seen the way Diego and his followers had studied their sur-roundings on visits to the exercise room, as though sizing up potential weaknesses — or potential hostages. He had no wish to see that dis-tressing experience inflicted on any others.

Yet when he consulted with the mediators and Arachnen leaders on the best way to avoid further attempts at violence, Churrlaya was surprised by Stephen Jacobs-Wong's proposal. "Put them in hibernation," the human said after a narr's thought. "Use their cus-tomized capsules aboard *Arachne*. It'll keep them safe and ensure they pose no threat. At least until we get settled in our new home."

L'chellin was clearly just as surprised. "Stephen… I am gratified that you are willing to cooperate in this, but that seems needlessly drastic. Their earlier escape attempt was a fluke."

"No. It was the result of human cunning and desperation. I picked the smartest, most determined people I could find for this expedition, L'chellin. They found a way to escape once, and they can do it again. And I'm afraid they may end up getting hurt or worse if they try.

"Besides, it might give them some peace of mind. In hibernation, they could dream, forget their reality for a while. Maybe that would give them a chance to heal emotionally. Make them a little more manageable when they come out."

"It is a reasonable suggestion," Broadwing put in. "It would certainly improve fleet security and free up resources and personnel."

"Agreed," L'chellin said after a moment's thought. "Thank you, Stephen, for the suggestion."

The Arachnen leader looked uncomfortable. "I know you're… trying to do what you think is best for us. And as you said, what matters is to look forward." L'chellin was visibly pleased by these words.

But Churrlaya was troubled. "Is it necessary to place them all in hibernation? Cecilia committed no violence. She deterred the others from violence, protecting Shilirrlaln lives even at the risk of undermining her comrades' trust in her. I think… she may be close to a breakthrough. I would like to keep working with her."

"But she did participate in the escape attempt," Broadwing countered. "She threatened you with a stolen plasma torch."

"She caused no injury."

"The threat alone is enough to concern the Antarean security staff. They do not wish to see this Star Palace's reputation for safety further undermined by human… unpredictability."

"He has a point," "Stephen said after an uneasy moment. "We don't want to alienate our new neighbors. I know the Chirrn's stance on mentoring isn't too popular with a lot of the locals. And the Unrenounced's actions have probably just reinforced that." He turned to Churrlaya. "It won't harm them. They may even enjoy it. And you can still work with Cecilia once we're settled at the colony."

Seeing that they were firm in their decision, Churrlaya left unhappily, angry that Cecilia was being treated so unfairly for something she hadn't done.

Then he realized how ironic it was that he of all people would think that.

Cecilia drifted weightless down an infinite corridor, pursued by lizard men and silver gargoyles that screamed at her in words she couldn't understand. She was naked and alone and there were no handholds within reach. She could do nothing to increase her pace as the monsters closed. All she could do was call for allies. "Ibrahim! Nik! Kahina! Help me!"

"You want us to help you?" She spun her head, and there was James drifting toward her, brandishing a fearsome plasma torch. "After you refused to help us? After you betrayed us to the enemy?"

"It's not true! I did it to protect all of us!"

"Liar!" It was Diego, grabbing her arm and spinning her to face him. "You're not one of us anymore, Cecilia. You've let the Frog Footman seduce you away from your own people. You apologized for his kind even after they drove Kweli to her death!"

"You're a traitor!" Amrita cried, advancing toward her with a toothed hunting knife. "And it's time to give you what you deserve." Diego twisted Cecilia around and held her tightly from behind as Amrita and James closed in on her. Evan hovered behind them at a safe distance, cackling in anticipation.

Cecilia flung her head back hard, taking Diego in the teeth, and shot her foot into Amrita's solar plexus. Evan yelped louder than they did. She broke Diego's grip, climbed around him, and kicked him into James, pushing herself away. But Amrita clambered over them and repeated the same maneuver, coming at Cecilia with the knifepoint thrust forward. Spotting an inviting archway of moldy, crumbling brick, Cecilia grabbed its edge and pulled herself into darkness.

She emerged onto the Fondamenta de la Misericordia, breathing a sigh of relief and joy as she soared above the canal, seeing herself reflected in its waters. *When did I become so gray and gaunt?* No matter. She was home! She angled northward, negotiating the narrow streets of Cannaregio until she reached her house. "Mamma! Papà!" she called as she floated through the door. "I'm home! I'm finally home!"

"Are you really?" Mamma said, looking up at her scornfully. "Then why do you float there like a spacewoman? Too good to touch the ground, eh? No weight. No roots! You've become just another tourist! Without even the courtesy to put any clothes on!"

"No, Mamma! I fly ships because I'm good at it, but I always come back. This is my home!"

"Liar! Tell that to your grandmother, to the mourners at her funeral! Where were you then, eh?"

"I couldn't get back! I was too far out!"

"Too far, yes. Too far gone to care! You abandon your family, you abandon Venezia like all the others."

"No, Mamma, I am a LoCarno like you raised me! I stay loyal to the city!"

"Staying loyal means staying here! Only we who stay keep Venezia a living city, not just a ruin for tourists! You make excuses, you make noises, but you abandoned us like all the others! Traitor! Seduced away from your own people! You're not one of us anymore!"

"No, Mamma, it's not true!" Cecilia reached for her, but she floated helplessly in space, out of reach, out of touch. She drifted up through the ceiling, through the roof, a ghost, dead to her family. *I didn't abandon you, Mamma. You abandoned me.*

Everyone's abandoned me.

She was alone with her tears until a voice intruded, startlingly clear. "Cecilia?"

She looked up and there he was, reaching out to her. "Stephen!" She grabbed his hand, pulled herself into his arms, and held him tightly. She vaguely remembered that she was angry at him, but that didn't matter. He'd come back. She was happier to see him than she'd ever thought she could be. "Oh, I've missed you. I should've told you last time—"

"I've missed you too," he said. "All of you. And I need to talk to you."

"I'm here, I'm right here."

"I'm speaking to you through the hibernation dream network. I'm sorry for putting you back in hibernation, but it was the only way I could think of to talk to you without the Chirrn overhearing. Arachne's keeping you in a light enough REM state that it should be like lucid dreaming. You'll be able to remember what I'm about to tell you."

Cecilia pulled back, gathering herself as she realized what he was saying. *Back in hibernation.* She remembered now: Stephen watching, cool and remote, as Joana Caravalho supervised the return of the Unrenounced to hibernation. Diego cursing him as a traitor.

Diego was here now, in the hibernation bay (or her dream image of it), though fully clothed, like the rest who were now appearing. Yet somehow Cecilia's image of herself remained naked, exposed, vulnerable. She hoped she was the only one who saw her that way.

"Why should we listen to you, traitor?" Diego said, and it took Cecilia a moment to realize he was addressing Stephen. She looked at James, at Amrita, but they were watching Stephen instead of her. Had their assault been only her private dream, or had they actually come after her through the shared dream network? She hadn't yet remembered she was dreaming, had been too afraid to think clearly, so she hadn't looked for the signs.

"We've all been betrayed, Diego," Stephen said. "It just took me longer to figure it out."

He told them what he hadn't been able to tell Cecilia before with Churrlaya watching, about Galactic civilization and the Mentoring Protocols. Then he revealed what he'd learned from the Zenith dissidents about the Chirrn's role in suspending the Protocols and the consequences to humanity. "None of it had to happen," Stephen concluded. "Cecilia, you were right all along, righter than you knew. The Chirrn brought the disaster on themselves by isolating us, hiding from us. We're the victims—we've been their victims since the dawn of history."

Diego and his clique were clearly pleased to see Stephen coming around to their point of view. But Cecilia was only thoughtful. "Because they let us be? Allowed us to find our own way? Hell, for the first time, I feel like thanking them."

"Thanking them?" Stephen was shocked. "For ten thousand years of war and cruelty, famine and plague?"

"None of which they caused."

"They could've helped us avoid it!"

"At what cost? How much of ourselves would we have lost?"

"It's not like that. The Protocols are subtle, delicate, giving mentored peoples as much independence as possible, just protecting them from the worst disasters and mistakes."

"Say the mentors themselves. Can we trust them? Any system can be abused. L'chellin even admitted it. How do you know we wouldn't have been worse off? Gelded and scattered like the Zenith? Weak and dependent, unable to think for ourselves?" Her dream self was clothed now, finally. She and Stephen were in his office back at Stargazer Enterprises in São Paulo, with its splendid view of the dense cityscape stretching clear to the horizon on all sides, the sky filled with an endless dance of quadrotor taxis and private helicopters flitting from rooftop to rooftop. This was where they'd had many of their best arguments, forging their friendship in the process. "Yes, we went through hell, but it was mostly of our own making. And we fought our way through it and survived. It made us stronger."

"It hardened us. Scarred us. That's not the same. We could've been spared so much insanity, so much trauma, so much loss. We could've grown up with a healthier strength, the strength that comes from balance and wisdom and serenity... and our loved ones by our side."

"But could we have had greatness?" Cecilia empathized with the pain in his voice, but she wasn't about to start coddling him now. She gestured around at the office, unleashing her Italian reflex to talk with her hands in a way she never could in free fall or cramped starships. "Look at yourself, Stephen. Look at what you built, what you achieved. Could you have done that if you'd had a peaceful, balanced childhood? If you'd never known hardship and suffering, would you have been so driven to make life better for tens of millions? To take humanity to a whole new world?"

"If Earth had been mentored, I wouldn't have needed to."

"Exactly. We would've been dependent on our mentors."

"We would've achieved just as much, but *together*. Not just a few rising out of the chaos, but everyone contributing their best. Not as romantic, maybe, but the cost would've been far, far less."

"And what about the cost if we had been mentored? You talk about avoiding mistakes. What about the beautiful mistakes? What about the glorious, offbeat, wonderful things we came up with because we were too stupid to know better and didn't have anyone to set us straight? What about Venezia?" She gestured out the window, where the steeples, domes, and low red-tiled roofs of her home had replaced the towering, modern São Paulo skyline. "Would the most beautiful city on Earth have ever been built if some wise, protective alien had said, 'No, don't build there, it'll sink into the marsh?'

"Maybe we did suffer more than most, but maybe that makes us special. Maybe we have things to show the galaxy they've never seen before because so few races have been allowed to develop entirely on their own. Maybe the other races are intimidated by us 'ferals' because they sense that we have something they don't. We could end up a power to be reckoned with in the galaxy, bring it a whole new Renaissance. And we'd have the Chirrn to thank for it."

"How can we achieve any of that," Stephen said, "while the Chirrn keep us imprisoned? You were right about that, Cecilia. Renunciation was just trading one prison for another, a subtler, more devious one. The Chirrn have kept us prisoner for our entire history, kept us isolated and ignorant. Even if you're right that some good came of that, the Chirrn never gave us a choice or an honest chance. Who knows if they'll ever let 'ferals' like humanity out into the galaxy? Programmable quark matter isn't easy to come by, and we know they have ways to cut off the supply to civilizations that cause trouble."

"So what are you proposing?" Diego asked from a corner of the office that still looked like the hibernation bay. Cecilia had almost forgotten the others were there.

"We're working on an escape plan," Stephen replied. "The convoy is getting ready to head out for the neutron star system called Lode Seven, and we have allies who will assist us there along with Broadwing. Once we arrive, I'll tell you more. But I'll need your help. I need us all together in this, working to gain our freedom."

"Yes!" Diego cried, coming forward to clasp Stephen's hand. "Glad to have you in the fight at last."

"I'd prefer it not to be a fight, Diego. We'll be striking back at the Chirrn in a way, don't worry about that. But we have to prove to the galaxy that we're not savages. I don't want this to become violent if we can avoid it."

"Of course not," Diego said, the insincerity subtle enough that Stephen didn't catch it—though Cecilia might have been projecting it onto him in her dream state. "But if we can't avoid it?"

Stephen was slow to respond. The expression Cecilia saw was only what she imagined, but it reflected what she'd sensed in his voice throughout, a depth of bitterness she'd never thought him capable of. "One way or another, we need to be free of the Chirrn."

"That's the spirit."

Cecilia moved in. "Stephen… be careful. I understand why you feel this way, believe me. But you're not used to it. It may be too heady a brew for you. Don't do anything rash."

He stared at her. "You of all people say this? I'm finally where you wanted me to be all along, and now you're objecting?"

"I just… don't like the way this anger looks on you." She knew how much his sense of self was built around hope and optimism. With that shattered, she feared he could lose everything he was. He'd achieved such great things in the name of hope; she shuddered to think what that drive and brilliance could be turned to in the name of rage. But she had trouble finding the words. She'd been angry at him for so long that it was hard to speak to him so intimately, to reconnect with the sisterly love and admiration she still felt for this man.

And so she missed her chance. "You've never approved of anything I did, Cecilia," Stephen said. "It's like a reflex with you. Either grow up or step aside."

He turned away, discussing plans with Diego, Nik, and the rest. Cecilia was alone again, a ghost drifting through the walls.

Haim Silbermann had been too distracted by all this mentoring business to study up on the PQM factory they were heading for. Normally, he was more practical than political, but Stephen's preoccupations had a way of rubbing off on the Arachnen, and it troubled Haim to see how much this one distressed his old friend.

He'd given the matter a lot of thought, but he hadn't arrived at any firm conclusions about where he stood. He did think the Chirrn had been wrong to isolate humanity completely. What made his and Tarik's shared homeland such a vital part of Earth history, a place where religions were born and great changes began, was that it was a crossroads where different cultures met and synergized. In society, as in engineering, potential differences caused energy to flow and work to be done. How much more could humanity have accomplished in interaction with the races of the galaxy? On the other hand, the more recent history of the Mideast was heavy with object lessons on the dangers of well-intentioned meddling in other people's societies. The Chirrn had tried to change the Zenith into copies of themselves and had ended up creating a lethal backlash—an all too familiar pattern. Haim may not have been sure where he stood on the Mentoring Protocols, but it did seem that the Chirrn had screwed up coming and going. Stephen said they couldn't risk staying dependent on the Chirrn, and Haim couldn't disagree.

Still, L'chellin was a stalwart sort once she warmed to you, and R'nilinnath was a real charmer. Yonchon, the Ryohoch starship engineer who had become Haim's mentor, was as alien as any creature Haim had ever encountered, yet had proven over and over that engineers were a universal fraternity. Haim wasn't comfortable thinking of any of them as the enemy. So he'd been uneasy when Stephen had requested his aid in committing a theft. He wasn't an activist like Stephen, but he had his principles. Still, he couldn't deny the cause was just. And it wasn't like there was no precedent. The Torah said the children of Israel had plundered the Egyptians before their Exodus from slavery—though divine intervention had enabled them to do so by asking politely. Haim doubted that would work in this case.

And Haim had to admit, he was intrigued by the technical challenge of pulling off such a heist. Which was nothing compared to the prospect of getting his hands on a large supply of PQM, taking it back to Solsys, and spending the rest of his life cracking its mysteries. Sure, he could study it while working to build the new habitat, but the Chirrn already had all the answers about the stuff, and where was the fun in that?

There were naturally some Arachnen who wanted nothing to do with the heist, Oyama Kazuko notable among them; though they'd grudgingly agreed not to report the others' plans to the authorities. Sita in particular had argued fiercely against it, insisting they'd be better off appealing to Velesh and the Shayal—who would be accompanying the migration fleet to Lode Seven for further "observation," much to L'chellin's annoyance—for assistance in winning liberation. Though Haim respected Sita's position, he regretted the schism that had formed between her and Stephen. Despite his own doubts, Haim knew that even if Stephen was making a mistake, he'd still need his loved ones' help and support to get through it.

One way or the other, Lode Seven would be where the next leg of their journey began. Haim had picked up a few of the basics: Lode Seven was deep in the Upper Scorpius group, where the Void Alliance's rough sphere of influence overlapped with those of neighboring powers, and was administered by a consortium of unaligned civilizations including the Zhalevey and a well-respected race of nocturnal quadrupeds called the Mykhshad. But that was just the politics. The trip was so brief, and he was so busy making sure Arachne and the hibernation pods were all battened down, that he'd had little opportunity for, as Diana had put it, "casing the joint" on a technical level before the heist. So he made sure to pay careful attention once the convoy arrived at Lode Seven, recording everything he saw into his buffer for later study.

When they emerged from the wormhole, the sky around them was far more subdued than the view from Antares; it seemed they were within a parsecs-wide dust cloud free of other habitation, native or otherwise. The wormhole terminal itself was a fair distance from the neutron star, for security and safety (since proximity to large masses and powerful EM fields could disrupt delicate wormhole metrics). Haim suspected that could be a problem for their escape, but Stephen said that Broadwing would be taking care of that end. Hearteningly, the convoy could approach the factory megastructure swiftly using their warp cages in sublight mode. At these speeds, the cage didn't need to be closed, so they had a naked-eye view through the ports. He had expected there to be nothing to see at first, since the star was a mere two dozen kilometers across and relatively cool, as one would expect from an older, radio-quiet neutron star.

But he was wrong. Soon after the warp cage unfurled, Haim beheld a cloudy shimmer of shifting, multihued light. It grew swiftly as they approached on gravitic drive, and with a little adjustment to his adaptive optics, it emerged as an intricate network of brilliant loops arcing along the magnetic field lines of the neutron star, cloaking it in a veil of iridescent threads. Arcs and sheets of energy jumped between the loops at lower altitudes. Brighter knots of light slid along the arcs in clusters like beads on an abacus, slowing as they reached the top of the arcs, then descending with increasing speed into the stellar remnant's immense gravitational field. Yet the blinding impacts he expected when they hit the surface at those speeds were nowhere to be seen, just gentle pulses of color rippling out like auroras. As the ships came closer still, he could discern intricate patterns of light and shading on the neutron star itself, fractal grids of shifting hues overlaid on its ember-orange surface.

"Behold metasapient technology," L'chellin told the awed Arachnen. "The shapes you see consist largely of PQM and nuclear-density superfluids accelerated along the field lines. On occasion, quantities of PQM are sloughed off from the structures and expelled onto the orbits from which we collect them — either a gift for our advancement or mere waste they are content to let us clean up, depending on the interpreter. We know that the structures affect the geometry of spacetime in their vicinity in unusual ways, but we can do little but conjecture as to their effect or purpose, and the conjectures are well beyond my expertise. Let their purpose be to make us wonder and keep us humble." Haim wondered what astronomers back home would have made of this sight if the dust hadn't hidden it from their view.

Lode Seven Station began to resolve alongside that stunning backdrop, initially just a faint string of lights that stayed centered in the viewport as the starscape drifted past behind them (for at the station's orbital distance of nearly half a million kilometers, its "year" was just under 45 *narr*, or 72 minutes). Soon it stretched clear across the sky but was still no more than a hair's breadth wide. This, the mediators explained, was a unique class of megastructure: a tidally stabilized bundle of tethers nearly 6800 kilometers from end to end, enough to spear Mars through both poles with length to spare. This close to a neutron star, the tidal gradient that kept it taut and radially aligned—with anything above its center of mass accelerated outward from the star and anything below it pulled down toward the star—was strong enough to provide habitable gravity inside the modules strung along its length at intervals from dozens to hundreds of kilometers. Moreover, the tethers generated their own electricity as they orbited through the neutron star's magnetic field—and the megastructure orbited in the star's narrow habitable zone, keeping it at a temperature suitable for water-based life. Everything—power, heat, gravity, not to mention PQM—came from the neutron star. It was a marvel of living off the land. In many ways it was so simple, based on elementary physics and technology well within human understanding. But the tension the tethers must be under was staggering. The structural engineering would have to be more advanced even than what he'd learned of Chirrn construction methods.

Haim laughed as he realized the perfect name for such a megas-tructure. "It's a Stringworld!"

R'nilinnath was mingling with the Arachnen, proud as always to show off her erudition as they *ooh*ed and *ahh*ed at the sight. "Everyone needs PQM," she explained, "so the station has modules with every possible environment and gravities. Well, at least those of all the starfarers in the Antispinward Void and neighboring space." She gestured toward the various habitat modules in turn, the pearls of the Stringworld. "There's something here for everyone."

"So people live here?" Haim asked.

"Oh, yes. Every starfaring power keeps an embassy to maintain access to PQM. Also for diplomatic reasons. Everyone comes here, so it's a natural meeting place for conferences or summits."

"Hunh. A watering hole."

"It also helps that exotic spacetime metrics aren't as stable this close to the star. Good for security. Nobody sneaking signals through wormholes or warping in and out for a theft."

Stephen looked at her carefully. "Do thefts happen a lot?"

Nilly mimicked a human shrug. "PQM is practically the only really rare resource, so it's very valuable. But don't worry. The security's very good."

Haim swallowed. "I, ah, I hope so."

The Stringworld was asymmetrical around its center of mass, the inner end half the length of the outer. Atop the radiation shield at the starward end was a large chunk of cometary matter serving as a counterweight and ice reserve. Above it were the automated levels where the PQM harvested from the neutron star's aura was processed, programmed, and prepared for shipping. The outer two-thirds held the residential modules, the "neighborhoods" of this linear megalopolis. This sensibly kept the people on the outer segment of the tether, where "down" was outward from the star; that way, anything or anyone that fell off would be flung into open space and could be recovered.

At the far outer end of the Stringworld was the docking structure that the migration fleet now approached. By docking at the outermost end and "climbing" inward, Haim realized, the ships would transfer momentum to the tether, raising it slightly in its orbit. They would then depart by simply "falling" down the Stringworld's length, the megastructure functioning as its own linear accelerator and giving that momentum back, keeping the ledger in balance.

The docking module was filled with ships of many sizes and designs, all within warp cages yet still displaying a wide variety of engineering and aesthetic philosophies. Haim only got tantalizing glimpses before the convoy docked, whereupon the ships and crews were subjected to an efficient yet thorough process of inspection by the Stringworld customs/security personnel. He strove to stay calm, reminding himself that any equipment for the heist would be brought in by Broadwing or provided by his local Zhalevey allies. Haim's job was simply to take advantage of his position on the engineering team to gain the necessary access.

Simply. Yeah, right. If he couldn't keep his cool during a customs check, he'd be a basket case in the actual heist.

Once the convoy was cleared for entry, *Arachne* was shuttled into a large elevator cage and began to ascend one of the great tethers that held the Stringworld together. There looked to be dozens of tethers running in parallel, each one as wide as a skyscraper and woven of vast fullerene-nanocellulose cables. The cage was evidently quantum-locked to the tether with a magnetohydrodynamic force field, allowing a high-speed frictionless ascent. It also let them slip past the anchor points of the monumental frameworks that ringed the habitat modules they passed, massive rings and arches that bore the immense tension the tethers were under. The module walls were coated in thick layers of aerogel, no doubt to shield their interiors in the event a cable snapped. The release of that kind of tension, Haim realized, would be like a meteoroid impact. He reminded himself that this was the product of a technology far more advanced and ancient than his own. Still, he wouldn't fully trust it until he knew how its safety features worked.

Each module was topped by its own radiation shield resembling a conical Chinese hat, in the event something hit the neutron star "above" them and caused a gamma-ray burst; they were so far from the inner radiation shield that it would be a mere pinprick, not wide enough to shade them if the Stringworld wobbled even the tiniest bit off the vertical. Which it undoubtedly would; no structure on this scale could be perfectly rigid. Looking down the length of the tether, Haim could see that it had a gentle curve, probably due to a very slow swaying motion driven by the movements of ships and elevators among the various modules. Haim wondered what kind of counterweight system was being used to keep the center of mass steady.

As they climbed, the number of parallel tethers increased, for the lower/outer portions of the Stringworld had less weight to support, and extra tethers would add needlessly to the weight the higher tethers had to bear. The modules had been somewhat sparsely distributed for much of the ascent, but were growing more numerous as the effective gravity decreased. The migration fleet finally docked with a large spheroidal module at about 1.3 g.

As they disembarked into the local port facility, the crew found themselves subject to a second inspection. "Security really is tight here," Diana observed, making it sound casual more successfully than Haim ever could. "So much for peaceful galactic society."

L'chellin gave a slight bow of agreement. "While it is true that mentored civilizations are generally less prone to war and savagery, there are other means by which civilizations compete and maneuver for gain," she said. "And there are still deadly threats in the galaxy, despite the best efforts of the mentoring powers to tame it. As the Zenith Cataclysm proved, mentoring can do more harm than good."

"But according to you," Stephen put in, "the Protocols don't apply in this part of space anymore."

"The Protocols were suspended less than four *yanarrach* ago. You are, as far as I know, the first unmentored civilization to reach a PQM lode in this octant since that time." L'chellin gave Stephen an amused glance. "And I trust you do not intend to set a precedent by becoming a security risk."

Haim fumbled and dropped the carrying case he was just receiving back from the customs inspector. *I'm not cut out for a life of crime.*

7

THE INTERIOR OF THE HABITAT MODULE HOUSING THE CHIRRN EMBASSY was a kilometer-wide cityscape segmented into districts, each dominated by a different species' architecture—yet as far as Sita could tell, there was little unity of style within any one district, and a good deal of overlap among them. It looked as though the module had begun as a planned cityscape, but had evolved and been rebuilt over centuries as styles changed and populations shifted—much like any city. Chirrn habitats had their share of such diversity, but it was harder to see, since their partitioned sense of order led them to maintain a fairly consistent style within any single sector, designing new buildings to mesh with those around them. Clearly the Chirrn were not the sole tenants of this module. Nor was this a tourist mecca designed for show like Antares B Star Palace. This was a living, working habitat with a history.

The Shayal embassy was in the same module, which Sita suspected was only partly because the two species had evolved in the same gravity and atmosphere and largely so that they could keep a close eye on each other. But the proximity had made it easier for Sita and Oyama Kazuko to slip away to meet with Velesh, with a little help from Lode Seven's Zhalevey contingent. Part of her still quailed at being surrounded by aliens, but the presence of the Zhalevey—and the relative physical harmlessness of the Shayal—eased Sita's fears enough that she could do what had to be done. Having Kazuko by her side brought her comfort as well, as it had in the weeks after their miscarriages. Though both women had acceded to the Arachnen's consensus to remain quiet about the heist, Sita was still determined to find a way to make it unnecessary. The Shayal may not have been a perfect option, but they did genuinely seem to be trying to make up for past mistakes by pressuring the Chirrn to alter their policies. Kazuko had readily agreed that if they could offer the Arachnen a legal path to freedom, it was surely worth investigating — even if it meant going behind Stephen's back.

The module's "Embassy Row" ringed a central mall/pavilion containing a cluster of open-sided white domes of various sizes, the smaller ones surrounding the large central dome in a fractal arrangement. Velesh and his two mates escorted the two diminutive women around the pavilion, showing them that each dome covered a recessed auditorium with tiered seats like a Greek amphitheater, where Stringworld denizens could gather to watch speeches and debates on the issues of the day. They could have attended virtually over Lode Seven's datanet, but as Velesh explained, "Those who are content to reside within their own minds are not the sort who travel the stars. The beings here are the kind who prefer to interact more directly with the universe and our neighbors within it."

Even so, the pavilion was linked by augreality to equivalent venues in other modules, so that sophonts from radically different environments could have the next best thing to a face-to-face meeting. Velesh's triad led the women into an auditorium hosting a speech transmitted from the Ocean Module high above their heads, positioned close to the Stringworld's center of mass to minimize the weight of the vast quantity of water it contained. Sita grinned in awe and delight at her first sight of the speakers, a pod of six large, long-necked beings like plesiosaurs with manta-ray wings and pronounced beaks. Sita promptly dubbed them "Concorde rays" from their resemblance to the antique European aircraft, though Kazuko didn't get the reference.

The pod collectively sang a trilling, scraping song that translated as a proposal to ecoform an uninhabited ocean planet for colonization by aquatic refugees from the Eta Carinae diaspora. Since such planets had no land of any kind — just pure ocean dozens of kilometers deep over thick mantles of high-pressure allotropic ice — their seas were usually barren, devoid of life-sustaining minerals. The Concorde rays' proposal involved a series of artificial floating land masses covered in nutrient-rich soil, the diversion and demolition of several thousand silicate asteroids to create a dense planetary ring that would rain new minerals down into the oceans on an ongoing basis, and the engineering of deep-dwelling microfauna that would consume the bodies of dying organisms and then rise to the surface to be consumed there, preventing nutrients from sinking out of the ecosystem. Sita had to struggle to remember that she was here to speak to Velesh; she would have been happy to stay here all day, learning more about galactic xenobiomes and their engineering.

The proposal faced some opposition from a conservative Gaurim faction within the Void Alliance, who argued that if it was the nature of an ocean planet to be barren, that nature should not be fundamentally altered. But this seemed to be a minority position; few in the Alliance disputed that the displaced aquatic sophonts had a right to a new home, and adapting an ocean planet was a safer long-term option than constructing a megastructure capable of containing the vast quantities of water they needed. Sita wondered aloud why the aquatics needed to migrate so far from their native Sagittarius Arm, given the abundance of ocean planets in the galaxy. Velesh explained that the intervening territories were already overloaded with refugees, and that interarm regions were the most populous areas of the disk to begin with, since many starfaring civilizations migrated there to avoid the turbulent starbirth zones and supernovae within the arms. A less crowded region would give these aquatic sophonts more breathing room, so to speak. "Although it may be a temporary gain at best," Velesh suggested. "Others are migrating here for similar reasons, so the population of the Four Voids is likely to increase still further in the future. All the more reason why your people would benefit from having prominent allies, lest you become marginalized in your own space."

"In the experience of both Mars and Earth," Kazuko replied coolly, "increased immigration is generally beneficial to a society, and rhetoric claiming the reverse is generally a self-serving political ploy. The Voids have gone this long without being repopulated; maybe it's high time they finally were."

"A fair point, and I apologize for implying otherwise," Velesh said. "Indeed, for some time after the Zenith Cataclysm, the Voids were too dangerous to resettle. The mad Zenith left hidden pockets of contagion which could lie dormant for generations, and combatants on both sides created booby traps and autonomous weapons that lingered long after the war. It was many generations before the last of these in the Antispinward, Outward, and Central Voids were sprung or defused, and some hazards still remain in Spinward, where the madness began. So the region's stigma has remained. You are correct to suggest that this has not been beneficial. Galactics are distantly aware that new civilizations in need of mentoring have arisen here, but the diaspora preoccupies the most powerful societies in this octant, and too many others have been slow to overcome their old fears."

Velesh's eyes rolled out to the sides, and Sita wondered if it conveyed shame in his species as it did in the Chirrn. "All because we were too proud of the Chirrn—too quick to believe they were ready to stand in our place. Because they were family and we forgave their faults too readily. Whole civilizations were rendered extinct as a consequence... and the civilizations that have since emerged in the Voids have paid an ongoing price. A price the Chirrn have forced them to pay in silence."

The Shayal emissary led the women back out onto the mall, his mates tagging along as always. They never seemed to say much; was it Shayal custom for the hermaphrodite to speak for the group, or was Velesh simply prone to monopolize the conversation? "But now the Lesshchi disaster has brought the plight of the Voids' young civilizations to the galaxy's attention," the emisssary went on. "More, the Chirrn are being judged for what they have done to you in the wake of that disaster. They have blamed and punished you for an accident that arose as much from their own choices as yours. You have repeatedly endured physical violence, even suffered deaths as a result of your captivity. Many find this unacceptable."

"Don't need to tell us, mate," Sita murmured without sound. She strove to remain patient with Velesh's incessant lecturing.

They passed into what looked like a sculpture garden, though the AR annotations identified the pieces as remnants of the Casimir cage that had held the first wormhole to reach this neutron star, the first crude habitat built in its orbit, and other historic artifacts. "This is why we have brought you here, Doctor Bhatiani, Administrator Oyama. We cannot unilaterally compel the Chirrn to surrender their custody of you. But we could arrange for Stephen and your fellow Arachnen to speak before the public. Your testimony about your experiences in Chirrn custody could help persuade the region's governments to bring pressure upon the Void Alliance and finally compel a change in their policies."

"I'm afraid that's something of a vicious cycle," Kazuko said. "What liberty we have is contingent upon being loyal, contributing members of Shilirrlaln society. Speaking out against them would violate our probation and subject us to penalties."

"That is why you must make your case publicly before the representatives here. If the Lode Seven administrative council can be convinced that the PQM ordered by the Chirrn would be used to support unethical practices, such as the coercion of human labor to construct a habitat in which human freedoms would be restricted, then the council might refuse delivery. If the Chirrn wish to strengthen their presence in this Void, they would be obligated to release your people."

Sita's heart raced. Was Velesh offering an alternative — and legal — path to freedom? But Kazuko caught her excitement and sent a cautioning eyetext. <*Galactic affairs sound very complicated. We need more context before we can judge.*> "Release us to what?" the poised Martian asked.

"The Nine Clusters Coalition would offer you sanctuary."

"Sanctuary," Sita echoed. "So you wouldn't take us home? Or let us settle on Cybele as we originally planned?"

Velesh's neck wattle puffed out briefly, an expression Sita hadn't yet learned to read. Pausing beneath an arch made from a fragment of Stringworld tether charred and pitted in some ancient construction mishap, he spent a few moments conferring with his mates (confirming that they could get a word in edgewise after all). "Potentially that could be arranged once we have managed to bring about changes in the Void Alliance's policies. Returning you to your homeworld is a desirable goal, but one that must be managed with care."

"'Managed,'" Kazuko echoed. "By you, I take it?"

"Please understand. Your people have been isolated for a long time. If knowledge of galactic civilization, and of the decisions that have damaged them over the *yanarrach*, were revealed to humanity too abruptly, without the proper context, their reaction could be... unpredictable. To avoid potentially harmful consequences in the long term, we would need to send emissaries to Sol System to mediate your people's initial engagement with galactic civilization."

Velesh's body language was enough like a Chirrn's that Sita could recognize him eyeing the two small women warily, as though handling half-tamed animals. *Not this shite again.* "You're afraid humanity might react violently."

"The concern is not primarily ours, Doctor Bhatiani. Your inadvertent role in the Lesshchi disaster reinforced long-standing fears regarding the indigenous peoples of the Four Voids. The Chirrn can use that to argue for your continued isolation, and that of other young local civilizations. If we are to bring lasting change for the benefit of your people and others, we must approach humanity's introduction to the galactic community judiciously. A degree of remedial mentoring would be expected."

Remedial mentoring? That had a rather Kiplingesque sound. She knew both sides of her cultural heritage well enough to recognize how dangerous it could be for one civilization to see another as unruly children in need of remediation. "Hang on, mate. We made it out here on our own, you know. We learned to stop blowing each other up—mostly—on our own. We may have learnt the hard way, but we're grownups now." *Even if we did make a hash of our driving test first time out,* she thought with grim humor.

"Your optimism is commendable, Doctor, but you are used to thinking on a briefer time scale than most. It was not long ago that you nearly destroyed yourselves, first with nuclear weapons, then with environmental neglect. It is too early to say that you would not fall back into old habits, especially if your development were disrupted by exposure to the Voids' history or by access to PQM and its potentials.

"Do not let pride override wisdom. Sponsorship by an established civilization would benefit your people. We could guide you through the transition to galactic life gently and peacefully. We could offer methods of self-mastery that have not occurred to your people, the collected wisdom of thousands of similar civilizations that could be adapted to serve your needs.

"And without such sponsorship," Velesh went on, "it would be difficult for humanity to win sympathy. We do not wish you to become a negative example that the Chirrn can use to promote their agenda."

<No,> Kazuko texted her. <*They want us to be an example to promote their agenda.*>

<*No kidding,*> Sita sent back. <*But is Meridian's agenda any better?*>

To Sita's surprise, Stephen was not angry at her or Kazuko when they returned. "I knew you had to follow your own consciences," he told them once the three were alone in his embassy quarters. "And I trusted you both not to betray our confidence." He turned to her. "Sita... I don't want us to be at odds."

He reached toward her, and she saw he was still wearing his wedding ring. But she maintained a coolly civil tone, nipping his gesture in the bud. He would have to earn the opportunity to win her back. "Then I hope you'll consider what we have to say."

His hand dropped, but his manner remained conciliatory. "Of course."

To his credit, he listened to the women's account of Velesh's offer with an open mind, taking the time to consider it before he replied. It reminded Sita how deeply she admired this man—though she was no longer sure if admiration was the same as love.

When he finally spoke, it was with regret. "No. There was a time, no question, that mentoring would have done us a great deal of good. Our exclusion from the Protocols cost us dearly. But Cecilia was right. *You* were right. We've learned from our hardships, fought our way to solutions that work for us. We became our own mentors out of necessity, and we've earned the right to be accepted into the galaxy as adults. The Shayal, these other privileged Galactics brought up within the mentoring system, they just can't understand that. They don't have the perspective to recognize their own prejudice and the impact it would have on us. Of all the species we've met, only the Zenith have that perspective."

"Look, I admit, Velesh's offer has its downside," Sita said. "But it's got to be better to be political pawns than wanted fugitives! Safer, at least!"

"Is it? The Galactics may not be prone to war, but like they say back home, diplomacy is war by other means. There are still plenty of conflicts among the powers of the galaxy; they just wage them through politics and public opinion, and you know how ugly a game that can be."

"But it's a game we have plenty of our own experience with," Kazuko pointed out. "Indeed, we're probably a lot more cutthroat about it than they're used to. We might have more of an advantage than you think. But not if we compound our already tenuous reputation with a deliberate crime."

"But it's not just about us, Kazuko. We've ended up as a *cause célèbre* at the heart of a major policy dispute. And we've seen how the mentoring process can be compromised by political agendas. If we ended up under the Shayal's 'remedial mentoring,' their choices could be influenced more by the fears and rivalries of the galactic community than by the best interests of humanity."

"At least we'd be in a position to win some trust and respect in the galaxy, even if it takes a while."

"Respect?" Stephen challenged. "We'd be seen as refugees, mistreated primitives in need of a handout. Human space would remain a backwater, dependent on the generosity of more powerful neighbors. Ask Tarik or Haim—how well did that work for the Middle East? You tell me, Sita, how well did it work for India under the Raj?"

"The Protocols wouldn't let them impose that much," Sita countered.

"Even so, do you think humanity would be content to be so weak and dependent?"

Sita ran a hand through her hair in frustration. "Well, what's the alternative? Become thieves, pirates?"

"We'd have the PQM. And we'd have the freedom to go wherever we wanted, to make our own choices without supervision."

"With the rest of the galaxy watching in terror to see what we'd do next!"

"And we'd prove," Stephen insisted, "that they have nothing to fear. I believe we'd use the PQM responsibly, apply the lessons we've learned the hard way. Maybe we could try some mentoring of our own, help other young civilizations in the Voids in accordance with the Protocols."

"Aren't you getting a little ahead of yourself there, Stephen?" Kazuko asked.

"Right," Sita put in. "Don't you think the Chirrn would try to stop us?"

"The Chirrn's standing has been weakened either way. As Meridian says, pulling off this heist will undermine them even more. Other races may even admire us for being able to get out from under the Chirrn on our own."

Sita scoffed. "Too right, on our own. Never mind the Zenith and the Zhalevey."

"The point is, we'll be independent, not subject to the Shayal's agendas. In their own way, they're just as responsible for all this as the Chirrn. How do we know we'd be any safer in their hands?

"Besides… we're already committed to helping Meridian. Her part of the plan is already in motion, and if we don't follow through with our part, it'll all be for nothing. Meridian's people deserve the freedom to pursue their dreams just as much as we do, and they're counting on us. We owe it to them and to ourselves to keep our word."

Sita stared at him, gobsmacked. "So you're going through with grand theft because you're too honorable not to?"

Stephen held her gaze. "It's civil disobedience. And a way to send a clear message to the Chirrn. I want that message to be ours, not the Shayal's."

"Do you?" Sita demanded. "Or do you just want to make the Chirrn pay?"

His hesitation was the last straw. She turned and strode from the room. A moment later, Kazuko jogged up behind her. "So that's it? End of discussion?"

"There's no changing his mind—trust me. If he's so bloody determined to commit this heist, I'll leave him to it—for better or worse."

"If you say so," Kazuko said after a moment. "Well, at least with Stephen in charge, the odds are that nobody will be hurt."

"Sure," Sita replied. "Except, just possibly, the entire human race."

"Stealing the PQM from the processing levels would be impossible," Broadwing told the group assembled in the passenger lounge.

Haim Silbermann was getting used to having conversations in space elevators—this time in a sightseeing car running up along the Stringworld's vast tethers, a trip the party was taking to get the lay of the land before the heist. In a way, Haim was perversely glad that Sita and Kazuko had failed to talk Stephen out of the theft. It would've been nice to have an easier way to win their freedom, but it would've been a shame to have done so much research and preparation for nothing.

"When launched from the star's surface," Broadwing went on, "it is too hot and traveling too fast to be intercepted before it reaches the capture tethers, and it would be useless to us without priming. The processing levels themselves are entirely cyber-controlled, for no organic life could survive in the conditions where the initial processing is done."

Broadwing's three eyes darted around to take in each co-conspirator in turn. Besides Stephen, Tarik, Haim, and Diana, they had been joined for this final review by Meridian's chief Zhalevey infiltrator, a nearly solid-colored greenish-tan male named Shthastya.

"That is why we must strike here," Broadwing went on, one wing-arm gesturing expansively at the tethers beyond the viewport. "The time when the PQM is in transit from the processing center to the migration fleet will be its only window of vulnerability."

"Tarik?" Stephen prompted.

"Haim, Diana, and I have successfully obtained clearance to accompany the freight lift for the pickup," Tarik said.

"All part of our rehabilitation as contributing members of society," Haim put in for Shthastya's benefit. "If we're gonna help build a habitat using this stuff, we need to learn all we can about it."

Broadwing called their attention to an occupied docking cradle on a tether several kilometers away, moving downward as they moved up. "Observe: one of the empty vessels assigned as counterweights for Stringworld attitude control. The Zhalevey stand ready to see that *Arachne*'s cradle is thus misallocated."

"Which will be my excuse to keep L'chellin distracted trying to track it down," Stephen said, frowning. "I'd rather be in the lift with all of you, but I'm the one who can draw the most attention elsewhere."

Haim turned to the Zhalevey. "And you'll make sure they don't find it, right, little fella?"

"At your service," Shthastya replied.

"There's one thing we need to be clear on," Tarik said to the tripedal sophont. "I know your people thrive on service, but don't you try to serve everyone equally? You're committing quite a betrayal against your employers here. Can we count on your loyalty to Meridian to take precedence?"

Shthastya seemed untroubled. "Service to Meridian led us to service to Stringworld. Service to Stringworld is subsumed to primary service to Meridian."

So they're moles, Haim realized. Meridian had been planning this for a long time; she just hadn't been able to find the right concatenation of allies and opportunity until now. *Just our luck.*

"Broadwing, can you be certain Meridian will time her little distraction to strike exactly when the lifts are in the right position?" Tarik asked. "What if she's late to the party?"

"I have received confirmation that Meridian is in-system," the Zenith said. "The optimal target object has already been selected."

One more reason she needed to wait, Haim thought. Meridian had cultivated or bribed enough allies at the Star Palace to get her smuggled past security and through the wormhole, but if she were spotted aboard the Stringworld itself, it would cost her people the deniability they needed. Instead, her small, short-range warp ship—better for relativistic in-system travel than FTL—had been snuck in as a support craft for a larger vessel, which had then jettisoned it between the wormhole exit and the Stringworld, whereupon the small ship had sped to the outskirts of the system to begin its crucial part of the operation.

"But I assume the Stringworld systems are shielded against that kind of radiation," Haim said. "This sort of thing has to happen naturally from time to time."

"Shielding has limits," Shthastya replied. "And can be subverted with advance knowledge of need."

"The damage won't be too bad," Tarik said, "but it should blind their sensors and scramble communications long enough for us to do the job, especially once the Zhalevey's viruses come into play. After all, you can't really harden EM sensors against EM."

"Is there any risk of a starquake?" Diana asked. "If that happened, we'd all be dead from the radiation in an instant."

"The metasapients stabilized the surface of the neutron star long ago," Broadwing assured her. "Otherwise it would not have been feasible for even them to settle it. Focus on your own responsibility, Diana."

The Vanguardian engineer sighed. "Hopefully, that'll just be moving the PQM."

Stephen squeezed her muscular forearm. "If you and Tarik handle the supervisors right, you won't need to get rough with them. Nobody wants that." Diana smiled back, appreciating his reassurance. For all her love of rough sports, hurting innocent bystanders was a very different matter.

"I'm still not clear on how we can fit it all on board *Arachne*, though," Diana went on.

"It is stored in concentrated form," Broadwing explained. "The quantity that will fit within *Arachne*'s cargo modules and the excess space within the warp cage should be sufficient to build dozens of vessels, or a wormhole and a smaller number of vessels. Also, we will not need to take the low-grade PQM slated for the habitat's maneuvering ring. That is the largest quantity by volume but the least useful for our purposes."

Diana nodded. "Makes it easier. Still… is it safe? I mean, the embryos are still aboard the ship."

Stephen frowned. "We have no choice there. We need to be able to make a swift getaway. But there's no reason to think they'll be in danger. If anything, their presence works in our favor—if we're discovered, the authorities won't risk endangering the embryos by taking rash action."

Haim frowned. "I don't like using them as hostages."

"If all goes well, it won't come to that, Haim. But none of this will matter if we don't neutralize that reference sample."

"Yeah, yeah. It's done." Haim sighed. "I can't say I enjoyed doing it, but I've hacked Yonchon's manipulator drones. I can intercept the control signals, make them do what we want while making it look to Yonchon's senses like they're doing what Yonchon wants." He held up a small emitter crafted from a portion of the smart matter that constituted Arachne's avatar. "And this little guy is ready to emit the fake signature once it's in place."

"But not before the system disruptions," Broadwing reminded him. "They must not learn of the sample's loss until it is too late to stop us."

"Of course. You just make sure the Unrenounced are awake and suited up so we can schlep the PQM over to *Arachne*."

"Do not take that lightly," Broadwing warned. "Remember, you will be outward from the center of mass, so acceleration will be present."

"But we'll still be as good as weightless."

"No such thing," Diana told him sternly. "If you let yourself think that way, if you don't keep track of which way you're moving at every moment, then before you realize it you could be falling too far and too fast to catch, and then you're vacked for good. Literally."

"Right," Haim realized. "Pardon an old dirtgrubber. That's what we're counting on, after all, isn't it?"

"That's right," Tarik said. "A few cut brakes on the docking cradle and *Arachne* will be free and clear to rendezvous with the rest of you."

"We can't get out through the wormhole, can we?" Diana asked. "They'd be ready for that."

"We can depart at warp," Broadwing told her. "It will take some time to reach another wormhole port, but we will be essentially untrackable."

Diana stared out the window, her expression buoyant in a way that had nothing to do with the diminishing tidal gravity. "And then... we can go anywhere we want."

"Sure," Haim said. "If we can pull off the impossible first."

8

"Course and velocity confirmed," chimed Mountain's Peak, her head lowered to Meridian. "Release in thirty-six hexapulses."

The subordinate female sounded a steady harmony with beats at three-hexapulse intervals, counting down to the release point. Meridian began to emit a stand-ready trill whose pace slowed as the countdown progressed; when it synchronized at zero point, their combined chord resolved into the command: "Release!" Mountain's Peak ducked her head with an obedient single-crest tone to indicate compliance. The command had technically been unnecessary, for their scout ship's computer had automatically dissipated the gravity pocket at precisely the right interval to release their chosen comet on its fated trajectory. But it did her subordinates good to feel they were playing their parts within the hierarchy.

Indeed, Mountain's Peak looked pleased. "The predator stoops toward its target," she whooped.

At Meridian's side, Apastron gave a warning tone. "You skirt blasphemy," the second chided.

Meridian leaned over and preened the featherfur on Apastron's neck to soothe her. "You know this will not harm the stardwellers. It will be like a refreshing rain to them. Were it not so, they would not permit this to happen."

"I aspire to that," Apastron keened in a skeptical minor key. "But what if we are wrong? I trust—I know that we can reach their level one day, if we achieve the means. But they are still so far above our comprehension."

"And we will never gain that comprehension if we do not dare, young one."

Meridian felt a twinge of regret. Apastron was reaching the age when a female would normally claim as many of her matron's males as she could win and branch off to begin her own harem. Her burgeoning rebellious streak was a symptom of that wanderlust. But as long as their clique was underground and forced to stay together, Apastron must either stay at her current rank, unable to climb, or challenge Meridian for leadership, which would surely leave her broken when she failed. Meridian had clawed her way back up from such a defeat long ago, building a new harem from scratch once she had discovered she could draw in the disenfranchised with the promise of metasapience. But she would not wish that long, lonely struggle on her second, even if she felt the young female had the determination and rhetorical skill to achieve it. No, Apastron's best hope was that the theft succeeded, so that Meridian and her followers could move to the Inner Disk, the heart of Galactic civilization, where the disasters and destruction that haunted the Four Voids were merely a distant rumor from the fringes. Once far enough away to be free of their stigma, they could branch out into separate harems and pursue multiple avenues of research.

Still, losing Apastron's trusted counsel would be a blow. They had been together for so long—but no. That was thinking like a lesser race, growing complacent. A Zenith thrived only by climbing upward, seeking change. And with so few positions at the top, other females would always be temporary allies at best. If Apastron were to continue to serve her, let it be as a rival forcing her to become better. Racing her to the pinnacle of metasapience.

For now, though, she needed her second as an ally, not a competitor. "Trust in the stardwellers, Apastron," she sang. "Remember, they wish us all to rise and join them. I do not doubt that our venture has their blessing."

Apastron echoed her phrases, chiming in accord to show she accepted Meridian's counsel. "But my doubts also extend lower, to the humans. I would rather you had entrusted that stage of the plan to Broadwing."

"Broadwing is easy to manipulate, but he has been too tamed by the Chirrn and has lost his hunter's instincts. He will accept it once he sees it is my will, but I think he would lack the determination to do it himself."

"But the humans? Crown of the Usurper King is even less a hunter, despite his name."

"I do not need his participation in that stage. From what Broadwing has told me of the Unrenounced, they are already primed for this task. Their ambition has been bottled for so long that they will seize the opportunity to strike."

"I aspire to that as well," Apastron chimed, though with an inverted counterpoint connoting ambivalence. "Yet I hope you are right that this is truly necessary."

Meridian clacked her mandibles together sharply. "Have you become too squeamish to stoop on prey?"

"To feed on prey is one thing. To extinguish minds… I would not do so more than I must."

"Then have no fear." Meridian preened her neck again. "For remember, the stardwellers are watching. We will extinguish no minds—we will simply free them to nourish the gods."

"L'chellin, we need to talk."

The mediator split her gaze, one eye on Stephen, the other on the party about to board the freight lift. "This is not an appropriate time, Stephen. I must supervise the processing and loading of our PQM order."

"Yonchon and Haim can handle that. And this is the only time. Velesh has invited us to request sanctuary for *Arachne*'s crew with the Nine Clusters Coalition. A lot of us think that sounds like a better offer than the life we'd have with you."

L'chellin ruffled her bristles with a sigh. Yonchon had entered the lift cab now, leaving one drone behind to watch her expectantly. The Lode Seven attendants, a pair of Zhalevey and a large Mykhshad, stood sentry alongside the doors. She gestured to them to wait.

"I had thought you had moved beyond these doubts," she told Stephen.

"I have doubts about a lot of things now. But Velesh's offer would let us reunite with the Unrenounced, set them free at last."

"If sanctuary were granted. The hearings would take *narruvh*."

"Which is why it would have to begin now."

"Would you abandon your oaths so easily?" L'chellin asked, saddened by the question.

"This isn't easy for me. But I have prior oaths to my own crew."

"That is why you should not hasten to align yourselves with the Shayal. They would use you as pawns. To us, you are family now."

"Then you need to convince me of that, L'chellin. And make it good enough that I can convince the Arachnen."

In her left-eye field, Haim hesitated on the lift threshold, tense with anticipation at the technological marvels he would witness on the processing levels. Diana appeared just as eager, her enthusiasm manifesting in more overt motion; she kept taking her measuring equipment out of her vest pockets to recheck it, even as she kept one eye on Stephen (though that phrase was only metaphorical for a human). Even Tarik stood ready — still bitter toward the Chirrn, L'chellin knew, but sworn to serve the Arachnen at all costs. He would go where Stephen led, so L'chellin needed to win Stephen back to the Chirrn's side, where his people would be nurtured to their full potential — not paraded as savages and victims, a cautionary tale to illustrate the so-called crimes of the Void Alliance.

L'chellin directed a small bow toward Yonchon's drone, instructing the Ryohoch to proceed without her.

"Then let us exchange words, Stephen — and resolve this with finality."

Sita hadn't slept well since the Arachnen's arrival at the String-world. She could swear she felt the habitat module swaying beneath her, disorienting her. Which didn't make sense; although the undulations of the megastructure were real, they took hours to propagate along its length, the motions too slow to feel.

So she was forced to admit the real reason: she was no longer used to sleeping alone. It wasn't just the sex; she missed Stephen's warm, comforting presence beside her at night. She missed…

No. She didn't miss falling in love with a fantasy and finding it too fragile to shore her up — to shore either of them up — through the harsh realities of the past two months. Beyond the surface distraction of their physical passions, she and Stephen had never truly been together. And she had surely proven to herself by now that she was capable of braving the Galactic community on her own.

But it would still take time to find her balance again without him. Fantasies could be very comforting in the dead of night.

The other thing keeping her awake was ambivalence about the insane scheme that Broadwing and his outlaw queen had roped the Arachnen into carrying out. Since the failure of her second attempt to talk Stephen out of it, she'd been debating what to do next, both within herself and with the other Arachnen. A few, including Joana Caravalho and Ravinder Pritam, had sided with her and Kazuko, warning the others of the dangers if any part of the overcomplicated plan went wrong. The Arachnen could all find themselves penalized as co-conspirators if they failed to come forward before it was too late. And though they all trusted Stephen to keep things nonviolent—especially with the embryos aboard *Arachne*—Sita wasn't so sure about Broadwing. True, it had been the mediator's dismay at the loss of Lesshchin life that had led him to this in the first place, but he was still a predator by nature.

Yet they'd been heavily outnumbered by the ones who sided with Stephen, swayed by his promises of freedom and a new beginning not just for them, but for all of humanity. These people wouldn't have been here if they hadn't already bought into Stephen's promises of hope and human achievement.

Justine Nguyen in particular was compelled by Broadwing's talk about the possibility of metasapients recording or capturing the minds of the dead. Sita could understand why the astrophysicist would grasp at straws to believe her lost baby could've been saved, but she resisted giving in to the same impulse—as did Ravinder, who insisted that an early second-trimester fetus would have no significant neural activity, certainly nothing resembling consciousness. But Justine had spun theories of her fetus's whole environment being simulated so it could develop and be born into a virtual posthuman life. It agonized Sita to see her buy so deeply into the delusion... although some part of her hoped that Justine might actually be right. Was it really any crazier than believing her own baby's soul would be reincarnated as part of the karmic cycle?

When Broadwing came to the Arachnen's embassy quarters to advise them that the plan was in motion, it crystallized her doubts. "Be sure to remain gathered here," the Zenith intoned to the group. He gestured to the Zhalevey attendants he'd brought with him. "When the system disruptions begin, these three will escort you to a ship that will smuggle you out to rendezvous with *Arachne* and Meridian's craft. Remember, you must stay together."

Once he left, Sita led Kazuko and Ravinder aside. "We've got to do something," she whispered, "and quickly."

"But what can we do?" Kazuko asked. "If we sneak off to warn someone, we risk being left behind if the escape goes off as planned."

"And *should* we try to stop this?" Ravinder added. "Don't we at least owe it to Stephen to let him try?"

"Maybe we owe it to him to stop him from making a terrible mistake," Sita replied.

"All right," Kazuko said patiently. "How?"

Sita stared back. "You're asking me? You're the administrator!"

"You know Stephen best, Sita. You know the Chirrn and Zenith best. Whatever you decide, we'll support."

Sita was moved by Kazuko's faith, but the answer to her question remained elusive. "Sod it, I need to know more about the Zenith. I need to know more about *Broadwing*." If she was going to trust him—or betray him—she had to know more. She had to talk to someone she could rely on to keep a secret—someone who'd known Broadwing longer than any human had.

Three minutes later, she was clambering over the embassy's balcony railing. Her old tree-climbing skills were still with her, though it was a near thing in this gravity. She managed to leap to an adjacent dendroid plant with branches like orange feather dusters, disturbing a swarm of silver-green, fingernail-sized avians to flutter away from their perches in a sparkling cloud. She startled a pair of Gaurim when she landed; she gave a quick apology she doubted they'd understand and ducked beneath their high, cantilevered torsos to get out to the pathway beyond.

As she ran, Kazuko's words echoed in her mind. If she wasn't with the others when they were evacuated, she could end up as the only human left in Chirrn custody. She could be condemning herself to spend the rest of her life alone among aliens.

So bloody what? she thought. She'd already lost her baby. If the worst day of her life was behind her, what did she have to be afraid of now?

As she ran through the crowded streets, feeling the giddy abandon of someone who'd just jumped off a cliff, she experienced a renewed thrill of wonder at the magnificently alien life forms that surrounded her. Having a lifetime to study them wouldn't be such a bad fate after all.

The discomfort in Haim's stomach had nothing to do with the shifting gravity in the freight lift over its lengthy climb, or the way the hemispherical cab mounted on the side had flipped 180 degrees as they passed the Stringworld's center of mass. He was worried about getting caught, worried about giving himself away *because* he was worried about getting caught, worried about betraying his friend Yonchon (though he still wasn't sure if Yonchon even had the concept of either friendship or betrayal), worried that the plan wouldn't work, worried that it would work.

So far, he had to admit, the scheme had gone swimmingly. It had been a relief and a bit of a surprise that the whole team had gotten clearance to start with; Haim had wondered if the administration would even let sophonts with a reputation like theirs anywhere near the highly secure factory levels. But in retrospect, it stood to reason that a society based in mentoring would be big on teaching opportunities. This was all being treated as part of a novice people's education in the ways of galactic life, an established practice that the Arachnen were able to slot into fairly well, despite the *tsuris* and *tumul* surrounding their emergence onto the scene.

Indeed, their attendants came off more as guides and instructors than guards—although Haim was aware that the freight lift was more than able to guard itself. The Zhalevey were helpful as ever, naturally. The chief attendant, a Mykhshad named something like Rysuth, was more physically formidable—a pony-sized quadruped with a teardrop-shaped body tapering to the rear, a prehensile trunk with fine manipulative tendrils at the end, and bulky forelimbs ending in strong grasping digits, which he could free for use by rearing up and resting his weight on his short hind legs and strong but flexible tail. His tiger-striped body was covered in bluish-gray sensory bristles resembling fur, and his face bore only the most rudimentary eyes; but the Geiger-counter ticking of his echolocation pulses and the way his bristles twitched in response to the slightest movement made it clear that he was watching his passengers closely. Haim recalled from Broadwing's briefing that a Mykhshad's sonar could be amplified to weapon force like a dolphin's. It would be less effective here than in their dense native atmosphere, but in this enclosed space it could still be loud enough to incapacitate. Haim hoped he would not have to find out.

Yet Rysuth seemed an amiable enough host, volubly explaining the PQM processing procedure to the group. Diana had played along as an eager student to get the Mykhshad off his guard, and as they now readied to observe the transfer operations, she made a show of fumblingly checking the equipment in her vest pockets. "Here, hold this," she said, briefly handing a coin-sized imaging unit to Haim. The senior engineer turned his back and deftly plugged in an extra component he had secreted in his hand. He let it slip from his grip when he tried to return it, but Tarik caught it; when he returned it to Diana, he nodded slightly, confirming that he'd plugged in his piece as well. The three components had been dormant to pass security; now the combined device would activate after the appropriate interval.

"I know this is asking a lot," Diana said to Rysuth, "but Yonchon already agreed to let me piggyback this image sensor on the drone Yonchon sends in for the registration, so long as you approve it. This is the first time humans have ever witnessed this — I want to record it on a medium designed for human senses."

Rysuth was only too happy to oblige Diana's curiosity. Haim was starting to get the impression that all the security around the factory levels was a holdover from earlier times when paranoia about pockets of surviving meta-Zenith was still rampant. The Stringworld staff seemed to be going through the motions without any serious concerns about theft. After all, why should they worry? If anyone tried to use a PQM supply illegally or destructively, it could always be neutralized as long as there was an entangled reference sample on file.

And that was the key to this part of the plan. In order for the new PQM to mesh properly with the migration fleet's existing stock, the two would need to be entangled and taken through a sort of handshake protocol to calibrate them with one another, and the security reference sample kept in the factory level would need to be entangled and calibrated with both. So Yonchon had brought along a sample of the fleet's PQM. Normally, the factory's own drones would take the sample into its uninhabitable innards for the process; but Yonchon, ever the individualist, had insisted on doing it personally. The manipulator drones that rode on the back of the Ryohoch engineer's massive, nine-legged body like birds on a hippo were effectively an extension of Yonchon's person, remote-controlled "hands" for a species with only rudimentary manipulative limbs. Apparently the Ryohoch were trusted enough that the request was accepted — or mysterious enough that nobody would suspect one of anything as quotidian as criminal motives.

Haim would've preferred to pay undivided attention to the registration and entanglement process (and he made sure his buffer was recording so he could study the memory later). Unfortunately, it was now his turn to play perhaps the most crucial role in the plan. While he pretended to make notes about the registration on his datapad, he was actually intercepting Yonchon's drone transmissions, making sure the registration code the drone entered in the new PQM supply was not the one Yonchon thought it was entering.

When that was done, Haim sent a command, and Diana's remote image sensor overloaded and burst. "Oh!" Diana cried in feigned surprise as the signal went dead. "What the vack was that?"

"Your device may have lacked the strength to survive the pressure and radiation within," Rysuth suggested.

"Oh, damn! Yonchon, did I hurt your drone?" she asked, placing a solicitous hand on the side of the Ryohoch's massive, peanut-shaped body.

"Sensation from drone in abeyance. Presumption is damage."

"I'm so sorry, I had no idea."

"Attrition occurs. This situation does not change."

"That means 'don't worry about it'," Haim interpreted.

"We have asked the factory to repair the drone," the taller, greener Zhalevey reported. "Its return shall precede your fleet's departure."

"Oh, what a relief," Diana said. But she didn't fully relax until Haim gave her a tiny nod. The debris from the explosion had included an array of transmitter nans, a portion of which had successfully attached to the capsule containing the reference sample. When the time came, they would activate.

Haim just had to hope their dormant state would fool the factory level's security — or he and his cohorts would be arrested before that could happen.

By the time the worried Arachnen called Broadwing to notify him that Sita Bhatiani had fled, it was too late to do anything about it. Meridian's will had been set inexorably into motion, and Broadwing had to do his part as reliably as orbital mechanics. He could only hope that Sita would be unable to reach Lode Seven's authorities in time to alert them to the theft. Soon enough, it would be too late for anyone to stop it — but only if Broadwing did his part and got *Arachne* underway.

So it was an unwelcome surprise when he and his Zhalevey accomplices arrived at *Arachne*'s docking bay to find Churrlaya there. The Lesshchin survivor eagerly accosted Broadwing. "Mediator, at last. I need your help."

"Apologies. I have urgent business aboard the ship."

"As have I. I must awaken Cecilia and speak with her."

"You may do so once we reach the settlement site."

"How long will it be before it is decided that we have the luxury of awakening them? We will be too busy to guard them; more than likely it will be deemed safer to keep them dormant until the habitat is functional, which could take two *narrenn* or more."

"They slept safely for far longer than that," Broadwing chimed impatiently. Seeing no choice, he allowed Churrlaya to follow him aboard *Arachne*.

"It is Cecilia's mental state that concerns me. I believe many of the other Unrenounced resent Cecilia for halting their escape attempt. Within their linked hibernation dreams, without conscious inhibitions, that resentment will most likely express itself openly, even violently. Cecilia may be traumatized, or coerced into submitting to the consensus. I believe she is on the verge of renunciation, of genuine healing at last. But if it is delayed, she may be lost to us."

"Have you not taken this up with the others?"

"I have tried. But the Lode authorities are pressing them not to awaken beings they consider proven threats. Mediator, the PQM is already on its way. We will be shipping out within *narrach*. This may be my last chance to save Cecilia."

Broadwing was surprised that the Lesshchin wished to help the commander of the ship responsible for destroying his world. But he had no time or attention to devote to that paradox. Instead, he considered that Churrlaya's request could be turned to his advantage. If the awakening of all the Unrenounced could be attributed to Churrlaya's mishandling of the primitive equipment in his effort to awaken just one, it would divert the subsequent investigation away from himself and Meridian. Besides, the young Chirrn was so fixated on Cecilia that he was not at all curious why Broadwing was here. Giving him his human pet to play with would keep him out of Broadwing's way without the need for any messy killing. Many of the Unrenounced wouldn't mind at all if he killed Churrlaya, but a few might balk at a time when their swift and efficient compliance would be essential. Not to mention that it would be difficult to kill Churrlaya in a way that would appear accidental yet be quick enough that no incriminating evidence would be recorded in his cloud memories.

"Agreed," Broadwing said. "I will assist you with the equipment."

"You have studied their hibernation system?"

He hesitated for only an instant. "Familiarity with their technology is one of my responsibilities as a mediator."

"Good. I am grateful for your actions, Mediator."

Broadwing chimed acknowledgment, while privately thinking a human idiom he had picked up: *Enjoy it while it lasts.*

Waking from hibernation was easier for Cecilia this time, for her short-term sleep had not required full immersion in life-support gel. Instead, she and the other loyalists had gone into *Arachne*'s hibernation pods wearing their standard inmate coveralls, which interfaced with the pods to monitor their vitals much as the gel did. This time, she still had her hair and some semblance of her dignity.

And waking was a relief after what she'd experienced in the dream state. There had been no repeat of the attempted assault she thought she remembered from the start of this hibernation; either she'd imagined it, or Diego's crew had been too preoccupied with Stephen's plan to steal the Chirrn's quark matter. From what Cecilia had picked up of their conversations, their dreamtime had been filled with fantasies ranging from humiliating the Chirrn to dragging them back to Solsys for war-crimes trials to simply murdering them *en masse.* In every case, Churrlaya had been the primary target of their imagined retributions, and when she'd found them engaging in a brutal torture session of their jailer — with James and Amrita describing everything in excruciating detail so that they could all share equally in the dream, compelling Cecilia's mind to visualize it as well — she'd been so disgusted that she'd isolated herself from the group, rebuffing every attempt at contact without caring if it was from a real crewmate or a phantasm. She'd envisioned herself back in Sol's Oort cloud, swimming in the subglacial water mantle of Aita, the Mars-sized ice planet they'd spent six months surveying. At first she'd imagined herself in a submersible, then a diving suit, then dreamed she was invulnerable enough to swim through it naked, populating it with benthic life from the fringes of her imagination… but no other people. She could think of no one right now that she could envision without mistrust or pain. In time, she even stopped thinking of herself as Cecilia LoCarno; she was one of the creatures of the deep, at home in the perpetual dark, safely ensconced within kilometers of ice, insulated by three light-months of empty space from the nearest trace of human presence.

When she awoke, she was crying.

Then she saw Churrlaya watching her. Reaching out a hand to help her up.

She stared at that hand for a long moment. Then she clasped it. It was surprisingly gentle.

Once she was sitting up, she squeezed her eyes shut and strove to discipline herself. She gave the memories of the dreamtime leave to fade, but they lingered more than she wanted. She struggled to focus on the here and now, to ready herself for whatever might be coming.

They were in a module positioned at a bit of a slant relative to the strong local gravity, so she needed to keep her grip on Churrlaya's hand as he guided her into its compact dining bay, then into a seat that Arachne had tilted to accommodate her. She envied the ease and grace with which the Chirrn negotiated the skewed environment. She realized that she had always seen something beautiful in them.

"Why did… you only wake me?" she asked.

"Because I do not believe you belong with the rest of the Unrenounced."

That reminded her to be on her guard. "If this is some sort of ploy…"

"No. I will attempt no more ploys. I will bear you only honest words—and an apology."

She didn't know what to say to that. She just studied Churrlaya as he continued. "My responsibility was to oversee your ordeal, yes. But not to punish you. Rather, the ordeal is a Chirrn custom of transition, to help us strip away the vestiges of an old life, an old affiliation, and leave ourselves open to a new one."

"Sounds like brainwashing."

"I grant that. One could also liken it to the procedures your militaries often employ to indoctrinate recruits. The purpose was rehabilitative." His eyes darted outward, then hesitantly refocused on her. "Moreover, it was meant to rehabilitate me. I was going through the same kind of transition, although my old ties had been torn from me by force. Perhaps that is why I made your transition harsher than it was meant to be, and hardened so many of you against us." He tapped his brows. "I was warned that my bias compromised my work, but I was determined to prove that I was better than you, that I could remain responsible and control my baser emotions."

Cecilia laughed in recognition, and Churrlaya's response was surprisingly insightful. "A familiar sentiment, is it not? But I think you achieved it better than I did. Perhaps if I had not fed the others' anger and fear so much, they would have been more swayed by your example."

Cecilia sighed. "I think you're giving me too much credit. Diego and his bunch… all this was more than they could take. If you thought they could ever make some 'transition' that was forced on them, you expected too much."

"Perhaps I did. But you have exceeded my expectations, Cecilia, and taught me much—not just about humanity. I think… we have both clung to old roots that we can never return to, and in so doing have both turned away from opportunities to become part of something new… to heal our incompleteness.

"Yet somehow… we two incomplete beings have complemented each other. In challenging one another, we have pushed each other to become better, to become stronger. I think it is time to acknowledge that, and to explore the possibility that we both may have found… at least the possibility of new roots in the last place we could have expected." His thick green fingers reached out and ever so lightly made contact with the side of her neck, just for half a second.

Cecilia didn't know what to say. The Frog Footman, her jailer and tormentor for the past six months or more, pledging his friendship? But even as she had the hostile thought, she knew it was a lie. She had come to look forward to their debates, the same way she had once enjoyed her philosophical and political arguments with Stephen. Those arguments back in Solsys, those opportunities to explore each other's very different minds and worldviews in depth, had been the foundation of a partnership as profound as any she'd ever known. Was she really feeling the same way about Churrlaya?

One thing she knew: she felt closer to him now than to her fellow loyalists. She remembered the impending heist. If Churrlaya was aboard, alone, when Diego's clique awoke…

She stopped herself from warning him. How could she trust what she was feeling now? Whatever distaste—whatever fear—she felt now toward Diego, James, and their group, didn't all of *Arachne's* crew deserve a chance at freedom? And Stephen would make sure no one was hurt…

Would he? As overcome as he was by bitterness and pain? She wasn't sure she knew him anymore. Could he really keep the others under control? Would he even try?

Arachne lurched into motion. Cecilia slipped sideways out of her chair, but Churrlaya was there in an instant and caught her. His hands were warm and strong. "Wait here," he said once he'd helped her regain her footing, more a request than a command. He did something to the cuffs of her confinement suit that made the mitts peel back, freeing her hands without the need to wrestle out of the sleeves. She stared at him in amazement. "For your safety should that happen again," he explained.

He still locked her in the dining bay, though. Never mind; she directed a thought at her comm implant, and the ready light blinked in her HUD. Arachne had reactivated the loyalists' comlinks, meaning the heist must already be underway. Cecilia tapped into the module's internal comms, closed her eyes, and moved her virtual field of view outside the bay to follow Churrlaya. "Broadwing, what is happening?" the Lesshchin called.

Calliope chimes sounded, and Arachne subtitled them: "A mishap with the lift allocation. The ship has been categorized as idle and cleared for use as ballast. A minor inconvenience; the Zhalevey are addressing it." *What the hell are Zhalevey?* Cecilia wondered, but then she noticed the floppy green tripeds with the elephant-meets-Yoda ears.

And then she noticed something else, just before Churrlaya did. "Why are the other Unrenounced awake?" the Lesshchin asked. "Why have their confinement suits been released?"

Cecilia choked on an impulsive warning cry as Diego, stripped to the waist, crept up behind Churrlaya and brandished a heavy wrench, swinging it low to smash into the Chirrn's right leg. The sound was very much like that of a human's bones breaking, though Churrlaya's screech of pain was unlike anything she'd ever heard. Diego struck again at Churrlaya's other leg, neutralizing the Chirrn's most formidable weapons. A similarly attired James moved in with another wrench to strike at his head. Cecilia froze in horror.

A fully nude Nik moved in and grabbed James's arm on the up-swing. "All right, that's enough! Just lock him in!"

"Agreed," Broadwing said. "Remember the schedule."

Moments later the door opened and they tossed Churrlaya back inside. "Captain!" Nik cried, looking somewhat happier to see her than Diego or James were. "It's okay, you can come with us now."

"Once we take care of the fucking Footman once and for all," James snarled, punctuating the syllable "Foot" with a vicious kick to Churrlaya's flank.

"Yes," Diego said, hefting his wrench.

"No, you heard Broadwing!" Nik protested.

"No alien tells me what to do!" Diego roared, cowing the doctor. "And this soulless beast has enslaved his last human." He lifted the wrench high.

Cecilia didn't make a conscious choice to throw herself on top of Churrlaya, shielding him with her own body. But that's where she found herself, and she didn't question it.

For a moment, she thought Diego was going to strike anyway. The wrench quivered in his tense grip, and his eyes went to her freed hands. "So this is your choice, *Captain*? I should have known."

"We are not the villains here, Narvaez. Not unless we choose to be."

"I choose to liberate my people! Evil must be destroyed, not appeased."

"This is supposed to be a robbery, not an inquisition!"

"Diego, come on," Nik urged. "We're on a timetable, remember? We need to suit up."

"Very well," the bigger man said after a moment, lowering the wrench. "But we will do it with eight—as I expected we would. And I'll be keeping my eye on you, Doctor! You need to pick a side once and for all!" He gazed down at Cecilia in grave disappointment. "And you... I always knew you were an appeaser at heart."

"And I would never have let you on my ship had I known you were such a coward."

He laughed. "You cannot make me waver," he said as he turned to the exit. "Not a man of true faith. Arachne, do not let her leave!"

"*Acknowledged*," Arachne said without affect, though with the tiniest of delays.

Then the door shut behind him, and Cecilia was well and truly alone.

Except for Churrlaya.

She retrieved the emergency medical kit from its cabinet and knelt to help him.

Sita found R'nilinnath in a module catering to nocturnal life forms, a darkened realm she was only able to navigate by having Arachne tap into the module's augreality system and feed her an enhancement of the available starlight. The main inhabitants seemed to be the tiger-striped, vaguely elephant-like Mykhshad, along with several unfamiliar species. They milled around a central pavilion matching the one in the Chirrn embassy's module, but with different vegetation, sparser and mostly black. As she approached the young Chirrn, she overheard a debate from the adjacent auditorium dome, something about a border dispute between diurnal and nocturnal settlers on a tidally locked planet. She switched off the automatic subtitles so they wouldn't distract her.

Nilly was seated on her tail before a large kinetic sculpture, an apparently free-floating sphere surrounded by a halo of intricate loops and prominences in a familiar pattern. The loops moved slowly as faster bulges swept around their curves like cars on racetracks, with occasional streamers or translucent sheets of material flowing between them. They vibrated as they moved, emitting an intricate, shifting, multitonal hum that Sita could've listened to for hours if she hadn't had more urgent business.

"Sita!" R'nilinnath drummed her toes and shook her mane in pleasure as she recognized the biologist. "Come and look! This is fascinating. It's an aural and textural representation of the halo effects around the neutron star in real time, for the benefit of species for whom vision is not a primary sense." She rolled an eye to gesture at the nearest pygmy elephant-tiger. "A Mykhshad artist designed it. Did you know? They evolved around a very small star whose radiant peak is in the infrared, and—"

"That's interesting, Nilly, but I need to ask you about something else."

"Ask anything. I am here to educate you."

"I need you to tell me about Broadwing."

Nilly jerked her head back. "Broadwing? You know him already."

"I need to know more. About his past. About his people. About... whether you trust him."

The Chirrn gave a delicate snort. "Sita. I thought you had moved well past these fears."

"No, it's not that. I'm trying to understand his character. What he might do in… situations where others relied on his… his agenda being what he told them. Ohh, how do I explain this…"

"Sita, you need not worry. Yes, Broadwing made a foolish mistake in his youth, but he repaid his debt long ago, just as you have. He earned his inclusion and has contributed meaningfully to the consensus of his guild." Nilly brushed her fingers across Sita's neck, ruffling her hair. "To an extent, you owe him your freedom. Back after Lesshchi, some said that, as ferals, you needed to be kept confined and repay your debt as subjects of study, like the Unrenounced. But Broadwing insisted that you deserved the same right as any civilized beings to repay your debt by joining the community."

"Then you have faith in his integrity? His… his principles?"

"I do. I know how it pains him to think he has done wrong, even when he is not to blame. He was as distraught as I was when he learned that taking you to the kiss dance had provoked the Lesshchin's retaliation. He could not have known that his suggestion would lead to that result, but he brooded with guilt for *narrissh*…. What is it?"

Sita felt as though the floor of the module had fallen out from under her. "That… was Broadwing's suggestion?"

"Yes, I thought you knew."

She clutched her hands to her womb, feeling the aching emptiness anew, like a black hole sucking her up from inside. "Oh, Krishna. He knew what would happen. He bloody knew!"

"What do you say, Sita?"

"He wanted… he wanted to bring us here."

"He proposed the migration, yes, but—"

"And he proposed the thing that created the need for it! *He knew!*" she cried, grabbing Nilly's shoulders and shaking her. "He knew… it would provoke them… they would attack… *he killed my baby!*"

Nilly pulled her away from the crowd around the sculpture and held her for a time, offering comfort, but twitching her tail in confusion. "I don't understand. Why would Broadwing want to provoke a migration?"

Sita told her about Meridian and the planned PQM theft. "All of this… all the way back to the trial. He's masterminded this whole thing to bring us here. All the violence… our babies… Kweli… none of it would have happened if not for him."

Nilly was panting through her nares. "I cannot believe Broadwing would want to kill babies. Maybe… maybe he didn't know the Lesshchin would go that far. Who could have known that?"

"It doesn't matter, Nilly," Sita said with growing resolve — growing rage. "He's the one responsible. He's manipulated Stephen and the rest of us, made us his pawns almost from the beginning! He's probably still manipulating, lying to us. Using us. He has to be stopped before Stephen and the rest are hurt."

She began to stride toward the exit, and Nilly loped after her, quickly catching up. "What are you going to do?"

"I'm going to find that fucking pterodactyl and kick his silver tail clear back to Shil—"

She was drowned out by a deafening clap of noise from the neutron-star model behind them. Reflexively clapping her hands against her ears, she spun to see a fountain of material erupting from the sphere near one of its poles, disrupting the delicate loops around it. The swarm of particles began to form a broad, diffuse ring around the sculpture.

Then she was half-blinded by a flash of actinic light through the module's star windows, and when her vision cleared, she saw the sculpture collapsing to the ground.

As it shattered, she felt the whole world convulse beneath her.

9

"WHAT HAPPENED?" STEPHEN ASKED, KNOWING EXACTLY WHAT HAD happened.

L'chellin had just returned from consultation with a group of Lode Seven infrastructure managers. Stephen had been playing his part, feigning dismay at *Arachne*'s misallocation to counterweight duty and keeping L'chellin preoccupied trying to hunt it down, until the moment came for the event that L'chellin now described. "A comet seems to have collided with the neutron star," said the aged mediator. "The resultant burst of hard radiation generated electromagnetic pulses in the tethers, creating some minor system disruptions. The tremor we felt was merely a shock wave from sudden thermal expansion."

Stephen pretended concern. "Are we at risk from the radiation?"

"The modules' shielding reduced any x-ray or gamma penetration to manageable levels." One of L'chellin's eyes briefly gestured upward to indicate the thick, wide shield mounted atop the module. Stephen reminded himself for the umpteenth time that the neutron star was above them relative to the local gravity. "Other protective systems seem less effective than they should be, but the disruption is mainly to inter-module communication, and some lift cars in transit are stalled."

"*Arachne*?" Stephen asked.

A puff of breath ruffled L'chellin's snout bristles. "Yes, Stephen," she answered. "It would appear that both *Arachne* and the freight lift conveying the PQM are somewhere along the central tract, though on this side of the center of mass. We are currently out of communication with both. But do not worry. Our people should be adequately shielded within their respective craft—particularly the Unrenounced in their hibernation chambers. And you know how well your embryos are shielded."

"That's good," said Stephen, fully aware that the Unrenounced must now be wide awake and suiting up for their hazardous spacewalk. He had balked at the risk when Meridian and Broadwing had detailed their plan, but the gamma and hard x-rays from a comet impact on the neutron star had been the only way to disrupt the Stringworld's sensors and communication long enough to achieve the heist. And all his people had received *D. radiodurans* gene therapy for radiation resistance; indeed, the Striders among them had been born with the trait. No human could thrive long in space without it.

Still, he sought a second opinion from L'chellin on another issue, prefacing it with a more basic question he felt he would plausibly ask in this situation. "Why wasn't the comet detected, steered away?"

"It came in at unusual speed and was unusually dark—perhaps an interstellar rogue. These things are not unprecedented in a star-formation zone, which is why the modules are shielded."

"Against radiation. But the tidal stress would've torn the comet apart before it hit, wouldn't it? There'll be an accretion disk."

"There is a debris disk, but the residual particles should decay onto the star's surface within a *narrach*," she said. "We should pass through it in about twenty *narr* and then once more before it dissipates, but it will thin rapidly. And the particles are ionized, so they can be easily deflected by the station's magnetic fields."

The lights flickered and the ground trembled as another, milder EMP went through the Stringworld, the product of one of the many secondary impacts that would be coming within the next hundred minutes. "If they've gotten these system disruptions under control by then," Stephen replied, aware that the Zhalevey's viruses would be working against that. Though surely the Zhalevey would keep the impact shields exempt from the malfunctions, wouldn't they?

"Do not worry. *Arachne* and the freight lift are on an inner tier of tethers, and lift cars generally ride on the trailing side, shielding them against anything intersecting our orbit. In all probability, they will be safe. But we will do all we can to reach them before the accretion disk passage."

"All right," Stephen said, nodding. "I… I trust you to make sure of that," he went on, trying not to make it seem too easy. "You understand all this better than I do, and I'd probably get in the way. I should go back down to the Arachnen and reassure them."

L'chellin straightened with pride and pleasure. "Most responsible, Stephen. Thank you. And I should do what I can to contact the other Shilirrlaln..." She trailed off, eyes rolling backward as often happened when Chirrn were interfacing with their datanet.

"What is it?"

"I cannot engage real-time communication with R'nilinnath... but her last locator ping indicates that she was in proximity to Sita."

Stephen froze. "Sita? What's she doing with Nilly?" He tried to mask his anger and concern. Was Sita trying to expose the plan?

"I do not know. I will ask the Zhalevey to track them down."

"No. No, I need to find her myself. Now."

"Stephen, she will be perfectly safe—"

He extemporized. "You know what she's been through, L'chellin. She's recovered well, but something like this... no telling how she'll react."

"True," L'chellin said. "But you do not need to birth bastard words. It is enough that you wish to be with your mate above all others. I will assist you."

If she were still my mate, Stephen thought, *she wouldn't have run off.* If anything, he was tempted to leave her to her own devices. If she'd made the choice to reject her own people in favor of the Chirrn, then so be it.

But he realized he couldn't let that happen. Whatever had occurred between them, she was still a member of his crew, and at least technically still his wife. He couldn't let her be stranded alone in an alien galaxy, the sole remaining prisoner of the Chirrn.

He didn't know if he could live with her anymore, but he wasn't ready to risk living without her.

Diana Thorne's far-from-feigned curiosity about PQM processing procedures had made it easy to keep Rysuth occupied during much of the ascent from the factory levels (or descent now, since they had passed the center of mass thirty kilometers back). So when the comet hit and the surge through the tethers shorted the freight lift's main power and security systems, she was easily able to snatch the Mykhshad's weapon from the holster strapped to his left forelimb, her Vanguardian reflexes letting her move faster than even his sensitive tendrils could react. She retreated to the exit as Tarik and Haim joined her to form a united front. "Okay, folks," Diana said, "this is a stickup." At the aliens'

total incomprehension, she elaborated, "We're taking the PQM. Don't interfere and you won't be harmed."

Rysuth's echolocation clicks grew louder, no doubt gathering a detailed picture of the humans' every move. "You will not be able to use that weapon."

"No, but neither will you," Tarik said. "And you won't risk a sonic attack in here, or you'd hurt the Zhalevey. But we're a race of fighters, as you may have heard. You don't want to make us angry." Following Tarik's lead, Diana posed as menacingly as she could in a fiftieth of a gee. Apparently it worked, since Rysuth, the Zhalevey, and even Yonchon flinched.

Yonchon's manipulator drones rose from the Ryohoch's back and moved toward the humans. "Sorry, pal," Haim said, working his pad with visible regret. "I can't let you do that." The drones swung around and began to circle the aliens. "Please, everyone, just stay calm and don't try to interfere."

"This action lacks reason," Yonchon intoned.

"We're taking this PQM on behalf of the human race," Tarik countered, playing his part in the script. "Our people have been held prisoner long enough." Diana knew he wasn't happy bringing down the blame on humanity, but those were Stephen's orders, so he obeyed.

Rysuth reached toward Diana with his trunk, its cilia rippling as if straining for answers. "You have not done this alone. Who has assisted you?"

"Let's just say there are a lot of people out there who aren't happy with the cost of the Chirrn's ban on mentoring. People who want humanity to be free at last." That was vague enough that the Chirrn would probably suspect the Shayal.

Haim's pad bleeped with the ready signal from *Arachne*. The humans began to back out of the cab. "Now, you all just stay nice and quiet and don't try anything," Diana said. "The drones will be watching."

Rysuth, Yonchon, and the Zhalevey remained calm. The Zenith had evidently been right; while PQM was valuable, it was not irreplaceable. But Rysuth had one more thing to say, and Diana almost laughed when Arachne chose to subtitle it as "You'll never get away with this." Well, perhaps that wasn't a cliché in Mykhshadese. No doubt Rysuth expected the PQM to be neutralized as soon as the Stringworld systems were back up and running.

Diana could only hope he was wrong. "Boss, can you confirm that the nans did their job?" she asked as they pulled themselves toward the airlock.

"Not yet," Haim replied, "but there's no reason they shouldn't. The factory security systems are much better shielded than the sensors and comms."

"They'd better be."

The nans planted on the reference sample by the drone explosion had been programmed to activate once the comet hit, whereupon they would emit the EM signature of a strange-quark chain reaction. Strange matter was naturally unstable and short-lived, but PQM could be programmed to produce a stable, negatively charged virtual strangelet, which would devour adjacent normal matter and turn it into more strange quarks. The stuff had many internal safeguards against that, but all they'd needed to do was fake the signature and the factory's security systems would have jettisoned the tainted sample to fall toward the neutron star, where the metasapients' halo fields would have captured and neutralized it, in the process destroying its entanglement with the stolen PQM and leaving the Stringworld authorities — and the Chirrn — with no way to deprive the thieves of a viable supply. This had been delayed until communications went out, so the authorities wouldn't know they'd lost the security sample and thus wouldn't feel this heist posed enough of a threat to warrant an aggressive response. Still, the lack of confirmation was worrisome.

Once they reached the airlock and Haim opened the inner hatch, Diego Narvaez and Evan Jiang emerged, leading to a happy reunion among the once and future crewmates. But Diego cut it short. "Suit up," he said, gesturing to the three EVA suits he and Evan had brought from *Arachne*'s stores. They would need to transfer the PQM across manually; it would have given away the game had Broadwing been seen smuggling any heavy equipment (including the kind of cumbersome EVA suit a Zenith needed to accommodate his wings) aboard the humans' ship.

Diana shed her Chirrn-style vest (it would pinch badly) and enjoyed Diego and Evan's appreciative stares as she climbed into her suit, which sealed itself and tightened against her body to keep her pressurized. Its helmet HUD signaled a positive seal, but still the group engaged in the age-old tradition of checking each other's suits before proceeding.

In the lift's cargo section, they found the PQM stored in several dozen upright hexagonal drums nearly four meters high and half that across. "Are you sure we'll be able to move these by hand?" Diego asked once Haim had blinded the lift's internal security and hacked the bay doors. "From what Arachne tells us, there's nuclear-density matter in there."

"Only partly," Haim replied. "It's a suspension of nucleonic processors in a superfluid substrate. Still pretty massive, but it's set by default to cancel most of its own inertia — don't ask me how or I'll start whimpering."

But when Diego, Evan, Tarik, and Diana applied themselves to moving the first drum, bracing their feet against the back wall of the cargo cell, it barely budged. "Most, but not enough," Evan groused.

Haim had already interfaced his pad with the drum's controls. "Hold on, I think I can set it to reduce its effective mass even further."

"You can do that?" Diego asked.

"I've been studying this stuff for weeks. The physics may be crazy, but at least I know what settings to change."

Diego moved to watch over his shoulder so he could repeat the process with other drums. "Okay, try it now," Haim said to the other three. "It should be light enough even one of you could move it."

"I've got this," Diana said, sticking her arms out to hold back the menfolk.

"Any of us could do it," Haim reminded her.

"You think," she pointed out. "You brought me along for muscle, okay? This is my thing." Bracing her feet, she gave it a push with one hand, and —

Nothing.

She tried again with both hands, putting her knees into it. All she felt was more resistance. This was getting embarrassing. "Oh, come on, Haim, who are you — " She broke off, realizing the drum was moving *toward* her. "Who's doing that?"

"Uh-oh."

"What uh-oh?" She flattened herself out in the diminishing space. Beside her, Tarik and Evan tried to catch it and push it away, but it seemed to be getting faster.

"I think I overshot. Set it to negative mass."

"That's impossible!" Diego cried. "It would disintegrate normal matter if it touched it!"

"What?!" Diana cried.

"That's okay, it's just virtually negative. It's a localized decrease in the Higgs—"

"HAIM!"

"Oh, sorry. Stop pushing, you two!" he cried. "Newton's Second Law! You push on negative mass, it accelerates *toward* you! Push on *this* side!"

The other men moved away, leaving just her between the drum and the wall. Diana tried to wriggle out, but she wasn't built for narrow spaces; her chest brushed the drum and it pinned her even more. *Uh-oh. Newton's Third Law. The harder it pushes against me, the harder I push back, and the more it accelerates.* She was about to get crushed into the wall. She fought her instinct to push against the drum, instead desperately feeling for a handhold she could *pull* on....

Finally she felt the pressure decrease and the drum moved away. "Careful, careful!" Haim kibitzed. "Now push it the other way to stop it. Don't forget!"

"We know!" Evan snarled.

Tarik was by her side. "Diana?"

"I'm good. And hey, there are worse ways to go down in history than 'first human killed by exotic physics.'"

Still, she was embarrassed. All she'd ever wanted was to challenge herself—to test the limits of the abilities that were her heritage as a Thorne. Her grandfather, Vanguard's first great leader, had dreamed that his people's augmented abilities and diversity would put them at the forefront of interstellar colonization. It was a matter of familial and national pride for Diana to be indispensable to this expedition. Yet time and again she'd found herself injured, sidelined, and humiliated. Were the others right when they told her she was trying too hard? Were her efforts to challenge herself ultimately self-defeating?

Haim proved reluctant to tamper with the settings again, so the group did their best to maneuver the negative-mass drum through space to *Arachne*, its docking cradle stopped along another tether some ninety meters away and twenty down, with a slender guide cable (non-conductive, for there were still periodic EMPs from the comet impacts) strung across the gap. "Remember," Diana told the others, "whatever it feels like, we're not weightless. Keep your suit lines clipped to the cable and watch your step."

That was easier said than done when trying to carry across a massive shipping crate that pushed back. Despite Evan's assurance, it was hard to remember to go against a lifetime of reflex and invert their pushes and pulls, especially while trying to keep gravity in mind at the same time. Diana made the mistake of looking down; the Stringworld stretched out thousands of kilometers below them, an incomprehensible drop that reduced the enormous habitat modules to near-invisibility… and below them was nothing but a starscape. Diana and the others were zip-lining across a literally bottomless abyss.

Her heart raced in sheer terror. And then she whooped out loud in her helmet, not caring that it hurt her own ears. Trying too hard? The vack with that. Pushing herself to the limits had brought her here. She whooped again. *"Thrill! Of! A! Lifetime!"*

Churrlaya had guided Cecilia through basic Chirrn first aid—as well as he could remember it with Broadwing jamming his connection to the fleet's data network. Luckily, all he had needed was to have his broken leg straightened and splinted, to take in some water and electrolytes, and to enter a somnolent state for a time, redirecting his energy and mental focus toward his internal repair systems.

Cecilia had then paced the room, searching for options, adjusting her stride as the gravity had diminished over the long ensuing minutes. The closer they had drawn to microgravity, the more relaxed she had felt, despite the circumstances.

"Where are we?" a voice finally asked. It was Churrlaya, his voice weak and scratchy; his healing must have used up a lot of fluids. She brought him a bulb of water. "I deliver gratitude. Where is the ship?"

Cecilia hesitated. "I'm not sure I should tell you."

He sighed, hands moving feebly in the direction of his brow ridges before dropping. "You still will not trust me. But how can you trust them now?"

"I don't know who to trust!" she exclaimed. "Least of all myself." His eyes simply held on her, and she couldn't remember how long ago she'd stopped seeing that as judgmental. "God, I don't know what to do, what's right or wrong. All my, all my life, I've tried to do what I thought was best, and I keep getting punished for it. I go to space to help my family, my mother calls me—calls me a traitor, says I've abandoned my home. I realize my husband will be happier without me, and he bleeds me dry in the divorce. I lead humanity to the stars, I get thrown in alien prison for—for an accident of fate. Even the universe punishes me. And Stephen... my one stalwart friend... hah!" It was a weak laugh, almost a sob.

Churrlaya considered her words. "So that is why you left the planet you felt yourself rooted in. You did not believe you were welcome there anymore."

She slashed her hand through the air. "It doesn't matter. I take my roots with me. I know who I am. I rely on myself. I've had to. And it's made me tough, made me effective."

"But is it self-reliance," the Lesshchin asked, "or self-flagellation? Cecilia... you are not to blame for how others have penalized you. Yet you close yourself off and live in a denial of your own making.

"That is what I did for too long—keeping myself apart, dwelling on my loss and pain instead of letting others heal me. I was afraid to let them become a part of me for fear of the pain I would suffer if I lost them again. And in so doing, I only hurt myself more. I did not begin to heal until I allowed myself to be open to another mind. To lower my defenses and make myself vulnerable... even to the very being whom I had blamed for the death of my world."

Cecilia winced, pained by what she knew was happening outside. "You can't trust humans, Churrlaya. Even with the best of intentions, we find new ways to do harm."

"I am... painfully aware of that risk. But I understand now that the young need to make mistakes as they grow... and perhaps the fault was ours for not being there to shelter you from the worst consequences of your mistakes.

"I understand... and so I forgive. In the name of Lesshchi, Cecilia LoCarno, I forgive you."

His words drove right into the core of her and turned her inside out. Hearing someone forgive her, most of all a Lesshchin, lifted a weight from her spirit that she hadn't realized she was carrying—or hadn't been able to face. She shuddered and wept as she let herself feel the guilt of the Lesshchi disaster for the first time. Eighty-eight thousand and four hundred living, thinking beings dead, sixty-four thousand and four hundred more left with gaping holes in their memory and identity, seven hundred and twenty thousand more made refugees. How could she ever face her responsibility for so much tragedy? How could anyone live with the guilt?

But now she had her answer: by not carrying it alone. By having a friend who understood. A friend who could forgive her and, just maybe, give her leave to begin forgiving herself.

If she'd only been that for Stephen, been there to support and balance him as she should have, maybe he wouldn't have gone so far astray. If they'd both been there, together, for Diego and James and Evan and Amrita, they could have helped them face the guilt they buried beneath rage and hatred.

But maybe now she'd found someone else to help her carry the burden. And maybe that could be the anchor she needed so she could reach out to the rest.

"Churrlaya," she said, "I hereby renounce my allegiance to the planet Earth." He showed no triumph, only understanding and acceptance. "My first allegiance should have always been to my crew. And so I need to betray them to you… and hope we can stop them from making a terrible mistake."

Arachne's EVA suits were as constricting in their own way as the Chirrn confinement suits, but Diego Narvaez knew which one he preferred to be in. At least the EVA suits had actual gloves complete with tactile feedback—an essential feature for the delicate task of maneuvering the negative-mass canisters of PQM across to *Arachne*. It was a relief to have his fingers free to manipulate things without having to strip half-naked first.

Diego's thoughts turned unbidden to his first actions after being freed from his confinement suit, and his sense of relief faded. Striking a blow against their jailer was one thing, but striking him down once he was defenseless was another. Churrlaya may have been a soulless animal, but Diego took no pleasure in being cruel to animals. He had allowed himself to give in to his anger and inflict unnecessary pain on the Frog Footman, and had almost allowed James to kill the creature in a fit of vindictive rage. Understandable, to be sure, but Diego feared he had jeopardized the support of less committed loyalists like Nik and Kahina. His coup against Cecilia clearly troubled them, even if the captain had all but abdicated on her own. Diego had reassured them that they would still bring Cecilia with them, and that these conflicts would blow over once they were free and reunited. But he was concerned that his lapse with Churrlaya, the gratuitous violence he had allowed himself, might scare them off from whatever further violence proved genuinely necessary to achieve that outcome.

On reaching *Arachne*, Diego brought Tarik aboard to coordinate with the loyalists. Kahina, Nik, and the others rushed to greet their old exec, and the Zenith collaborator — Broadwing, as Stephen had called it — came down from the cockpit to observe. "The others are securing the PQM drum in the cargo module," Tarik told them afterward. "They'll be in shortly, and they'll show you how to do it on subsequent runs. We need to be fast and efficient; we've got no more than forty minutes to get this done."

Two of the three-armed green teddy-bear aliens — Zhalevey — approached Diego, carrying an unmarked container. "Special instructions and equipment are delivered to you," they told him.

Broadwing's head snapped around. "Special instructions? Explain."

"Meridian sends them. A refinement of the plan." The Zenith lowered its head obediently, and the Zhalevey turned back to Diego. "You may interface with the case to receive instructions."

Diego took the case and stared at it, and his eyes widened at the new instructions that uploaded into his buffer. No wonder the interface had been kept private. He knew that Kahina or Nik would never agree to this, let alone any of the ones who'd been living with the aliens for months, subject to Stephen's weakening influence. Diego had to give the pterosaur things some credit — they'd been able to recognize the differences between the humans' agendas and identify which ones were capable of what needed to be done. Sometimes animals could behave in ways that were almost human.

Diego caught himself. This was no time for doubt or irrational qualms. Granted, the devices whose specifications he now read were marvels of engineering, but so was a spider's web. Mindless instinct could produce the appearance of amazing sophistication. Diego strove to keep that in mind as he girded himself for what must now be done.

On the second trip to the freight lift, Haim Silbermann figured out how to reset the PQM drums to a low but positive virtual mass, enabling the thirteen humans to shuttle them across to *Arachne* with relative ease. Diego appreciated this, for once the group had moved a few more drums and gotten a steady rhythm established, it gave him an opportunity to draw his three most trusted allies aside within the lift's cargo bay and brief them on Meridian's amended plan over a private, short-range suit channel. James, Amrita, and Evan curiously studied the long, flexible tubular instruments he handed out to them. "Are you sure these little things will have enough power to do the job?" Evan asked.

"Once they're loaded with the quark matter," Diego said, then demonstrated the procedure for tapping the drum and drawing off a fraction of its contents, as per his uploaded instructions. "Keep in mind, there's nuclear-density matter suspended in there. With enough speed, that stuff can penetrate anything."

James frowned. "I don't know. Taking orders from those gargoyles… Who knows what their real intentions are?"

Amrita glared at him. "Not getting squeamish, are you?"

"I just want to be sure this serves us, not them. If we're going to do something this… this big, I want it to be for the right reasons. Last time, we were tricked into it, remember?"

"Last time," Diego corrected him patiently, "was an accident. This time, we're striking a blow for human freedom. This will ensure the local authorities will be too busy to chase us. And it'll be a crippling setback to the Chirrn, weakening their whole civilization."

"And it'll be revenge," Amrita added, her voice shaking. "For Kweli. For the babies. Those monsters will finally pay."

"And all our people will be safe," Diego reminded them. "Remember that. And remember how powerful these are. Set the timers carefully, and wait to plant them until I give the word. We want them to go as soon as we and the humans below are in clear space, but not before. You hear me?"

He met each of their eyes, making sure they understood. Diego Felipe Narvaez Duarte would not compromise his morals for anything. The fate of the aliens would be a regrettable but acceptable sacrifice. They could play at immortality and metasapience, but there was nothing truly eternal within them, no soul that could genuinely know suffering. But every human soul aboard *Arachne* was precious beyond measure. Even traitors like Stephen, like Cecilia, like the others who'd let their fear or selfishness corrupt them, were precious, every one of their souls worth more than a trillion alien lives.

Though Diego took some comfort in knowing that the death toll wouldn't be quite that high today.

10

Once Cecilia had finished explaining the plan to Churrlaya, he covered his eyes in dismay. "I would not have believed Stephen capable of this."

"He's hurting," she said in his defense. "He blames himself for what happened to his kid, to the others, to Kweli. And blaming you is easier to face."

Churrlaya met her gaze, acknowledging his understanding that she spoke from experience. "But Broadwing… He has been a proper citizen for many years."

"Churrlaya, nobody could've witnessed the death of Lesshchi and not been changed. We're all proof of that."

"Yes. Yes, what matters is stopping this before it is too late."

"Look, I know you're afraid of these Zenith because of what happened in the past, but what if their leader's right? What if they have learned enough to ascend or evolve or whatever without going mad this time?"

"While that possibility exists, my concerns are not so futureward. I know of Meridian's movement, and they are capable of shocking violence. They once bombed the PQM girdle of the habitat where my friend Ruzhalu was born, though the habitat was saved with no complete or permanent deaths. But they have killed entire ship crews to steal their PQM. They even attempted to accelerate an asteroid into a populated Star Palace to penetrate to its gravity core, even though the bulk grade PQM therein would be of little use to them."

"If she's so dangerous," Cecilia countered, "why would they ever let her onto a Star Palace?"

"Her involvement in these crimes has never been adequately proven. She tends to work through proxies and subordinates, and none of her captured accomplices have ever verified her complicity. Normally, Zenith loyalty tends toward whoever holds the greatest status, but Meridian has an exceptional hold over her followers, whether through her personal charisma or her promises of immortality. They have all been convinced that metasapient civilizations record and capture the minds of all sapient beings. In their certainty, they believe that by killing, they send their victims to a higher existence and nourish the metasapients at the same time.

"If Meridian told Stephen that she was willing to carry out this theft without loss of life, then her words were bastards. Here in particular, in the direct sight of a metasapient population, Meridian will not miss the opportunity to make an offering of lives."

"Stephen would have no part of anything like that."

"But Diego would, where nonhumans are concerned. And if communications are disrupted, Stephen would have no way to stop him."

"Oh, my God." Cecilia raised her voice. "Arachne, I know you're listening! You need to let us out of here!"

"I'm sorry, Cecilia," the cyber's voice came over the intercom. "Stephen is still the leader of this expedition."

"But I'm the captain of your goddamn body!"

"I'm afraid you forfeited that responsibility some time ago. As a prisoner, you have no command authority."

"All right, forget regulations! Use your judgment. After what you've heard—"

"With all due respect to Churrlaya, I have heard only that Meridian was implicated in the incidents he described. That is a matter of concern, but in the absence of proof, I can't let it outweigh my duty to my crew."

Cecilia hated to voice her next thought, but this was no time to pull punches. "Remember what happened last time you put the good of your crew over what you assumed was a low-probability hypothesis? Ninety thousand people died! Are you willing to take that chance again?"

Arachne hesitated long enough that Cecilia actually noticed the pause. "There is little I could do even if I agreed. My avatar is running in detached mode down with the Arachnen. And I'm not ready to violate Stephen's orders without more to go on.

"The most I am willing to do at this point is to allow you to speak to the others who are here. But the Arachnen are currently outside the ship, transferring PQM from the freight lift, and comms are subject to interference due to the currents induced in the tethers by the on-going radiation bursts from the neutron star. For now, I can only put you in contact with Broadwing and the Zhalevey in the cockpit."

Cecilia traded a look with Churrlaya. "I'll take what I can get right now, Arachne. And... thank you."

"Cecilia," her former captor said, "Meridian's followers are fiercely loyal. Trying to reason with Broadwing will be sending our words to futile deaths."

She laughed. "Look at us, Churrlaya. You and I changed each others' minds with just our words. After that, reasoning with a fanatic should be a snap."

Thanks to the system disruptions and the imminent accretion-disk passage, travel between modules was restricted to official use only. Stephen had made arrangements with Shthastya, their Zhalevey accomplice, to get shuttled down to the Arachnen's module, but going up to find Sita was another matter. Fortunately, L'chellin was able to pull some strings with the transportation managers — "This is what media-tors do," as she put it — and got herself and Stephen on a lift going up to the Night Module, where Sita and R'nilinnath were located.

Less fortunately, when they boarded the lift, they found Velesh already aboard, seeking to speak with them both. Stephen had almost forgotten his cover story of considering the Shayal's offer, but L'chellin was quick to lash into her distant relative for attempting to subvert the Chirrn justice system, reminding Velesh in no uncertain terms that the Chirrn were not under their mentoring anymore. It was uncannily like listening to a teenager assert independence from an overprotective parent — although once they fell into arguing over the good of the Arachnen, Stephen felt more like he was the child at stake in a custody battle.

When they reached the Night Module, it didn't take long to locate Sita and Nilly. They were already at the administrative lift terminal, loudly insisting on being permitted to go upward. As Stephen drew closer, he realized to his horror that they were telling the local Mykhshad administrator about the heist in progress. "No, you don't understand, they have a way around the bloody entanglement thing! The Zenith are helping them, and they've got Zhalevey moles here on the Stringworld!… Moles. They're, they're infiltrators.… It's a metaphor! See, they're animals that dig underground so you can't… look, the point is—"

"Sita!" Stephen grabbed her arm and spun her around. "What the hell do you think you're doing?"

"I invite an answer to that question myself," added L'chellin, whose long limbs had let her easily keep pace with him. Velesh lagged some distance behind. "You are speaking of an attempted theft?"

Sita responded to Stephen instead. "Listen, you have to call it off. Broadwing is using you! This whole thing was orchestrated to get us here as Meridian's puppets!"

"Meridian?" L'chellin was stunned. "Here?"

"Sita, you don't know what you're—"

"*He knew*, Stephen!" Her fierceness silenced everyone. "Broadwing was the one who sent us to the Lesshchin kiss dance. He knew it would provoke them. He wanted an incident that would give him an excuse to propose this migration. So he set us up to be attacked." At Stephen's bewildered stare, she went on: "Do you understand what I'm saying to you? Broadwing got our baby killed!"

He couldn't let himself accept it. "Why would you think that? What would make you think…"

Nilly came forward, an arm moving protectively around Sita's shoulders. "She's right, Stephen. Broadwing was the one who gave me the idea of taking them to the kiss dance. He convinced me it would be all right."

"We should've seen it," Sita said. "Nilly told us that she'd cleared it with Broadwing, but I thought that just meant it was her idea and she'd consulted him on the specifics."

"Even so," a puzzled L'chellin said, "a mediator of Broadwing's experience should have understood that it was a procreative kiss dance rather than a mere recreation, and that an Arachnen presence would thus be provocative."

Velesh had arrived moments earlier. "Are you saying," he asked L'chellin, "that you entrusted the care of the humans to an individual with known ties to the Meridian organization?"

"There is no record of any such ties in Broadwing's past!"

While they argued, Stephen confronted Sita. "I can't believe you'd do this. All you have is circumstantial. You can't know Broadwing did it on purpose! Maybe it was like Nilly said, that she misheard his advice. Maybe he regretted his mistake and wanted to free us to make amends!"

"And it's just coincidence that Broadwing pushed for us to be allowed to renounce in the first place? He set us up from the beginning!"

"Sita, do you hear what that sounds like?"

"Oh, come on, Stephen! This is our baby we're talking about!"

"You don't have to remind me about our baby. Everything I'm doing to free our people is in her name!"

"Is that why you can't face the fact that you were used? That what you're doing, playing Broadwing's game, is a betrayal of her memory?"

"I can't accept that. Not on such flimsy evidence. There's too much at stake."

"Oh, right, I'm only your wife, why the hell should you listen to me?"

He stared at her. "I wasn't sure you still thought of yourself that way."

Sita scoffed. "Honestly, I'm not sure you *ever* thought of me that way. Not really."

"I loved you. I've loved you since the dreams."

"Yes, and it was the dream you loved! *Your* dream, of building a community and a future, of churning out babies for a stable population base! You and me, it was all just part of your grand master plan. It was never really *about* you and me, was it?"

"I always tried to do right by you."

She sighed, softening her tone. "Of course you did. You always try to do right by bloody everyone. That's just it. You're always trying to fix everything. Always spinning grandiose schemes to save the world. You try so hard to be everyone's best mate that you don't really let any one person get close to you. Not close like family, close where you let your guard down and risk getting hurt." She shook her head, laying a hand on his arm. "I don't know, maybe after you lost Benjamin and your mum, you were afraid to let anyone else get that close. You built up all your dreams and ambitions as your defenses and nobody else can breach those walls."

"Excuse me," L'chellin interrupted. "Stephen, is this true? Did you agree to assist Meridian's organization in the theft of our PQM order?"

Stephen hesitated, but ultimately he couldn't bring himself to lie to a direct question. "Yes. After what happened to Kweli, after learning about the Protocols, I couldn't trust you with my people's safety."

"You pledged yourself to serve our community. To make amends for the losses you inflicted."

"The Chirrn inflicted unfathomable losses on humanity by cutting us off from the stars! If anything, you were responsible for your own losses. Cecilia was right about that all along."

"I tend to agree," Velesh interposed. "Indeed, your choices have left the humans so dysfunctional that they choose to react with crime rather than pursuing the more peaceful avenues we offered them. Moreover, they have allied with the victims of your previous mentoring errors!"

"Look at yourself, Velesh!" Stephen exclaimed. "You're no better. You're not interested in helping us, you just want to use us to score points against the Chirrn."

"Exactly," L'chellin added. "You accuse us to divert attention from your own culpability! The Zenith Cataclysm would never have happened had you not pushed us into mentoring prematurely!"

"You were the ones who pushed! Our only mistake was trusting you because you resembled us! We overestimated your ability to grow beyond your primitive tribalism."

"*Oi!*" Sita cried at the top of her lungs. "Belt up, the lot of you! Stop blaming each other for ancient sodding history and start taking responsibility for what's going on right now!"

Stephen spun to her, meeting her vast dark eyes. *Responsibility…* The word echoed in his mind, in his own voice. *"And what about your responsibility for your own ship's wake?"* He had been the one to urge Cecilia to stop blaming others as a way to hide from her own guilt. He'd taken such pride in his ability to own up to his mistakes, his acceptance of the burden of responsibility for all the lives lost because of his choices.

But responsibility for a choice that had taken ninety thousand other lives was one thing to bear. Responsibility for a choice that took ninety thousand other lives plus one's own unborn daughter? That was intolerable. So much easier, then, to find an excuse to blame the Chirrn for all of it, and throw in Benjamin and Mama and everyone who'd died and suffered in Florida, and for ten thousand years before. After all, he didn't have to face the personal losses if he could bury them in a mass grave, in an anger based on abstract moral principle rather than firsthand grief and pain.

He reached out for Sita's hand, and with only the slightest hesitation, she grasped it, squeezed it with a strength he hadn't known she possessed. "She's right," he told the chirrnids. "I've made a serious mistake—allowed others to take advantage of my anger and denial and manipulate me into—"

Sita socked him in the arm. "To hell with the ruddy speeches already! Let's get up there before it's too late!"

Broadwing had tried not to heed the entreaties of Churrlaya and Cecilia LoCarno, tried to dismiss their lies about Meridian. All they knew was the propaganda of those who had opposed Zenith metasapience for so long, who had oppressed Meridian and her followers and forced them to employ extreme methods. Yes, Meridian taught, and Broadwing believed, that the metasapients recorded and preserved the minds of the dead. But that did not mean that Meridian actively sought to kill *en masse*. Surely the longer a mind lived, the more experience it gained, and thus the more complexity it could provide to the metasapients recording it both during its life and after its corporeal death. Meridian's conviction of the dead's survival was a source of comfort when killing was unavoidable, not an incentive to maximize casualties as an end in itself.

Still, he had seen the devices the Zhalevey had given to Diego Narvaez. He had seen that human and his followers breaking off from the group just *narr* ago and moving to attach them to Lode Seven Station's tethers. He had picked up enough radio chatter through the interference to know that Diego had claimed they were monitors to warn of approaching lift cars. But Broadwing could see that their intended targets were the main structural tether bundles of the megastructure, and that the devices resembled PQM-based heavy demolition charges that he had seen in replayed memories during the Lesshchi trial. The nucleonic matter in PQM, if released from superfluid suspension and accelerated with sufficient force, could tear through even the strongest non-degenerate matter as easily as through air. At Lesshchi, the charges had been used to rescue trapped survivors or cut through to hazardous equipment that needed to be secured. Here, placed against the tethers, their only possible use would be to slice the heavy fullerene bundles clean through.

But Broadwing was not the only one to realize this, for Arachne interrupted Churrlaya and the human to inform them of it. According to her, given the number of charges and the strategic positions of their target bundles, their detonation could potentially sever enough tethers that the tidal stress could tear the entire megastructure in two.

"I am sure it is only a precaution," Broadwing told them.

"Is it?" Cecilia challenged. "Your Meridian doesn't seem the type to leave anything to chance. The plan to take out the security sample always struck me as sketchy. But if they cut the Stringworld in two, drop the whole PQM factory into the neutron star, then it's a sure thing. Not to mention that the loss of a main PQM supplier will weaken the whole Chirrn state and make it harder for them to hunt your people down."

Broadwing didn't want to admit that he'd realized the same things himself. "Even if that were so, the megastructure is designed so that the inhabited sections will fall away from the neutron star should the tethers fail. At most there would be injuries due to the abrupt loss of gravity."

"You forget," Churrlaya said, "that cometary matter is still falling onto the neutron star. The habitat modules are only fully shielded on the side facing it. If the tension on the cables is lost, then the modules will tumble and their inhabitants will be exposed to lethal doses of radiation. Thousands could die. Moreover, the magnetic deflection will fail and particles from the accretion disk could penetrate the modules! It could be a repeat of Lesshchi!"

Broadwing's diaphragms contracted at the thought of witnessing such a disaster a second time. But he shook off the anxiety. "The radiation and accretion disk will be gone within six *narredj*. There would be no reason to detonate the devices before then."

"Wouldn't there?" Cecilia asked. "If the Stringworld breaks, the local authorities will have to devote all their ships and attention to evacuating as many people as they can. A perfect opportunity for you to slip away in the confusion."

"Why risk a long, slow series of warp hops," Churrlaya added, "if you can simply blend in with the crowd of ships escaping through the wormhole?"

"And what about the occupants in the lift car?" Arachne asked. "If they are still trapped there when the tether snaps, they would be immediately killed by the shock."

"We could evacuate them to *Arachne*."

"You would not have time to do that and still fulfill the plan."

"Broadwing, please adopt my words," Churrlaya said. "Remember how it felt when you learned of Lesshchi's death. Remember what it was like to hear the survivors' testimony in the trial, to experience our memories. That event

changed all our lives forever, and not for the better. Do you wish to inflict that on so many others?"

"Take it from a human," Cecilia interposed. *"Violence goes in cycles. People react to death by causing more death, and that makes more people react the same, and it just keeps branching out. It never stops unless someone breaks the chain. Unless someone recognizes that any pain or death they cause to others is their own responsibility, their own choice, not just a payback for something done to them.*

"Broadwing, I helped kill ninety thousand people, and I can hardly live with the guilt of it. But if I'd gone on hiding from that guilt, then I would've joined the others and I'd be part of something that could kill thousands more. Guilt is there to make us stop. To shame us when we're wrong. We have to listen to it or we just keep making ourselves worse and worse."

Broadwing's head sank below his shoulders, his whole stance lowering. His folded wing dactyls twitched against his forearms. He thought of the guilt he bore already. He had not expected the Lesshchin's retaliation to go as far as it had. He had thought he would provoke an attack, swoop in to frighten the attackers off, be hailed as the Arachnen's savior, then use the incident as an excuse to propose migration. He had not expected the Lesshchin mob to be large and organized enough to overpower him — or perhaps he was simply not as formidable a raptor as he had imagined. Because of his miscalculation, Sita, Kweli, Kazuko, and Justine had lost their babies… and Kweli had ended her life. Meridian had consoled him, assured him that he could not have anticipated or prevented it, and that their minds would be saved to live on forever (though what mind did a fetus have for the metasapients to record?). She had assured him that the good his efforts would ultimately do — freeing the Zenith from oppression, weakening the Chirrn's grip on power — would more than make amends for the harm.

But she had also assured him that no lives would be lost here today. He tried not to doubt his matriarch's word, to convince himself that the charges would not be detonated before the radiation had faded. There was no reason the plan couldn't still go off without permanent loss of life. But that was what he had thought before, and look what had happened. What factors might he be overlooking now?

He cursed himself for his disloyalty. Meridian was his love, his inspiration, the one being he happily called his superior. She had made him hers in the most intense mating flight of his life. She had offered him, of all people, the chance to become her primary mate. How could he even contemplate letting her down?

But he thought of Yonchon, trapped in the freight lift—an enigmatic, aloof being, but still a part of Broadwing's guild, a contributor to the consensus memory that was part of Broadwing's current identity almost as much as any Chirrn's. He thought of L'chellin and the rest of his guildmates, who might not all be able to evacuate in time or escape the radiation.

And he thought of Sita, who had fled the Arachnen compound and was lost somewhere on Lode Seven. Sita, who had already paid an intolerable price for his miscalculation.

"Arachne, release the prisoners," he chimed even as his mandibles clacked together in pain. "We must stop the planting of the demolition charges."

Maybe the plan could still succeed without them. Maybe the thieves could still get away at warp and trust that the security sample had been properly destroyed. Maybe Meridian would only demote him to a lower-tier husband, or at worst an odalisque, with the opportunity to work his way back up.

Or maybe she would rip his throat out and he would wake up in metasapient paradise.

Either way, he had to try. How could he strive to the highest in his matriarch's name if he saw himself as the lowest of the low?

But then again… if he had done all this in Meridian's name, if she now wished to do far worse, was she not with him in the depths? He still believed in the goal—but was he following the wrong person?

After he and Diana finished securing the latest drum to *Arachne*'s warp cage (for the cargo modules were already filled, and even the cage had limited room left for more), Tarik was pleasantly surprised when he recognized Cecilia LoCarno's coltish figure emerging from the lock. She was leaner than he remembered, but he knew her by the way she moved, with the discipline of a longtime spacer balanced with the boldness of a natural leader. At first he hoped she had changed her mind about participating in the heist; but then he saw Churrlaya in the lock behind her, clad only in a skintight full-body sheath of the kind Chirrn used for emergency EVAs. Tarik had heard from the other Unrenounced that Cecilia had apparently fallen prey to full-bore

Stockholm syndrome, so he steeled himself for whatever she might say.

But the story she told, backed up by Broadwing's staticky transmissions from inside the ship, was one he never could have anticipated. "You?" he cried to the Zenith, his rage engulfing him as he had never allowed it to before. "You were responsible for my son's death? My wife's..." He trailed off.

"*I never intended that,*" the monster chimed in that deceptively melodious voice. "*I tried to ensure no permanent harm was done.*" A pause. "*But yes. I am responsible.*"

"You lying demon! First you manipulate us into fighting your *jihad*, now you betray your own side! Why should I help you?"

"*Avenge yourself on me if you wish, Tarik Hüseyin Bahar. You are entitled to that, for I owe you two lives. But other lives are at stake, including Sita Bhatiani's. Let the culpability for lost lives fall only on me, not yourself.*"

Tarik wanted to toss all other concerns aside to slake his vengeance. But he couldn't. He remembered Kweli's kindness, remembered how much kindness she had received in turn from Sita and the others—even from R'nilinnath, and from L'chellin in her own matronly way. He remembered that his highest duty in life was to Allah and then to his community, his crew, and that anger was one of the sins that undermined those duties. He could not protect his community if he could not master himself.

He had too much anger to contain in full, but that was all right, for it could be useful. "Diego!" he cried over the open channel. "James! Amrita! Evan! Do you read?" There was no reply. "Stop what you're doing this instant! That's an order!" Still nothing. "We know about the bombs! This is not part of our plan!"

"Arachne, can they hear us?" Cecilia asked.

"*I am boosting the signal to maximum, since there is no more need for stealth. I don't think they're inclined to listen. I have received requests for clarification from the others and have filled them in.*"

Cecilia met Tarik's eyes, communicating volumes, just like old times. "Arachne, have you tracked their movements?" In this forest of cables, they could be difficult to find.

"*They've disconnected their trackers, but from what I've been able to detect, I'd say they've planted two devices already, on the structural tether bundles closest to the freight lift. From what I can extrapolate about the charges, I can estimate where they'll need to place them for maximum effectiveness. Sending you maps now."*

"Then let's move," Cecilia said to him and Diana — and to Churrlaya too, he realized. The Lesshchin's emergency sheath had no air supply, but as Chirrn space crew, Churrlaya had surely been modded to survive virtually naked in vacuum for a limited period.

As they pushed away from the ship, Cecilia spoke loudly. "All Arachnen, this is LoCarno. I intend to stop all personnel involved in planting bombs on the tethers. Everyone who agrees, rendezvous at the crossover cable. Everyone else, be advised that we will be dismantling those bombs, so you'd be best off standing down now and getting the fuck out of our way."

"We won't listen to traitors, Cecilia," came Diego's reply to her challenge. *"Everyone still loyal to humanity — to* Earth *— I ask you to stand with us now! Striking this blow is the only way to ensure our freedom!"*

"It will make us hunted!" Cecilia fired back. "And cost us everything we are, everything we've striven so hard to become!"

No reply came from Diego or his followers, though Tarik had no doubt they were strategizing on a separate channel. But Tarik, Cecilia, Diana, and Churrlaya were soon joined at the rendezvous point by Haim and three of the remaining Unrenounced: Nik Zacharias, Kahina Amrouche, and Zhao Changkun. There was no sign of Ibrahim al-Bakri. "He went off to join the others," Nik explained, keeping his eyes on Cecilia. "Diego can be very persuasive. But don't worry, Captain — I'm with you all the way. We can't let them do this."

Kahina was less certain. "I don't want to fight my own people. I'm still not sure they're wrong."

"And I can't fight," Changkun said. "I won't."

Haim just shrugged — he was too old to get into a physical confrontation. The small, slightly plump Kahina and the lanky, gray-haired Changkun weren't exactly suited for it either. "Very well," Tarik said. "We need a team at the freight lift anyway, to either get it moving down out of the danger zone or evacuate the people inside."

"We can detach the cab, use it as a lifeboat," Haim said.

"What people?" Kahina asked. "Who's left?"

"The Shilirrlaln's engineer, a Mykhshad supervisor, and two Zhalevey."

She stared. "Oh. You mean… people."

"Is that going to be a problem?" Tarik asked.

"*No,*" Changkun replied, holding Kahina's gaze and her hand until she nodded.

"All right," Cecilia said, "you three deal with the freight lift. That leaves us even, five to five."

"But we outmuscle them," Diana said. "Hell, *I* outmuscle them."

"Don't get cocky," Cecilia warned her and the other Arachnen. "They're not the people you remember. They've clung to hate for so long, I'm not sure they have anything else left in them. They're angry and desperate and more dangerous than you can imagine.

"And they're about to make us guilty for another Lesshchi. We can't let that happen, no matter the cost."

After that, nothing more had to be said. The team broke and spread out into the fray.

Though circumstances had forced him to become a revolutionary, Diego Narvaez was still an engineer at heart. So it comforted him that this blow against the aliens was such a methodical demolition job. He may have been at peace with the necessity of having to kill so many intelligent animals for the protection of humans, but it was still an unpleasant chore. So much better, then, to focus on the logistics of the task and take pleasure in the careful engineering of the planned results.

The tethers holding this alien Tower of Babel together were arranged in a triangular lattice, each one surrounded by a hexagon of neighbors at equal distances. The thick tether bundles that provided structural support were spaced nearly a kilometer apart, with narrower tethers in between—some for transportation, others for drawing power from the neutron star's magnetic field or generating current to thrust against it for attitude control. Those flimsier cables would not be strong enough to hold the so-called "Stringworld" together if enough of the main structural members were cut—and many of them would become collateral damage in any case.

The demolition charges, Diego had to admit, were marvels of engineering. The PQM within them was somehow configured to function as a shaped charge, expelling the tiny quark-matter nuggets it contained in a directional burst (and he hadn't yet figured out how the action and reaction balanced out). These particular devices were cutting charges, sending out the PQM in a razor-thin, expanding wedge, perfect for slicing through bundles of fullerene cable. Eventually, Diego assumed, the unleashed nucleonic material would expand back into normal matter. But these charges had been amped up well beyond their proper safety limits, so the PQM "blades" would travel far and fast, cutting through whole swaths of tether bundles before re-expanding—and that expansion would be explosive enough in its own right. Six of the charges aimed in different directions should be enough to slice through the majority of the support tethers, and most of those remaining would probably be snapped once the cut tethers went flying and crashed into them. Diego tried to estimate the amount of potential energy those vast tethers stored in the form of tension, supporting the mass of dozens of habitat modules against the acceleration of a neutron star. The answer was downright terrifying. He thanked God that *Arachne* would be well away from the megastructure before the detonation.

Two charges had been planted when the challenges came from Tarik and Cecilia, and Diego was on his way to plant a third. He had ordered Evan to come assist him, mainly so he could keep an eye on the erratic planetologist. When Ibrahim declared his continued loyalty, Diego sent him to protect the first charge while sending James to defend the second and Amrita on ahead to plant the fourth. That was the most pivotal one of all, to be mounted on a tether bundle close to the much thicker bundle at the center of the Stringworld and aimed directly at it. Even that great mass of tethers would barely slow the quark matter down as it tore through. Diego felt that Amrita deserved to strike that critical blow more than any of them. He found James's paranoia and Evan's raging xenophobia useful as sources of energy to be directed, but distastefully petty. Amrita had suffered more at the Chirrn's hands than any of them, her captivity reawakening her childhood memories of imprisonment and torture, of her father's murder before her eyes. Her hate was truly righteous, and Diego hoped that striking the *coup de grace* would help her purge it and begin to heal at last.

"Remember," Diego told them, "deluded or not, these are still humans. Restrain or disable them if you can, but don't get carried away."

"Nice principles, Diego," James called, *"but if they're working for the enemy, then anything that happens to them is their own fault."*

"Damn right," Amrita added.

"What about the Footman?" Evan asked, breathing fast. *"If he comes after me…"*

"Churrlaya is another matter, of course," Diego confirmed. "But don't go out of your way for revenge. Focus on the mission first."

As he pushed up and off from a vacant lift cable and fired his thrusters to boost him toward the first charge, he spotted a familiar kangaroo shape soaring toward him past the freight lift, with a wiry female figure clinging to his tail. "Never mind," he announced. "The Frog Footman is about to greet me personally. Evan, get here fast. Keep your cool. And remember we're in orbit—you can't point straight at what you're aiming for. Trust your suit to navigate."

But the first charge was closest to *Arachne*, so Ibrahim intercepted Tarik before anything else occurred. Diego saw the blips in his HUD and heard the *"Oof"* of impact as Ibrahim collided with the larger man, trying to knock him off course. But Tarik had a considerable mass advantage, so he was able to catch the edge of the tether bundle, about ten meters down from the demolition charge and twenty over. Ibrahim was badly outmatched and had no training in EVA combat. He tried words instead. *"I don't want to fight you, Tarik. Please, you should stand with me."*

"You should stand with me! Does the Prophet tell us we can kill innocents in jihad*? No! You disgrace Islam like the fanatics of the past. Now stand aside!"*

A few moments later Ibrahim reported: *"I'm sorry, Diego, I couldn't do it. He's heading for the bomb."*

Diego couldn't fault the man for his piety, but it had manifested in an unfortunate way. "That's all right," he said. It was one of the less essential charges, its arc directed outward and intercepting relatively few structural bundles. Even without it, they could do enough damage that the surviving cables would be unable to hold the strain for long. "You go back up James at charge two."

"But Diana's heading there!" Ibrahim cried.

"All the more reason to reinforce him! Now, go!" The Vanguardian was the biggest threat the other side possessed. He could only pray that the two of them could overpower her—or, more realistically, delay her long enough.

Evan soon arrived at the tether bundle, meeting Diego's eyes through their visors and nodding to confirm that he wouldn't collapse as easily as Ibrahim. Diego smiled and nodded back. He would have preferred a more emotionally stable wingman, but he hoped that by keeping Evan calm and confident, he could encourage the younger man to direct his xenophobia usefully against Churrlaya. "Run interference while I plant the charge," he ordered.

But Churrlaya came in faster than Diego expected, shooting right past Evan and straight for him. Even on the injured list, the Footman's prowess in ultra-low gravity was formidable. Still, no matter how efficient his internal repair mechanisms were, his legs and left flank would be weak from his earlier injuries. And the heavy, flexible demolition charge would make a very effective cosh. Diego let himself drop, then pushed off toward Churrlaya's underbelly as the alien reached the tether bundle. Diego swung the charge and put himself into a spin in reaction, but the swing was good enough to take Churrlaya in his bruised ribs, or whatever he had there, and double him over in pain. Diego saw no sign of damage to the thin, clear sheath Churrlaya wore, but he had the chance to try again. He stopped himself from spinning away by grabbing the kanger's broken leg, which he yanked on fiercely, sending himself back up and past the Chirrn toward the tether. He tried to aim a kick at that froglike head, hoping to impart enough momentum and loss of consciousness to send his jailer plummeting, helpless to save himself. But Diego wasn't trained in space combat either, and the blow only grazed a brow ridge. Still, the renewed leg injury seemed to have taken its toll; the Footman was moving slowly, barely able to catch a tether. When he finally brought himself to a halt several meters down, he simply clung there, leaving Diego free to begin attaching the charge.

As he climbed up and around to the optimal placement point, Diego caught sight of Evan engaging their ex-captain. The planetologist had intercepted her in open space between tethers, and now they tumbled, drifting slowly downward and away from Diego as they grappled. Evan was slight relative to Cecilia but had an edge in body mass, and he was angry. *"Traitor!"* he cried between heaving breaths. *"You were supposed to be our leader! You promised us we'd stand together no matter what! That we'd never give in to the monsters!"*

Cecilia had nothing to say in return. Maybe she knew she could offer no defense. More likely she was saving her breath and attention for the struggle. Either way, they would have to resolve the fight soon; they were accelerating downward ever so slowly, but already visibly picking up speed. Before much longer, they'd be falling too fast for their suits' low-powered thrusters to stop them.

But Diego couldn't concern himself with that; he had to get the charge placed before Churrlaya recovered. He willed himself to turn away from the fight and focus solely on the task at hand. But as he attached the charge, he silently prayed that Evan would survive.

He didn't even realize that he'd omitted Cecilia from his prayer.

Tarik was grateful that Nik Zacharias had switched sides. The doctor was young and robust, with a Strider's instinct for functioning in space. He'd shot out faster and straighter than any of the others and was about to intercept Amrita before Tarik could finish deactivating the first charge or Diana could even reach the second. *"Amrita, stop!"* Nik called. *"I know you don't have any reason to trust me, but just think! It's the Chirrn you blame, not all these innocents. We can steal the PQM and humiliate the Chirrn without all this needless death!"*

But Amrita was a Strider too. In Tarik's visor-magnified view, the Trojan native clipped her line to a lift tether, planted her feet against it to meet Nik's approach, then caught him and redirected his momentum to send him down and away, forcing him to expend thruster fuel just to catch himself. *"That's always been your problem, Nik. So focused on your goal you don't pay enough attention to a woman's whole body!"*

"Well, your problem is that you can't resist dragging people down! And I'm not letting you do that to me anymore." Nik thrust upward to reach the lift cable several meters above Amrita, then secured his own line's molecular-adhesion clip to its surface, halfway around its tree-trunk girth from her. He was able to stay out of range as she swung at him with her unplanted charge, but he'd positioned himself to be in her way if she tried for the structural bundle.

Reassured, Tarik finished deactivating and releasing his charge, though he kept half his attention on the fight as he did so. "One charge down," he broadcast as he secured it to a suit clip. "Repeat, one charge down."

Amrita swung at Nik more and more angrily until she lost her footing. She got in a couple of good blows, but he managed to fire his thrusters to loop around the cable on his line and slam into her from behind, sending the charge flying. Amrita recovered quickly, detaching her line and thrusting after it. Nik was dazed from the impacts, but he had bought some time.

Moments later, Diana's proud voice came over the comm. *"Yes!"* she cried, drawing Tarik's eyes toward her. As she waved a freshly detached demolition charge above her head, she crowed, *"That's two down, boys and — "*

That was when James Oates sprang from behind the tether bundle and began flailing at her with a charge of his own. His legs wrapped around her waist to keep them from flying apart as he struck at her. Only her helmet saved her from having her skull caved in before she could raise her captured charge to block his.

Tarik hesitated only a moment before launching himself toward Diana. She had twenty centimeters on James and several times his strength, but it looked like his surprise attack had left her dazed, and he had the advantage of leverage. Not to mention sheer deranged fury. *"It was you, wasn't it?"* James screamed. *"I never bought their story that* you *had trouble coming out of hibernation. They took you, didn't they? Took the strongest one of us, dumped their thoughts into your brain, sent you back to spy on us! This whole mission was a trap to lure us out here, admit it! You genetic freak, you're not even human! You were in league with the kangers all along!"*

Although his strikes with the heavy charge were as random as his accusations, a lucky blow to Diana's left wrist knocked her own charge loose. It tumbled down and away, end over end, and Tarik hoped it was sturdy enough to withstand any tether impacts on the way down. Surely it couldn't be set off by impact, but if it broke open, the dense matter inside could do some real damage as it fell.

More urgently, James was now ahead by one weapon, and he was more than willing to use it. Still anchored around her waist, he struck at her head and torso repeatedly, dazing her. Diana triggered her helmet lantern to full brightness, dazzling James so she could grab for his arm. But the reflected glare from his visor must have dazzled her too, for she missed. Cackling madly, James lifted his arm over her head, luring her to reach up for it… then slapped the demolition charge across her wrist, activating the device's magnetic adhesion. Diana shrieked as her wrist was clamped hard between the charge and the tether—not just from the pain, no doubt, but from the realization of what James intended to do.

"That's right, whatever you are," Oates cried as he set the timer. *"This will take care of you. Of all of you! Oh, I'm sure you could survive losing a hand, but when this goes off, the hydraulic shock in your bloodstream will make your heart explode!"*

That, at least, was not insane ranting, Tarik knew. He'd seen people struck by meteoroids. "Diana!" he cried. "I'm coming!"

"In that case…" James adjusted the timer. *"There! Think he can get you out in under a minute?"* He laughed and pushed himself away at high speed, opposite the direction it would fire.

"No!" came Diego's voice. *"It's too soon! James, do you realize what you've done? Go back and stop it!"* But James was past listening.

Diana strained futilely against the charge. Even her strength was insufficient to overcome its magnetic adhesion, and she had no leverage anyway; but she kept trying regardless. "I'm almost there!" he cried to her.

"No, Tarik!" she grated back. *"You're carrying a charge! If it's hit, it'll worsen the damage!"*

He reached her at last, pulling himself alongside her. "Then I'll just have to get you out before it goes off."

"I tried that! It won't shut down! You have to get away. I can handle this!"

"No, you can't!" He took Diana's helmet in his hands, making her face him. "You have nothing to prove to us, Diana. Nothing to lose by asking for help. So set aside your damn stubborn pride in your body and use that engineer's brain! Work the problem!"

She fell silent. Though he knew it was futile, he braced his legs on the tether and began to pull on the charge with all his might. After a few seconds, Diana called his name. Holding his gaze, she said: "I'm releasing my glove. You do the rest."

At her wordless command, her suit unsealed at the wrist. Tarik yanked her glove free. She gasped in pain as the vacuum struck her bare skin, as her blood swelled out her hand from within. But the suit tightened around her wrist, minimizing the swelling. Tarik grabbed her firmly and fired his thrusters at full power to pull her away. She screamed in agony, but managed to turn it into words: "Keep… pulling!"

A normal human would have come free easily, though painfully. But Diana's Vanguardian bones resisted breaking, and Tarik feared that the superior durability she took such pride in was about to get them both killed.

"Tarik!" It was Nik's voice. *"Hang on, I'm coming your way."*

"No time, Nik! Veer off!"

"Nothing doing! I lost Amrita — at least I can help you!"

Finally her hand began to fracture, her wrist slipping through as the skin tore and her blood lubricated the charge. Then they were free and thrusting away, and Tarik desperately tried to get distance from the blast arc in the few precious seconds remaining. "Told you… I could do it," Diana rasped, and Tarik swallowed a laugh.

"Nik, she's free! Get away! Repeat, get—"

Then the world tore apart around them.

11

The effects of the detonation unfolded so quickly that only Arachne was able to process them almost as they happened. The charge James had placed was misaligned, but still the molecules-thick "blade" of PQM that spread outward in a fifty-six-degree arc was easily able to slice through thirteen structural tether bundles and dozens of adjacent lift and dynamo tethers. Arachne glimpsed the mirror smoothness of the severed ends before the released tension sent the cables flailing in unpredictable directions at extreme velocities.

Her children were out there. And all she could do was watch.

The arc of destruction encompassed the tether where the first charge had been attached, though at a lower altitude. Tarik and Diana had thrust in the opposite direction, taking them far enough out of the blast zone to avoid the deadly tethers. The arc came dangerously close to the freight lift's tether, but Haim's team had already detached the cab hemisphere, which had begun descending the tether on its emergency quantum-lock magnets.

Evan and Cecilia had been wrestling well below the arc of the charge, in the opposite direction from the blast. But Nikolos's attempt to redeem himself by aiding Tarik and Diana had placed him in the worst possible position. The PQM missed him… but the end of a tether struck his lower body with enough kinetic energy that the bonding energy holding his molecules together was trivial by comparison. Arachne had to watch as half of him simply turned to mist and the rest of him was torn apart by the resulting shock wave.

There was no human concept for what Arachne did instead of screaming. She did it just the same.

It had been her work, her purpose, to protect her crew. Again and again, she had failed. Again and again, she'd been helpless to fulfill that purpose, doomed to let her children down due to circumstances beyond her control. She'd always been overly attached to the physical world, a world that many cybers considered boringly slow and inflexible. But it was the world where humans lived, and they needed help so much. She'd thought she could give that help, but she was just too limited.

Why hadn't she defied Stephen earlier? He'd chosen her because he'd wanted a cyber who would disobey him if he endangered his crew. Had she been so blind to the possibility that the heist could go violently wrong? Or perhaps she'd simply been afraid to risk taking that step a second time, after the first had taken her career and her first body from her, and all for nothing.

No… more likely, she'd simply loved her children too much to believe they could be capable of this. And now she had to bear the weight of another death, another failure — all before the rest of them even realized Nikolos was gone. All too often, that was all she could do: endure the weight on their behalf.

The car carrying Stephen, Sita, and the others had been passing through the Stringworld's highest residential module — a low-gee aerial habitat populated mainly by Zenith and other fliers — when the disaster alert had activated and forced them to a stop. The human and chirrnid passengers insisted on listening in as Orshym, the Mykhshad administrator escorting them, was briefed. At first, there was no physical effect to be felt from the detonation up above; a fair number of the Stringworld's support cables had been severed, but their lower portions were still in the process of contracting around their new centers of mass, so they continued to exert force to hold the module up. The shock from the detonation and abrupt relaxation would take a few minutes to travel down through the cable. This gave the authorities enough time to sever the cables at the base and activate their self-disintegration safeguards before the immense weight of them crashed down onto the module or tore adjacent cables free. Their dissociated fullerene shreds trailed off to antiorbitward and fell clear, and the occupants of the module had time to brace themselves before it started to sway from the loss of support on one side. Enough cables remained that it held essentially upright.

"But it is worse than it should have been," L'chellin relayed to the others. "Apparently, a second charge had somehow fallen and affixed itself to a tether nearly a kilometer lower. A severed tether must have struck it and ruptured its containment. The force accelerated the PQM at sufficient velocity to sever or damage a number of other cables, though not as efficiently as it was designed to. More cables are giving way from the strain."

"What about *Arachne*'s cable?" Stephen asked.

"It and the freight lift cable are intact… for now."

"L'chellin… you need to understand, I would never have gone along with Meridian and Broadwing if I'd known they planned to do… *this*. They guaranteed me no one would be harmed."

The mediator's gaze was stony. "Stephen, Broadwing's vacuum suit is accounted for. He is not the one planting the charges. It must be your own people."

Stephen squeezed his eyes shut. "Diego. I never thought he'd take it this far."

Breath ruffled L'chellin's bristles. "Perhaps that is to your credit," she conceded.

Orshym turned her head and emitted a burst of echolocation clicks to get their attention. "There is no cause for alarm," the Mykhshad told them. "We shall simply send current through the dynamo tethers. This will accelerate Lode Seven outward from the star. This will reduce the tidal load upon the tethers to a safe level."

"Can you do that fast enough?" Sita asked.

"Provided no other charges are detonated. We are about to issue an evacuation order. This is a precaution only." Velesh's eyes convulsed in alarm at the word "evacuation."

"Precaution, my ass," Stephen exclaimed, confusing their translators. "There's still a fight going on up there between my people. Is there any way to punch a signal through so I can talk to them?"

"We have identified the system sabotage. A purge is underway. However, the impact event is ongoing. The interference remains considerable."

"Then you've got to get me up there so I can put a stop to this, order them to stand down. Please," he went on when Orshym hesitated. "This is my fault. My responsibility. I have to do this."

"You should allow this," Velesh said. "These events are the consequence of a failure of mentoring. And our responsibility as mentors is to help younger races help themselves." Stephen looked at the Shayal in surprise and gratitude.

"The wisdom of the Nine Clusters is recognized," the administrator said. "There is a high-acceleration emergency lift. It can reach the area within two *narr*." She hit Stephen with another echolocation burst. "Your body structure may not endure such acceleration undamaged."

He realized Orshym had just given him a quick sonogram. "I'm tougher than I look, believe me," Stephen said. "And I've never let risk stop me from trying."

"Noted. You may accompany me."

"Of course," Velesh added, deflating Stephen's hopes for him, "I insist on joining you to offer guidance."

L'chellin snorted in annoyance. "You can offer no meaningful guidance. You do not know the Arachnen as individuals, only as an abstract cause. They are members of my guild and have been my direct responsibility for *narrenn*. More — Stephen is my friend. I will accompany him."

"Only one of you may accompany the human," Orshym snapped. "Choose quickly!"

Stephen met L'chellin's eyes. "I choose the mediator."

Velesh wanted to protest, but the Mykhshad overrode him. "Noted. Come now!"

Stephen turned to his estranged wife. "Sita…"

She smiled. "It's okay. Like you said, this is our responsibility. I'm not just going to tag along to watch you work. I intend to help with the evacuation."

"*We* intend to help," R'nilinnath added, taking Sita's hand.

Stephen took her other hand, and they both moved in for a brief but heartfelt kiss. Then he and the others hustled for the lift, and as the door closed between them, he hoped that he would see Sita again.

"*Nik! No!!*" Diego's scream rang in Cecilia's helmet. "*James, what did you do?*"

"*It was an accident!*"

Cecilia was furious, but she had no time to indulge it. Nik Zacharias was beyond help; her duty was to the others. "Diana, status?"

"*I can manage, Captain.*"

"*The hell with that,*" Tarik insisted. "*I'm getting you back to* Arachne."

"He's right, Diana," Cecilia said. "No arguments." She checked her HUD. Amrita had recovered her charge and was heading for her near-central target bundle, with James moving toward her at a fair clip to provide reinforcement. "Belay that. Tarik, you need to intercept James and Amrita. You're the only one close enough. Ibrahim, if you're really with us, then get Diana back to the ship and into a medbed."

"*Yes, Captain,*" Ib replied humbly.

"*Very well,*" Tarik said, his voice tight. "*I won't let James get away with what he did.*"

"No revenge. Just get the job done."

A brief pause. "*Acknowledged.*"

Cecilia began climbing toward Diego, who was hanging from his tether in shock, holding the charge loosely in his hand. If she could get up there quickly enough… "Churrlaya, status?" she sent on a private channel.

<*Recovering,*> he texted to her eyes, for his tight sheath wouldn't let him move his mouth. <*I am pursuing Amrita. I believe I have the best chance of reaching her.*>

"You're in no shape for more fighting."

<*Neither is Lode Seven Station. I am substantially outnumbered.*> A pause. <*Do not worry about me, my friend. At worst, a portion of who I am will survive.*>

In the wake of that, it took Cecilia a moment to realize that someone was missing. "I've lost track of Evan," she broadcast. "Did he…"

"*Look down,*" Arachne instructed.

Diego spoke again. "*No… Evan, slow down! Use your thrusters!*"

Cecilia followed Arachne's instruction, finding Evan's blip on her visor. He was hundreds of meters below them now and visibly falling. The blast must have disoriented him long enough to let him pick up significant speed. "*I tried. I'm going too fast.*"

"*No. Not you too.*"

Cecilia felt exactly the same. Her mind raced. She was lower, closer to Evan… but she would have to go faster than him to catch up, and then she'd be even worse off than he was. She could do nothing.

"*It's okay,*" Evan said, his voice quavering. "*Some good can come of this. I'm coming up on the freight cab with the aliens in it. If I time it just right, I can take them out.*"

"*No! There are humans in there too!*" Diego was losing control of his people.

"*Please, Diego! This is my last chance to stand up to those freaks. I can do this… I can…*"

Cecilia braced for the worst. If he was aiming at the freight tether, the charge's arc might intersect the bundle she was tethered to, in which case the explosive release of tension would kill her before she knew it. Instead, when the cables again snapped and flew faster than her mind could process, leaving behind sparkling clouds of shrapnel and carbon dust, the destruction missed her tether and the ones bearing the freight lift and *Arachne*. *"He tumbled,"* the cyber reported in an affectless voice. *"The charge went off in the wrong direction."*

"And Evan?" Diana asked.

"Gone."

Cecilia could feel the tether bundle she gripped trembling from the suddenly added strain. To her left, over a kilometer away at the edge of the first severed section, several damaged tether bundles snapped as they were forced past their limits. Cecilia was too focused — and too angry — to mourn Evan now. "Arachne, if another charge goes off..."

"Lode Seven is undergoing magnetic acceleration into a higher orbit, easing the tension. But it's moving too slowly. Another correctly aimed detonation will almost certainly be fatal, especially if Amrita succeeds in severing the central bundle."

Cecilia looked around. Ibrahim was still helping Diana back to the ship. Even if he abandoned her, he'd be too far away. Tarik was pursuing James, and would not reach Amrita in time to stop her in any case.

So it was up to her and Churrlaya to stop this.

Stephen would probably remark on the symbolism. Cecilia just found it contrived. But she began climbing toward Diego.

"Be advised of another concern," Arachne's voice came over Tarik's radio. *"We are seventy seconds from passing through the accretion disk from Meridian's comet. The loss of tethers has weakened the magnetic shields in this section. The disk is thinning, but there is still a particulate impact hazard. Please take cover behind the tethers as indicated."* Directional markers appeared in Tarik's visor to show where the cometary dust and vapor would come from and how to get safely alee of a tether or bundle.

But he couldn't break off now, not when he was moments from intercepting his quarry and making him pay for Nik's death. He wasn't sure what he would do when he caught James, but he knew the murderous lunatic had to be stopped. He had sworn to protect his crew at all costs, but had only watched helplessly as Mehmet and the other babies had died, as Kweli had died, as Nik and Evan had died. And he had been more than a mere bystander. If he hadn't agreed to go along with this insane heist… if he hadn't persuaded Kweli to start a family so soon… none of this would have happened. He had failed to fulfill his oaths to Cecilia and the crew. But this time, no matter what, he had to succeed.

He couldn't have aborted anyway, for James was now turning and decelerating to intercept him. Tarik tried to slow for the rendezvous, but James was closing at full thrust. Luckily, he was forgetting the fractional gravity pulling him off course, and he passed below Tarik. Still, he managed to snag the larger man's legs on the way past and clung with manic strength. The two of them went into a spin from their clashing thruster fire. "James, stand down thrusters! We need to get in the lee!" There was a lift cable nearby, one he could find if they would only stop spinning. Perhaps if he pushed James away, into the path of the oncoming debris…

"You don't tell me what to do!" James screamed. "You're another sellout. An alien plant like that bitch Diana! I bet they replaced all of you who woke up first!" James was clambering up his body, trying to strike at Tarik's groin, but the wild, shifting accelerations threw off his aim (and the suit automatically hardened against impacts anyway).

"James, look around you! We need to stop this!" But James had become completely irrational, maybe even suffered a psychotic break. What had he been through in the seven months of his captivity? What personal demons had driven him to this while others like Cecilia had remained strong?

Any thoughts of revenge evaporated from Tarik's mind. This was a sick person who needed help. More: This was a member of his crew. One of the people he had sworn to protect… no matter what.

But first he had to get him to safety. He grabbed at James' arms, hoping to haul him into a restraining grip and get to his thruster controls. But an alarm went off in his helmet and he saw small eruptions of dust and gas on the stormward side of multiple tethers. They were in the accretion disk! The impacts weren't as frequent as Tarik feared, but it would only take one. "James, come on!"

A tether spun into view, almost within reach. He thrust toward it, stretched out a hand—but a spurt of carbon dust and water vapor erupted practically in his face before he was swept away. A particle had missed his head by centimeters.

He redoubled his struggle—but realized James's grip had gone limp, only his thrusters pushing him against Tarik now. He caught the smaller man before he could slide off, found and deactivated his thruster controls, and quickly looked him over. The inside of James's helmet was spattered with blood. Sealant oozed into the puncture in the visor, and no doubt the opposite one on the back of the helmet. His status lights showed he was still alive, but barely.

Tarik studied James for a moment. Two minutes ago, he would've been willing to let the man drop. Now, he felt only pity—and he still had an oath to fulfill. Recognizing that the accretion disk passage was over, Tarik began thrusting back to *Arachne*, hoping he could get James into a medbed in time.

Amrita, like most of the other humans, had had the good sense to duck behind her destination tether bundle during the disk passage. Churrlaya, on the other hand, had risked staying in the open, taking the opportunity to close with her. He had little left to lose at this point. He had been luckier than James, though, suffering only a minor erosion of his sheath from a high-velocity cloud of water vapor. Just one more point against his success in the impending confrontation. No matter, in any case; his internal rebreather was close to its limits, the carbon dioxide already starting to build in his circulatory stream. Either way, this would have to end soon.

Even with the gap reduced, he failed to close with Amrita before she reached her target site. "Stay away, Frog," she warned. "If you touch me, I'll set this charge off right now! I mean it!"

<*I believe that you do,*> he texted. He changed direction, coming to land on the tether a few meters away from her. <*Please consider all the lives you will take if you do.*>

"Alien lives. It serves you all right for what you did to us!"

<*Amrita. I have done much to wrong you. I harmed you with intent, to avenge a harm you had no conscious part in. The culpability is mine, and I must live with that. I implore you — do not make yourself as wrong as I was. Do not punish others for what I and my fellow Lesshchin have done. Let compensation fall only on me. Let me help you to rebuild yourself, as I should have done all along.*>

Amrita scoffed. "I've heard it all before. You'll say anything to get me to submit to what the state wants."

<Then do what you want. Come and kill me. I am the only one here who has oppressed you. Take my life in exchange for theirs.>

A pause. "That I can do," Amrita said, and lunged for him.

Cecilia's throat seized up at the sound of Amrita's screams and grunts as she beat the eerily silent Churrlaya. "Is this what you wanted, Diego?" she screamed as she climbed the tether toward him. They had both circled to the lee side to dodge the comet debris, which had also shielded them from fragments of one more snapped tether bundle for which the debris was the final straw. Now they were racing for the charge placement point, and Diego had both the lead and the high ground. "Our own people dying! Killing each other! Killing themselves! What happened to the sanctity of the human soul?"

"None of this was supposed to happen!" Diego screamed down at her. "This wasn't the plan!"

"Are you vacking kidding me?!" Her fury at his words spurred her to climb faster, kicking off the tether bundle to assist her thrusters. "You encouraged all of this! James's paranoia, Evan's bigotry, Amrita's rage. You spent months teaching them to cultivate the worst in themselves, and you have the gall to say you're surprised that this was the result?"

He braced himself above her, his suit cable anchored to the tether. He spun the demolition charge slowly, ready to strike. She ducked beneath it, taking the blow on her left forearm so she could anchor her line with her right hand. "This is your fault!" he cried. "This wouldn't have happened if you'd led us as you were supposed to!"

He swung for her head with killing force. She ducked it, taking a grazing strike to her helmet that left her ears ringing. "Now the truth comes out! You'll kill a human as easily as anyone else!"

He kicked her in the side, sending her flying out from the tether. Her line held, but she ended up dangling upside-down from it, and Diego took advantage of her position to get her in a leg hold and force the charge toward her neck. She caught it with her hands, but his strength was greater, his leverage better.

"You call yourself human?" he cried. "You sold your soul to these devils! At least they were born soulless! You are an abomination, and I'll end you even if I have to set this charge off here and now!"

"Diego Felipe Narvaez Duarte!" Cecilia was stunned. It was Stephen's voice, staticky but recognizable. *"Listen to yourself, Diego! Look at what's happening around you!"*

"Stephen? This wasn't my fault! The Frog got to them, turned them against us! You understand, right? You're still with me, aren't you, Stephen?"

"Oh, I wish I still were, Diego. Do you know why I wanted you with me in the first place?"

"What?" Diego asked. The charge pressed closer to her throat. She could feel its magnetic field straining toward the tether, trying to break her wrists and crush her windpipe.

"Growing up where I did, I had a lot of reason to fear and mistrust Christians. But I quickly learned you were nothing like the militias."

"Of course not, I'm Catholic."

"More than that," Stephen pressed. *"You weren't just using piety as a weapon against others, a tool for power, an excuse for hate. You genuinely believed in the good your faith could do. I saw a kindred spirit in you, Diego, a man of deep conviction."*

"That's right, Stephen! That's what this is all about!"

"The thing about the people with the deepest convictions, though, is that we have the most trouble figuring out what to do when our convictions fail us. But you know what I've realized, Diego?" The pressure against her throat wavered, but only slightly. A few more centimeters and the field would grip too strongly to break. *"I realized that's exactly when we need to hold onto our convictions the hardest. To take a good, close look at them and think about what they really mean.*

"Is the sanctity of the soul just about who you're allowed to kill, Diego? What about the things the soul has to endure? What about causing it pain? Causing it guilt? Diego, what happens to your soul if you commit suicide in order to commit mass murder? What will you have become?"

"It's no sin to sacrifice myself to save my people!"

"Diego, your people are down in the Chirrn embassy right now, not knowing if they can get out in time. Your people include Sita, who's down there somewhere, I don't even know where, risking her own safety to help evacuate others. Your people, Diego Felipe, include the six hundred embryos on Arachne that are in mortal danger every time a tether snaps!"

Inside his helmet, Diego looked lost, confused. His grip on the charge loosened, and Cecilia was able to push it away. She tucked her legs, braced her feet on the tether, headbutted Diego (her head was already ringing, so why not?), and ripped the charge from his hand. Then she slammed him in the gut with it and he was down for the count. Her chest heaved as she gasped for breath.

"Cecilia? Are you all right?"

"Oh… damn… it's good to hear your voice, partner. Position secure. That leaves only Amrita. Are you in position to reach her?"

A pause. *"I… don't think that will be necessary."*

Cecilia checked in on that channel. Amrita's screams had stopped. Now she was only weeping, bawling it out like she never had in all the months of captivity. "Churrlaya?" Cecilia sent tentatively. "Are you…"

<*Damaged,*> he replied. <*But my job is done.*>

"The charge is secured?"

<*More than that. I think I have made another breakthrough.*>

When Stephen boarded *Arachne* along with L'chellin and Administrator Orshym, he found himself having to fend off an aggressive, rambling apology from Cecilia, which he finally interrupted by the expedient of giving her a tight hug that she only gradually relaxed into. "I think I owe more apologies than you do now," he murmured in her ear. "I set them loose. You stopped them."

She shook her head. "I couldn't have without you."

Finally he had mercy on her and let her go, but her grip lingered on him for a few moments more. She pulled away, blushing, and he gave her refuge in a companionably rough slap on the shoulder. "I'm glad we're a team again. Let's keep it that way, okay?"

"May your words forgive me for supplanting them," L'chellin interposed, "but it is not yet time for celebration. Lode Seven Station is still in serious danger."

"Too many tethers are lost. The rest cannot support the tidal weight at this altitude," Orshym clarified, her sensory hairs rippling across her flanks—a sign of nervousness? "As more give way, the load increases on the rest. We accelerate outward at the best rate possible. But the damage impairs this. I must recommend evacuation." They reached the cockpit where Broadwing and the Zhalevey conspirators (now ready to cooperate with the group around them, as was their way) stood waiting, along with Tarik and Diana. Churrlaya and the three surviving human conspirators were in medbeds, with Ibrahim sitting vigil. Diana should have been in one too, Stephen thought, rather than just having a healing-gel sheath around her crushed hand, but there was no way she'd allow herself to be out of action at a time like this.

Orshym turned to the Zhalevey. "Do you control this vessel's docking cradle?"

"Yes," Shthastya replied.

"Then please begin descent. We will rendezvous with the freight cab. We will take it within the warp cage. Then we will launch."

"What about our people down below?" Cecilia asked just before Stephen could.

"A general evacuation order has gone out," Orshym said.

"They were already prepared to depart at a moment's notice," Broadwing put in, looking unwontedly sheepish.

"But Sita isn't with them," Stephen reminded them.

"She and the apprentice assist with the evacuation," said the Mykhshad. "They may leave with those they assist."

"How many people reside on this megastructure?" Broadwing demanded. "How long would it take to evacuate even a fraction of them? Have you thought that through? I have done little else since the first charge went off. The cables will split and the habitats will flip over before the radiation surges end. Only a fraction can get away. We cannot guarantee anyone's safety. We cannot even guarantee this lift cable will hold long enough to launch us."

"Isn't there anything more we can do?" Diana's voice was strong but rough; she was clearly weak and in pain, but effectively ignoring it. "Any way to thrust faster than magnetically? All the PQM tech you have..."

Orshym waved her trunk in Diana's direction as though sniffing at her. "We are instructing the factory core. It will jettison its PQM from the antispinward hatches. This will reduce the mass of the inner core. It will also accelerate it closer to orbital velocity."

"But will it be enough?" Tarik asked.

"It will grant us time. We can evacuate a higher percentage of the population."

"That's it?"

"It is all we can do. We are close to the neutron star. The PQM is little more than dead weight here."

"Weight," Diana echoed—or was it "Wait?" "Listen—don't jettison the PQM. Set all of it to simulate negative mass!"

Stephen and Cecilia both stared. "What?" the latter asked.

"Negative mass. It reacts opposite to the way you push it. I almost got crushed by it when we stole the first drum. If we set all that PQM to negative mass, won't it fall up instead of down? Push it away from the star?"

"That's for force, not acceleration," Arachne's voice pointed out. "Solve for acceleration and only the star's mass counts. Negative mass would fall like everything else."

Diana looked embarrassed not to have realized that, but set it aside with surprising ease. "Okay, okay, then make it a force! You've got all that machinery in the factory levels—have it push down on the negative-mass PQM, and it'll push back up. It'll push up against the weight, reduce the strain on the tethers. Won't it?"

"It would reduce the weight as you say," Arachne confirmed.

Orshym was agitated. "It would also place great strain on the factory facilities. The force would keep building. Finally the PQM would tear through. It might not be long enough for ascent to a safe altitude."

"But it's got to work longer than just tossing all the stuff out the side, right? And reversing its mass shrinks the total weight more than just removing it."

"It is not a particularly rational proposal."

Cecilia stepped forward. "This isn't a rational situation! Take it from a feral human—if there's one useful thing we've gotten out of our history of disastrously bad choices, it's a knack for desperate, last-ditch solutions. We may not have a billion years of precedent to solve every problem, but that makes us gifted improvisers."

"Please," Stephen urged. "The factory will be lost anyway if the tethers snap. This way we can at least save a greater number."

To her credit, Orshym decided promptly. "Agreed. I have transmitted the order."

After that, it was only a long, tense wait. Once *Arachne* caught up with the freight-lift cockpit and took it inside the already-crowded warp cage along with Haim, Kahina, Changkun, and the other four sophonts inside, they released the docking cradle's brakes and began to fall. From their current altitude, it would take ten minutes or more of free fall to reach the bottom and be launched clear of the Stringworld and the neutron star. If the tether snapped before then, they would likely be killed by the sudden, convulsive release of tension. If it snapped far enough above them, they might be spared, but if the Stringworld gave way, the whole structure would lose rigidity and twist, and a safe launch would be impossible.

And what might await Sita and Nilly, and the countless other beings inside the Stringworld, was too much to contemplate. Stephen's eyes met Cecilia's, the look conveying a depth of feeling. Neither of them could bear being responsible for a second disaster of this magnitude. Stephen knew, though, that the burden of responsibility would fall entirely on him. The fact that Meridian had manipulated and lied to him was of no consequence. He had chosen to act rashly out of pain, to do something that he knew could endanger others because he was too angry to care. He had cloaked it in self-righteous rationalizations, but the power-hungry governors, robber barons, and fundamentalist militias who had turned the Gulf States into a decaying ruin had done no less.

Cecilia took his hand, and he could tell from her face that she saw right through him, as she always did. "Don't you dare try to fall on your sword for the rest of us again. Whatever happens, I'm in this with you."

"So are we all," Tarik affirmed, and the others — even L'chellin and Broadwing — gave gestures of agreement.

"Everyone?" Arachne spoke up. "Would you look outside, please? I think you'll want to see this."

Stephen moved to the ports, Cecilia at his side, the others close behind. Beyond the transparent crystal, beyond the tethers flying past and the occasional habitat whose bulk blocked their view as they passed through it, the Stringworld was surrounded by light. Shimmering, iridescent filaments wrapped around it, flowing along its edges, sending out darting, electric-arc tongues that jumped and danced across its surface. Beyond was a meshwork of intricate auroral patterns stretching into the distance.

Arachne gave them video feeds from cameras on the Stringworld, from ships already launched, even from the wormhole terminus beyond. The enigmatic halo that surrounded the neutron star had extended a set of loops outward like a pseudopod to engird the megastructure. "The tension is diminishing!" Orshym cried, listening to reports from below. "This is unexpected, shocking. The metasapients have intervened on our behalf! The star's magnetic field has been altered! It is guiding us into a higher orbit! I never imagined to know such a privilege!"

"The hell with privilege," Tarik asked, "are we safe?"

"At worst, the modules will not flip until after the radiation bursts end. And we have time to mount a full evacuation. However, the acceleration shows no sign of halting. Shortly, the remaining tethers will be in no danger of breaking. We will be unable to operate under normal weight until repairs are completed. But Lode Seven will survive."

"Were there any casualties?" Stephen asked, dreading the answer.

"I think you should hear this report yourself." A link from Orshym blinked in his inbox display, and he opened it.

Sita's face appeared in his field of view. Her hair was drifting around her beautiful face in the extreme low gravity, and she was grinning. *"Everyone's okay down here. Some injuries from the swaying and the rush, but nothing that won't heal. Nobody died, Stephen. Not even temporarily."* He didn't have the heart to tell her about Nik, Evan, and James yet.

Nilly drifted by upside-down in the background, halfway through a slow midair flip. *"You should've seen her in action, Stephen! She was so commanding. She helped a lot of people stay calm. She should be a mediator, like me!"*

"But how did this happen?" L'chellin asked, her eyes staring out opposite viewports in bewilderment at the dancing filaments of light outside. "For metasapients to directly intervene in sophont affairs is virtually unprecedented. They are not even aware of us as individuals."

"No," Broadwing said. "But Lode Seven Station is a collective entity — a community that has value to the galaxy beyond. Its importance is great enough to draw their attention."

"It is more likely," Orshym put in, "that they reacted to the negative-mass signature from the PQM below. Negative masses striking the surface might have done more damage than ordinary matter. They may have only acted to save themselves."

Diana grinned widely. "So… it was my idea that saved everybody? Just so we're clear."

"Perhaps that was all it was," Broadwing observed, gazing out at the luminous hand of his saviors. "But I prefer to believe… that they wish us to live."

12

Apastron had been complaining of the cold, but Meridian knew it was just a manifestation of her second's instinct to challenge. To minimize their chances of detection, the ship had burrowed beneath the loose agglomeration of ice boulders that made up the surface of a small comet and powered down. The physical contact with the frigid matter had drawn away their ship's heat far faster than the emptiness of space could. But Zenith were bred to fly high and endure extremes. Meridian found the cold invigorating.

Still, when Mountain's Peak reported the readings from their optical sensors on the comet's surface, Meridian felt the chill within her. Lode Seven Station had not been destroyed, simply moved to a higher orbit, apparently through the stardwellers' intervention. Mountain's Peak found the latter miraculous, but Meridian was distraught that the stardwellers had rejected her offering of lives. Had the humans done something to foul it?

It was a partial relief when the human ship arrived under sublight warp only mildly behind schedule, with telemetry and their transmissions confirming that it carried not quite ten-twelfths of the expected PQM shipment and only some of the humans. Apastron did her job, ordering Mountain's Peak to power up and rise to rendezvous with *Arachne*.

Meridian's new concubine soon arrived across the docking tube, accompanied by the human with the name-sound Stephen Jacobs-Wong. She greeted them in turn, chiming their names in her own tongue. "Broadwing. Crown of the Usurper King. You are welcome. But why is the shipment incomplete?"

"The Unrenounced proved too volatile," Broadwing explained after bowing his head in obeisance. "They detonated the charges early and incompetently. We were forced to depart prematurely. With respect, Matriarch, why did you not entrust me with the full plan?"

"You know I wished no mark of Zenith talons on this deed."

"Even so, could I not have passed on your instructions?"

She leaned down and preened his cheek featherfur to show her continued favor. "You understand that trust must be earned. I do not doubt your loyalty, but you have lived among the Chirrn for way too long. You might have hesitated in what was necessary."

"You may be right. Even now, I have trouble seeing your intentions."

"I intended to ensure the reference samples were destroyed. I intended to hurt and humiliate the Void Alliance far worse than by a mere theft."

"For what it's worth," the human said, "we did inflict considerable harm, and not just to the tethers. They saved Lode Seven by setting the PQM to negative mass to reduce the strain on the tethers, but that caused significant damage to the factory. It'll be a good while before they get things up and running again."

"That is but a token blow. It was not enough to ensure the stardwellers' favor."

"I don't understand."

"As a groundwalker, you would not," Broadwing said. "Courtesy requires an offering of nourishment to those whose favor we wish. Is that not right, Matriarch?"

"You do understand," Meridian chimed, pleased that Broadwing's years in the wilderness had not led him to forget too much. "Lode Seven Station would have been a great offering to the stardwellers."

"An offering?" Stephen Jacobs-Wong asked. "In what way?"

Stars above, the human was slow-witted. "The stardwellers thrive on complexity. The more minds they are fed, the more they are nourished. As it is, we have given them nothing. Worse, they rejected our offering."

"More than nothing, Matriarch," Broadwing said. "Two of the humans lost their lives from the premature detonations, and another has lost much of his mind."

"It is not enough! They would not even notice two or three lives! I meant to send them thousands to bless this beginning of our quest." She spun on the human. "Curse you primitives! I gave you people clear and simple orders. Are you too incompetent to follow them?"

"Orders to do what again?" the stupid male asked.

"Orders to sever the cables cleanly! Did you damage your brain in the upheaval?"

Rather than taking offense, the human leader relaxed and released a sigh, the corners of his mouth turning upward. "No, my lady. If anything, I feel whole for the first time in quite a while."

"Matriarch!" Mountain's Peak cried. "Multiple vessels have just emerged from warp bubbles. It is the Chirrn migration fleet! They will soon surround us!"

Meridian sang an undertone of shock and disbelief while her other crests chimed, "Get us out of here! Crown of the Usurper King, tell your ship to follow!"

"We cannot form a warp metric!" Mountain's Peak cried a few moments later. "They are bombarding us with radiation and shifting gravity fields."

Meridian spun on the human. "What has happened? What have you done?"

"It's an old human tradition," Stephen Jacobs-Wong said. "It's called wearing a wire. And you just gave us the confession we were fishing for. Every word you said has been recorded and broadcast to the Stringworld authorities."

Meridian whirled on Broadwing. "You were part of this? How could you betray me?"

The male faced her without bowing, a shocking breach. "You betrayed the cause, Meridian. The stardwellers do not want us to kill for them. They saved Lode Seven Station. Some may think they acted only to protect themselves from the negative masses, but they could have done so after the megastructure was severed. They chose to preserve lives, not consume them. Meridian... you were wrong."

"How dare you speak to me in that tone, you low-status male!" She spread her mandibles, preparing to lunge for his throat.

But Apastron leapt in her way. "Then *I* will speak to you thus," her second trilled. "He is right—the failure is yours. You promised to lead us to glory. But instead you have led us directly into the capture we have eluded for decades, because you let yourself be tricked by a primitive groundling!" She rose to a full combat stance and uttered the shrill cry of challenge.

So this was it. Apastron, admirably, had watched for the first sign of weakness from Meridian and struck without hesitation when it presented itself. But Meridian had broken or killed all prior challengers, and though she bore Apastron no malice for her legitimate ambition, she would win this fight as she had all others.

But when she leapt up and swept at Apastron with her lower talons, something went wrong. The timing of her leap had been off, ever so slightly tentative, and Apastron dodged it easily. Meridian struggled to banish any hint of doubt from her mind. She had not been defeated yet! She would make it up to the stardwellers somehow — no! If she let herself feel she had failed…

Before she realized what was happening, Apastron was upon her, striking with the speed and fury of youth. Fire raked across Meridian's wing as its glorious smoothness was ripped clean through, rendering her unable to fly. To add insult to injury, Apastron bent back the dactyls and snapped them, leaving the tattered wing hanging limp and ugly. Meridian screamed with all three crests, hoping to stun Apastron with the volume, for after all, her crests were the largest, the loudest, the most resplendently feminine.…

But Apastron leapt up and struck with her powerful leg, the talons coming straight at Meridian's left eye. The next thing she knew, she was lying on the floor, staring up at the sharp corner of a console, which was stained with blue Zenith blood and fragments of a material that shimmered with prismatic light.…

In horror, Meridian tried chiming, and only two tones sounded, the third replaced by a hollow hiss. Her intact arm shot up to her head — but even as she felt the void, she caught sight of her long, beautiful right crest lying broken on the floor. Meridian couldn't stop herself from keening, though it was a claw through her throat to hear the incomplete chords that resulted. Apastron had ruined her beauty, her voice. No one would follow her now.

But she was so proud of her beautiful second-in-command. Apastron had won fairly, with a ruthlessness Meridian had to admire. Meridian had failed, had brought shame on herself, but the cause would still be well-tended.

She dragged herself forward, prostrating herself before her new matriarch. She laid her broken head on its side, eyes away from Apastron, the soft back of her neck exposed to the victor's talons. Meridian waited silently for Apastron to grasp her throat in her talons — the lowliest part of the victor surmounting the highest part of the loser — and claim her rightful dominance.

But then she heard her former second chime: "No. In truth, it was not I who defeated you. Not in the way that matters most. Not in the way that will get us all arrested, our cause defeated. That honor," she finished with a disturbingly smug and cruel tone entering her chimes, "belongs to another."

Out of the corner of two eyes, Meridian saw Apastron step aside… and beckon Broadwing to take her place. Meridian's digestive system heaved as though she were falling from a great height without functional wings. Broadwing hesitated at first, but then stepped forward with confidence and determination, positioning himself for the ritual. "No," Meridian cried, unable to keep her silence any longer. "No, please! Not a male! Kill me instead, please! No!!"

But no mercy was coming, and she knew that even death would not grant her release. The stardwellers had rejected her offering and they would reject her soul. She could not escape her fate. She could only keen like a baby as Broadwing's cold, filthy masculine foot pressed her neck into the ground.

Within a day, the frenzy of the evacuation had settled down, although the occupants of the Stringworld were still vacating it at a less harried pace to make room for the extensive repairs needed to restore it to full function. Thus, the surviving Arachnen were now reunited aboard the largest ship of the Chirrn migration fleet, save only James Oates, who was in stable but critical condition aboard *Arachne*. Joana Caravalho and Doctor Mh'lellish had reported that James's brain damage could be healed, but the resulting mind would have lost much of its memory and personality, including most of what had occurred since Lesshchi. Stephen held out hope that this would allow James to make a fresh start, free of the baggage that had driven him to become what he had. Churrlaya had promised to do what he could to help in that process. "It is a state of being I understand well," the former Lesshchin assured him, before resuming his counseling of Amrita Dhillon.

The Lode Seven authorities saw Meridian as the prime culprit and were thrilled to have her under arrest at long last, so they were content to leave her human accomplices in Chirrn custody. That placed them right back in the hands of the Shilirrlaln justice system—or what there was of it aboard this fleet.

L'chellin assembled a mediators' hearing to determine the facts of the case. Since Broadwing was an admitted conspirator, R'nilinnath had to join L'chellin on the panel. As they listened to testimony from the witnesses, Nilly sat stiffly and tried to look solemn and disciplined, with little success.

Now, with the testimony concluded, Stephen sat before the panel accompanied by Cecilia, Tarik, Haim, Diana, Broadwing, Diego, Amrita, and Arachne's avatar, with the rest of the Arachnen in the audience. He was grateful that Ibrahim, Kahina, and Changkun had not been charged, for their only crime had been to assist in ferrying the stolen PQM to *Arachne*. L'chellin had not required Cecilia to stand with the conspirators either, for she had played no role in the crime; yet she had insisted on taking responsibility for the acts of her crew. For his part, Stephen had confessed all his actions and choices freely, as had all the others, save only Diego. Though he was subdued and clearly grieving, Diego still refused to acknowledge the Chirrn's authority or participate in the proceeding. At least Amrita was beginning to make progress. There was still bitterness in her toward the Chirrn, but it seemed she had begun to realize that Diego had exploited her more.

At length, L'chellin spoke. "We now have many factors to weigh in determining the extent to which the balance has been disrupted and what must be done to restore it. Your willing cooperation in establishing the facts of these events, and the declared repentance of most of you, is appreciated and noted for the record. However, much damage was inflicted upon Lode Seven Station, and the supply of PQM to the Antispinward Void will be disrupted for some time.

"Far more importantly, your actions led to the irreversible deaths of Nikolos Zacharias and Evan Jiang Erfan, and the partial death of James Albert Oates. The fact that the two individuals directly responsible for those deaths are themselves partly or completely dead does not mitigate the loss, but worsens it. In death, they cannot work to repay the community for what they have taken from it." Stephen blinked away tears, moved by her words. "James can be restored, but the person he becomes will not be the same person who killed Nikolos, so would it be fair to demand compensation from him?

"In addition," L'chellin went on, her voice heavy with disappointment, "Mediator Broadwing's violation of his oaths led to the deaths of the unborn children of mated progenitors Sita Bhatiani and Stephen Jacobs-Wong, mated progenitors Kweli Ndege and Tarik Hüseyin

Bahar, unmated progenitors Oyama Kazuko and Ravinder Pritam, and surrogate progenitor Justine Nguyen, and contributed to the self-inflicted irreversible death of Kweli Ndege." Broadwing lowered his head. No trace remained of the pride and triumph he'd shown when he'd clutched Meridian's neck in his talons.

"On the other hand, Mediator Broadwing, you have contributed to the restoration of balance by assisting in the rescue of Lode Seven Station and the arrest of Meridian. Your voluntary confession and readiness to repent are also noted. Yet you will need at least a lifetime to repay your debts in full."

"I submit fully and without challenge to the judgment of Shilirrlal," Broadwing intoned in a minor key.

L'chellin puffed a breath through her nares and turned her eyes to Stephen. "As for most of the culpable Arachnen, you have already taken decisive and heroic action to correct your mistakes before the worst was done. Your imaginative thinking saved thousands of lives. And you helped us bring one of the worst criminals in the Four Voids to justice." Stephen bowed his head in acknowledgment of her generosity. He didn't feel he deserved it.

"Yet we must still examine what led you to betray your oaths in the first place — a betrayal without which the events here at Lode Seven could not have occurred, and which I know to be an offense against your own personal convictions as well as Chirrn laws." She leaned forward pleadingly. "Why, Stephen? You had my trust and my friendship. You had worked so hard to contribute meaningfully to the community. Why did you feel compelled to attempt such an act against us?"

After a careful pause, he replied: "Because when I learned the truth about mentoring, I blamed the Chirrn for the destruction of Lesshchi, for all human suffering, and became convinced that our incarceration was unjust and oppressive. Because ultimately it was easier to blame you than to live with my own culpability for Lesshchi — and my own inability to save my brother and my mother so long ago."

Cecilia grabbed his shoulder. "No. Stephen, I told you not to fall on your sword alone."

"Cecilia —"

"Let her speak," L'chellin said. Nilly gave a half-hearted gesture of agreement, trying to look like she served a purpose.

Cecilia rose and threw a look at Churrlaya. "Look. For months I was doing just what Stephen said — blaming you to hide from my own guilt.

I'm ready now to accept something else he said to me once, about taking responsibility for the consequences of your own actions no matter who or what may have goaded you into them. What happened here, what happened to Kweli and Nik and Evan and James and the rest, that's on all of us, and I'm as ready as Stephen to do whatever we can to make amends.

"But in the name of fairness, shouldn't the same principle apply to the Chirrn? You had a hand in what happened here as well. You pushed the Zenith to seek metasapience too soon and triggered everything that followed. You cut Earth off from the galaxy. Now, personally I think you did us a favor, all things considered." She met Stephen's eyes. "But that doesn't mean it didn't come at a terrible cost. It left us both unprepared to meet each other. It forced humanity to develop starflight on our own and use dangerous methods to do so." She glanced at Diego. "It left some of us unable to face alien life without panic or xenophobia.

"I'm not saying you should let us off the hook for our mistakes. But if the Chirrn don't face up to their own mistakes and accept responsibility for the consequences, nothing will change in the long run, and sooner or later there will be another disaster, another attempted genocide. Maybe even another interstellar war, if the Void Alliance and the other powers all keep refusing to budge."

Her eyes took in L'chellin, R'nilinnath, and all the other Chirrn in the audience. "It took me months to learn that denying culpability for our bad decisions is ultimately a self-destructive path. I'm asking the Chirrn not to make the same mistake. Now, I don't know if mentoring is a good idea or not, but I think it's a question you need to open again. You went too far in one direction, and to fix it maybe you went too far in the other. Maybe there's a better solution in the middle somewhere. But you need to start looking for it, see what you can fix in yourselves to keep things like this from happening again. Or maybe..." She reached down and clasped Stephen's hand. "What you can learn from listening to others who see things differently."

L'chellin considered her words for some moments. "You have learned wisdom," the mediator finally said. "And the Chirrn must not be averse to doing the same. If nothing else, consider our pride." Her unwonted (but typically dry) humor helped ease the tension, punctuating the moment before she continued. "You are correct, Cecilia. This has become a referendum not merely on the Arachnen's fate, but on the Void Alliance's policy toward humanity itself—for it is only within that context that the Arachnen's actions here can be understood and judged.

"Our forebears four *yanarrach* ago believed that we could best serve the nascent civilizations in the Four Voids by leaving them alone. But now we must acknowledge that even in trying to avoid interference, we have affected you profoundly. We have still made choices on your behalf, choices that have consequences to you but in which you were denied a say. That is an unjust and ultimately harmful imposition.

"And yet," L'chellin went on with pride, "you have managed to thrive and advance entirely through your own choice and effort. You are prone to monumental errors, but as recent events have shown, you have a remarkable capacity for correcting those errors—even if you do tend to postpone such correction until the last desperate *narr*. I now believe that you have the maturity and the right to make choices on your own behalf as a species.

"Moreover, I believe only you, and your fellow unmentored civilizations in the Voids, are qualified to know what is best for your own species, for your nature is outside the experience of the mentored galaxy. If it is your judgment that you deserve to participate in the community of the galaxy, we have no right to isolate you for what we imagine to be your own good."

After a moment, Nilly made a hesitant snuffling noise, akin to clearing her throat. "But Mediator… what about the Shayal? They don't think humans are ready. They think they're scary ferals who need to be mentored and tamed. What happened here will only make people more afraid of humans than they already are, and make it easier for the Shayal to get what they want."

"You spawn robust and well-formed words, Apprentice Mediator," L'chellin said, and Nilly raised her head and gaped in pride—then gave a startled jump and closed her mouth, realizing she'd shown a bit too much tongue. "And they have captured the essence of our dilemma. Whatever penalty we impose on the Arachnen, it will not resolve the larger political issues that could still enfold them and jeopardize their future standing as members of our community. Nor will it prevent others from treating the rest of humanity in ways that could provoke dangerous consequences."

L'chellin's eyes swivelled and she hissed across her tongue. Her fingers tapped repeatedly on her brows, and her tail twitched and thumped against her perch. Stephen had never seen her so agitated. "I can see one possible recourse, but it is highly… unorthodox. It is only possible under the current turbulent circumstances at Lode Seven." A sigh ruffled her snout bristles. "With all that has happened, the stolen PQM has not yet been unloaded from Arachne. If that PQM were somehow to… somehow to come into the possession of the humans of Sol System… it could enable them to develop their own interstellar technology. They would then be in a stronger position to resist interference, to gain allies.…" She trailed off.

Stephen rose. "L'chellin… are you inviting us to steal the PQM *again*?"

"I do not spawn these words lightly. But if the Chirrn have wronged you, then we are obligated to restore the balance. We have left you vulnerable, and now you are exposed. Something must be done to grant you strength. That PQM aboard *Arachne* is immune to neutralization, since you successfully destroyed the reference sample. If humanity gained possession of it, no one could take it from them. It is a unique and limited opportunity, so the decision must be made now."

"You need that PQM to build the colony, though," Cecilia said. "And Lode Seven won't be up and running for a while."

"We still have the bulk-grade PQM for the habitat collar, and the ships we have should be adequate to do the work with only a limited delay. We can make do until a replacement supply can be obtained."

"But how would we get away with it?" Stephen asked.

"I can persuade the other fleet alphas to delay reporting the theft. This would allow *Arachne* to traverse the wormhole to Antares among the other evacuating ships, then return to Sol."

"Even so," Haim put in, "it would take us decades to get a handle on the PQM and start building our own warp or Casimir cages."

"We can provide Arachne with complete specifications to save you time. And the Void Alliance will not wish to act in haste toward you once you have that potential. I believe it will force us all to reevaluate our mentoring policies and their consequences, and that debate could easily fill that interval. As for the Shayal and others… the Voids are still our responsibility, and if we invite them to participate in the debate in good faith, they are likely to respect our independence in turn — at least until humanity is strong enough that the matter is rendered moot."

Stephen and Cecilia met each other's eyes. "What do you think?" she asked him, though she hardly needed to.

He sighed. "L'chellin… I think it's a generous offer, but it troubles me. I've compromised my oaths and my integrity enough already. I don't want to see you doing the same."

"He's right," Cecilia said. "We've all agreed to renounce our ties to Earth. It took me a long time to get to that point, and a lot of people suffered as a result." She looked to Churrlaya in the audience. "I can't go back on that word, not so easily. If anyone else wants to go, they have my blessing, but I'm staying here to pay my debt."

"We both are," Stephen said.

"But there's more than that," Cecilia went on. "Talk about political maneuvering all you want, but if humanity shows up on the galactic stage with warp ships so soon after Lode Seven, it'll just make us thieves in the eyes of the galaxy. And that's at best. At worst, we'll be linked with Meridian, and all the irrational terror you Galactics have about metasapient plagues will fall onto us. We'll be mistrusted, feared, even hunted."

Stephen squeezed her hand. "And just giving humanity PQM wouldn't help us stand on our own. We'd still be dependent on out-siders. We'd be seen as a charity case, not true equals. Any accom-plishments we made in the future would be seen as an indulgence from others, and we'd be judged only by our past mistakes.

"Too much of what's happened here these past months, these past millennia, is the result of people being unable to look beyond the mistakes and abuses of the past. Maybe it's because your civilizations have lived so long, have so much history. Maybe our young civilization has the potential to break that cycle. But to do that, to move beyond the trap of the past, we need to take responsibility for our own future. We need to find our own path to the stars."

L'chellin was visibly moved and impressed. "These words are also well-spawned. Yet I admit I do not see how what you propose can happen. Relativistic travel is a dead end, and PQM is only available from neutron stars. It would take you many *yanarr* at least to reach the nearest lode. The PQM aboard *Arachne* right now is your best, perhaps only hope to grant your people self-determination."

R'nilinnath made another attention-seeking snuffle. "Ahh… I have a very strange and probably very stupid idea."

L'chellin looked at her. "Do not let the words die on your tongue."

"Well… we need to give them the PQM… but it mustn't be obvious that it came from this theft… and we can't just tell them how to build warp ships because then they won't be independent. And the Arachnen don't want to break their oaths by renewing contact with Earth. Right?"

"An adequately efficient summary."

"Then maybe… what if we just… *left* the PQM where they could find it? Like in their outer cometary cloud, or somewhere in a system they've already colonized but barely begun to explore. Then the Arachnen could keep their oaths, and the Soln — the humans — they could study the PQM and figure it out on their own. Find their own answers, like they've learned how to do so well. Who knows? Maybe they could discover something new about how to use it, test out some crazy idea we're all too smart to try. Plus it would probably take them a yanarr or two to invent superluminal ships, enough time that the connection to the heist would fade in people's minds. After all, they wouldn't know where they got it, so they couldn't be blamed."

"I don't know, Nilly," Haim said. "Is that supply enough to sustain a whole civilization?"

"Enough to give them a good start, at least. Once the Soln have achieved that, they could find out where to get more."

Stephen considered Nilly's proposal and nodded. "Yes. I think it's a good compromise. Humanity deserves its independence in the galaxy, but it doesn't deserve to fall victim to the bad press we Arachnen have garnered. A delay will give us time to earn our repentance and build a better image of humanity in the galaxy's eyes."

"But you know what this means, don't you?" Tarik asked. "This only works if the Shilirrlaln have deniability, if there's no clear link from them to Solar humanity. If some of us leave in *Arachne* to drop off the PQM in human space… then it would be permanent. We couldn't come back to the fleet, or to the new habitat."

"You could go back to Earth," Nilly suggested.

"No," Tarik said. "Cecilia's right. We swore an oath. We have a debt to repay. We can't make a good beginning of this if we do it without honor."

Stephen's heart sank, and he shook his head. "I can't ask anyone to do that. To be an exile, adrift in the galaxy."

Tarik laughed, surprising him. "You needn't ask, Stephen. I volunteer! To command a ship that could take me anywhere in the galaxy? It would be the adventure of a lifetime!"

Cecilia clasped his hand. "Are you sure, Tarik? You've been so important to this community…"

He gave a wistful smile. "I held them together as best I could in your absence. And it took almost everything I had. Now you're here, back with Stephen, so I know the Arachnen are in good hands. And I…" He sighed. "I need to get away. To make my own *hijra*… and try to find what is left of myself."

The captain squeezed his hand. "All right. But I can't let you go off with only Arachne for companionship. You'll need others too, enough to make a working crew."

"Very well," L'chellin said after a moment. "I would prefer to deliberate longer, but there is limited time to carry out R'nilinnath's plan successfully." Nilly beamed at the attribution. "I will permit a small party to depart aboard *Arachne*, no more than the minimum necessary to function as a crew."

"Then I'm going too," R'nilinnath said.

L'chellin was stunned. "No! I cannot allow that."

The young Chirrn faced her without wavering. "You can't just let a bunch of children wander around the galaxy. They need *some* adult supervision! They're still our responsibility. And they need a mediator to help them interact with the sophonts they'll meet." She bounced up and down a bit. "And it'll be fun!"

L'chellin hesitated. "I suppose they do still owe a debt to the Chirrn. Someone should accompany them to oversee their repayment of it. But R'nilinnath, are you sure…"

"Mediator, this was my idea. I have to take responsibility for the consequences."

"But you would be alone, the only Chirrn. You would have no consensus knowledge to share. You would be fragmentary."

"I prefer to think I would be closer to human," Nilly replied. "It will make me more a part of *their* community, and that is what I need in that context."

"I am learning not to underestimate the wisdom of the young," L'chellin finally said. "I grant you permission." She took a hop toward R'nilinnath, brushed necks with her, and clasped her hands. "But I will miss you, child."

Not many other Arachnen volunteered. For some, the idea just seemed too insane. Others, including all the expectant mothers, had too many commitments to the community. Diana Thorne would normally have jumped at the challenge, but after her complicity in the near-disaster, she felt obligated to stay at Lode Seven and help repair the Stringworld. Haim, meanwhile, felt he owed it to Yonchon to resume his apprenticeship and make amends for almost getting his Ryohoch mentor killed—although Yonchon behaved as though none of it had ever happened. But enough people came forward to make up a reasonable skeleton crew, including Ravinder Pritam to tend to *Arachne* and Justine Nguyen to provide astrophysical knowledge. It made sense that so many volunteers came from the group that had lost their babies, for they had little keeping them here and every reason to want to leave recent events behind.

So perhaps Stephen should not have been so surprised and saddened when Sita stepped forward to join them. He quickly realized that he should have seen it coming all along. But he wasn't sure he was ready to accept this ending. "Does this mean our marriage is over?"

She kissed him gently, almost platonically. "I'm not sure it ever really began. I got swept up in your fantasies, your ambitions. It was wrong for both of us.

"But I can't define my own life as long as I'm stuck in a small community with you. And this—the adventure of traveling the galaxy, exploring all the forms life has taken—that is who I really am."

Tears filled his eyes. "It'll be dangerous out there. You could be killed."

Sita rolled her eyes. "I'm not as fragile as I look, you know. And I'll have good backup. Turns out Nilly and I make a wicked team."

"That's—that's not what I meant," he assured her. "I meant it would hurt… it *does* hurt to lose you."

"How many times have you lost me already, Stephen? Best to make a clean break, so you can move on and find someone more suited to you." She winked. "Come on, I've seen the way you look at Diana."

"Everyone looks at Diana like that."

"And everyone looks at you like that. Think about it, okay?"

She took his hand, held it gingerly. "I've already asked Arachne to enter our divorce in the records. I don't need any of our property beyond my files. All that's left is your formal acceptance."

He took a shaky breath, nodded, and asked Arachne to upload the form to his window. Clicking his confirmation wasn't as painful as he'd expected. If anything, he felt relieved, and more on Sita's behalf than his own.

The most beautiful woman he'd ever seen stood on tiptoes to kiss his cheek, and he felt the warmth and pressure of her slim, supple body against him for the last time. Then she turned and walked away to begin her new life.

EPILOGUE

"JAMES IS GETTING BETTER," CECILIA TOLD DIEGO AS SHE SAT ACROSS FROM him in his cell. There was no visible barrier between them, but they both knew—from experience—that the utility fog would block him if he attempted to assault her. "He's breathing on his own now. Moving his fingers and toes."

"You should have let him die," Diego said. "His soul has already gone to its judgment. Restoring his body is a travesty." She noticed he didn't say "to Heaven."

"What makes you the expert on who has a soul and who doesn't, eh? Are you really still so sure of your own judgment?"

Diego simply stared. Finally he said, "You're so convinced that I'm the one who needs redemption. It was your betrayal that killed two of our own."

She heard a variation of the same charge from him every day, so she let it slide. "Are you so convinced that everyone else—everyone who isn't dead—is morally inferior to you? Do you have so little faith in the judgment of every last one of your colleagues, your friends, the people you were willing to entrust your life to?"

"Someone must stand firm. Someone must stand for humanity."

"Humanity isn't about staying inside limits, Diego! It's about growing beyond them! If you'd only look... we have a chance to change the Chirrn, not just let them change us."

He met her with silence again, and she growled in frustration. "Damn it, Diego! You're the only one left! You can't spend the rest of your life alone!"

"San Diego de Alcalá spent the last decade of his life in seclusion and contemplation."

"Aren't you forgetting the penance?"

But he would say no more. Frustrated, Cecilia emerged to meet Churrlaya, who had waited for her. "Still no luck," she said, her shoulders sagging. "I'm not sure we'll ever get through to him."

Churrlaya brushed his mane against Cecilia's cheek to comfort her. His scent was already starting to change; he had decided it was time to embrace his new community fully by bearing a child for it, so he had initiated the hormonal shift and would soon become a *she*. "I have confidence that we will in time. I doubt any human could ultimately be more stubborn than you."

Cecilia laughed and hugged his neck, returning the nuzzle. Then she grew more somber. "He's in denial. He can't live with the guilt of Evan and Nik's deaths, so he blames me. It was hard enough for me to face that burden. For someone as pious as he is…"

"I understand," Churrlaya said. "But this time we will help him. All of us." Isolation had proven a colossal failure in dealing with humans, so now they tried engagement, offering Diego the support of the community so he wouldn't have to bear his guilt alone. But Cecilia suspected it would be some time before he was willing to accept it.

She thought of Broadwing, who had so much more guilt to bear, but whose faith had helped him to face it and make amends. He had been returned to Antares a couple of days—rather, a few *narrissh*—ago to give evidence against Meridian and her organization. He had revealed many secrets that would enable the detention of offshoot groups that might seek to follow in Meridian's wingbeats. Yet at the same time, he had sung eloquently of the mercy the metasapients had shown, and how wrong it was to equate the Zenith pursuit of metasapience with death and destruction. He had urged the civilizations of the Voids and beyond not to penalize all Zenith for the mistakes of their distant ancestors and the fanaticism of Meridian. Had metasapience research by Zenith not been treated as taboo, it would not have been driven underground and could have been pursued with optimal care and safeguards, and without prompting the kind of resentment that led to Meridian's genocidal efforts. Apastron, the new matriarch of Meridian's former clan, had backed him up, affirming that she too had seen the revelation at Lode Seven and pledging that once she had served her time, she would lead her clan in rejecting Meridian's violence and finding a better path to ascension. Cecilia suspected that Broadwing would be by her side the whole time; she had already made him her first concubine.

Some people get all the luck, Cecilia thought. There weren't a lot of unattached men remaining among the Arachnen to choose from. As she met Stephen outside the security area, she momentarily found herself noticing how sexy he was before she recoiled at the incestuous feeling the concept gave her. *I must be getting desperate.* Mercifully, she found herself reflecting instead on her intense lovemaking with Diego in times gone by. If he could be redeemed, maybe....

"Any luck?" Stephen asked, anticipating the answer.

"No," she told him, smiling wistfully. "But that just makes me more determined to try."

He smiled back without ambivalence. "That's why I partnered with you in the first place, Cecilia. Your gift for tackling the impossible challenges."

She shook her head and laughed. "What?" Stephen asked.

"I was just thinking… not so long ago, we thought that building a colony on an alien world with no other intelligent life—one with auxon-built cities already waiting for us when we landed, mind you, and an army of self-replicating servants at our beck and call—would be the greatest challenge of our lives. Now I think of it and it seems so… amateurish."

They passed a viewport, and she stopped to gaze out at the ice dwarf which the Migration guild was already beginning to mine for construction material, and at the unfamiliar stars that dotted its sky—her home sky, from now on. "Look how far we've come. I can't even *see* Gamma Leporis from here." She sighed, growing subdued.

He understood. "Let alone Sol." He clasped her shoulder. "I miss Earth too, sometimes. I miss what we were."

"Yeah," she said. "But life is change. The past is part of us." *Oh, my beautiful city.* "It always will be, no matter how far we go. So we can move beyond it without losing it."

"And we can keep it without letting it hold us back."

"All right, yes. You always belabor the point."

"Sorry."

She smiled. "But there's no one else I'd rather build a world with."

"Me neither."

They began to stride away, leaving the view toward the past behind. "One thing, though," Cecilia said. "If you ever need to plot another heist, consult me next time. That plan was way too complicated...."

Arachne loved being a starship again. Traveling by warp cage still scared the hell out of her, to be sure. But she loved having a purpose once more—having the freedom to act and the power to make a difference. It was rewarding to have her body filled with lively, raucous humans (and one especially raucous Chirrn), acting out their silly hormone-driven melodramas and keeping Arachne endlessly entertained. Tarik, Sita, and the others argued endlessly about how to deliver the PQM to humanity and how much warning to give them about what they would find in the Four Voids and beyond. Arachne could read the undercurrents of sexual tension forming between Sita and her new captain. Was the biologist about to repeat the same mistake of falling for the leader? Or would Tarik respond to Ravinder's attempts to attract his interest? It certainly added spice to the ongoing debates about where to go after they dropped off the PQM. Would they survey or contact the other unmentored civilizations of the Four Voids? Would they investigate the resettlement efforts along the Eta Carinae diaspora front? Would they head for the densely populated Inner Disk where the most ancient civilizations resided? Whatever they chose, it would be something that made a difference, and Arachne could be a part of it. Hopefully, it would give her opportunities to make amends for her past failures.

She found herself contemplating her namesake, the Arachne of myth. What was often overlooked was that Arachne's transformation at Athena's hands was not just a punishment for her hubris in challenging the gods, but an act of mercy. When the defeated weaver tried to hang herself in shame, Athena let her live on as a spider—condemned for her crimes, trapped forever in penance, yet still alive and in a form that let her continue to ply her greatest skill.

All in all, there were worse fates. Whatever form she was now trapped in, she had been given another chance, and she was still in a position to do what mattered most to her. Wherever Arachne went, wherever the web of wormholes took her across the galaxy, she would keep her children safe.

APPENDIX 1: DRAMATIS PERSONAE

Arachnen (incomplete list)
Arachne: shipmind
Bahar, Tarik Hüseyin: acting captain
Bhatiani, Sita: biologist, behaviorist
Caravalho, Joana: physician, neurologist
Jacobs-Wong, Stephen: expedition leader
Ndege, Kweli: chief surgeon
Nguyen, Justine: astrophysicist, mathematician
Oyama Kazuko: political scientist, legal scholar
Pritam, Ravinder: senior cyberneticist, programmer
Silbermann, Haim: chief engineer
Thorne, Diana: construction engineer

Unrenounced/Loyalists
al-Bakri, Ibrahim: geneticist, ecologist
Amrouche, Kahina: mathematician, programmer
Dhillon, Amrita: geologist, mining engineer
Jiang Erfan, Evan: planetologist, meteorologist
LoCarno, Cecilia: ship commander
Narvaez Duarte, Diego Felipe: assistant chief engineer, pilot
Oates, James Albert: industrial engineer, cyberneticist
Zacharias, Nikolos: physician, psychologist
Zhao Changkun: programmer, systems analyst

Migration guild members (Chirrn unless otherwise specified)
L'chellin: senior mediator, Intersocietal guild
Churrlaya: xenopsychologist, formerly Lesshchin biologist
Broadwing (Zenith male): junior mediator

R'nilinnath: apprentice mediator
Yonchon (Ryohoch): starship engineer
Mh'lellissh: physician assigned to Arachnen

Nine Clusters Coalition representatives (Shayal)
Commissioner Velesh (hermaphrodite): diplomat
Velesh's triad mates (male, female): aides, bodyguards

Antares B Star Palace personnel
Rauhoc (Gaurim male): physician
Phlrntsya, aka Fred (Zhalevey female): concierge

Zenith dissidents
Meridian (female): matriarch
Apastron (female): second-in-command
Mountain's Peak (female): pilot
Sunflash (female): medical orderly, infiltrator

Lode Seven Station personnel
Orshym (Mykhshad female): administrator
Rysuth (Mykhshad male): freight lift attendant
Shthastya et al. (Zhalevey): assorted station personnel

APPENDIX 2: CHIRRN TIME UNITS

THE BASIC UNIT OF CHIRRN TIME MEASUREMENT, THE NARR, IS ONE STANDARD habitat rotation, equal to 96.64 seconds. Chirrn employ base 8 mathematics, so their time units are derived as follows:

1/64 narr	=	*narrat*	=	1.51 seconds	
1/8 narr	=	*narreth*	=	12.08 s	
1 narr	=	*narr*	=	96.64 s	=	1.61 minutes
8 narr	=	*narredj*	=	12.89 min	
64 narr	=	*narrach*	=	103.08 min	=	1.72 hours
512 narr	=	*narrissh*	=	13.74 h	
4096 narr	=	*narruvh*	=	109.95 h	=	4.58 days
8^5 narr	=	*narrenn*	=	36.65 d	
8^6 narr	=	*narranl*	=	293.21 d	
8^7 narr	=	*narrayth*	=	2345 d	=	6.42 years
8^8 narr	=	*yanarr*	=	51.38 y	
8^9 narr	=	*yanarredj*	=	411.03 y	
8^{10} narr	=	*yanarrach*	=	3288.2 y	
8^{11} narr	=	*yanarrissh*	=	26,306 y	

APPENDIX 3: SPACE HABITAT PARAMETERS

Antares Star Palace:

Although the Star Palace's gravity is artificial, we can calculate its effective gravitational mass by:

$$g = GM/r^2, \text{ so } M = gr^2/G$$

where g = surface gravity, $G = 6.67 \times 10^{-11}$ m^3/kg·s^2, M = Star Palace mass, and r = orbital radius.

To calculate the synchronous orbital altitude R, where w = angular velocity and p = rotational period:

$$w = 2\pi/p$$
$$R^3 = GM/w^2 = gr^2/w^2 = g(rp/2\pi)^2$$

The formula for horizon distance d for a sphere of radius R as seen by an observer of height h is:

$$d = (2(hR+h))^{1/2}$$

Results for Antares Star Palace:

Radius (at datum):	24.237 km
Horizon (at datum, for h = 2m):	311.36 m
Surface gravity (at datum):	0.68 g = 6.66 m/s^2
Rotational period:	81.73 min = 4904 sec = 50.75 narr
Effective mass:	5.85 x 10^{19} kg
Docking ring (synchronous) altitude:	133.571 km

Lode Seven Stringworld:

Where M = neutron star mass, d = Stringworld center of mass distance from star (in meters), a = tidal acceleration (i.e. "gravity"), and Δr = distance from Stringworld CoM, we get:

$$\Delta F = (3GMm/d^3)\Delta r$$

and

$$a = F/m = (3GM/d^3)\Delta r$$

$$\text{Therefore } \Delta r = ad^3/3GM$$

Gravity varies linearly with Δr; for instance, at twice the distance from the center of mass you feel twice the gravity.

$$\text{Orbital period } P = ((4\pi^2/GM)d^3)^{1/2}$$

To calculate insolation Q (thermal heating) where T is the neutron star's surface temperature, R is its radius, and d the Stringworld's distance (in kilometers):

$$Q = T((1-albedo)^{1/4})(R/2d)^{1/2}$$

$$\text{If albedo} = 0.5, Q = 0.84T(R/2d)^{1/2}.$$

Results for Lode Seven:

Neutron star:

Mass:	3.26×10^{30} kg
Radius:	12 km
Surface temperature:	98,000 K

Stringworld:

11	Center of mass orbital radius:	467814 km
	Total length:	6783 km
	Outer endpoint:	4522 km from CoM; gravity 2.94 g
	Inner endpoint:	2261 km from CoM; gravity 1.47 g
	Insolation temperature:	Inner end: 296 K = 23 C
		Midpoint: 295 K = 22 C
		Outer end: 293.5 K = 20.5 C
	Orbital period:	4311 s = 71 min, 51 sec = 44.6 narr

ACKNOWLEDGMENTS

Thanks again to the people whose advice guided me in structuring and revising this work and strengthening its characters, including Michael A. Burstein, Greg Cox, David Mack, Sam Morgan, and Marco Palmieri.

Research by Radu D. Rugescu and Daniele Mortari ("Ultra Long Orbital Tethers Behave Highly Non-Keplerian and Unstable", *WSEAS Transactions on Mathematics*, Vol. 7, No. 3, March 2008, pp. 87-94) suggests that the Stringworld's length relative to the neutron star could make it unstable. However, "Stabilization of Electrodynamic Tethers" by Robert P. Hoyt, online at http://www.tethers.com/papers/ED_Stabilization.pdf, shows that electrodynamic feedback could stabilize it.

For the specifics of the comet impact on the neutron star, I relied on "Radiation from Comets Near Neutron Stars" by Harwit, M. & Salpeter, E. E., *Astrophysical Journal*, vol. 186, p. L37 and "A possible mechanism for the generation of cosmic gamma-ray bursts and ultra-high-energy particles" by Zaidel', R.M. [sic] and Kurt, V.G., *Astronomy Reports*, Volume 42, Issue 6, pp.779-786.

The Zenith concept of metasapient consciousness preservation is inspired by a conjecture of Robert L. Forward in the "Future Speculations" chapter of *Indistinguishable from Magic* (Baen Books, September 1995), specifically pp. 312-9. Diego's suggestion of confining degenerate matter in synthetic diamond comes from pp. 154-5 of the same book.

The passage on anger quoted by Tarik in chapter 3 paraphrases a saying attributed to the Prophet Muhammad (peace be unto him) by the *hadith* scholar Al-Tabarani. Since *hadith* are considered revelations of the Prophet's words rather than the verbatim word of God like the *Qur'an*, they are not required to be learned in Arabic, hence Tarik reciting in Turkish.

ABOUT THE AUTHOR

CHRISTOPHER L. BENNETT IS A LIFELONG RESIDENT OF CINCINNATI, OHIO, with a B.S. in Physics and a B.A. in History from the University of Cincinnati. A fan of science and science fiction since age five, he has spent the past two decades selling original short fiction to magazines such as *Analog Science Fiction and Fact* and *BuzzyMag*. For the past dozen years, he has been one of Pocket Books' most prolific and popular authors of Star Trek tie-in fiction, including the epic Next Generation prequel *The Buried Age*, the *Star Trek: Department of Temporal Investigations* series, and the *Star Trek: Enterprise — Rise of the Federation* series. His original novel *Only Superhuman*, perhaps the first hard science fiction superhero novel, was voted Library Journal's SF/Fantasy Debut of the Month for October 2012. His short story collections *Hub Space: Tales from the Greater Galaxy* and *Crimes of the Hub* are available in e-book and print formats from Mystique Press.

Christopher's homepage, fiction annotations, and blog can be found at christopherlbennett.wordpress.com, and his Facebook author page is at www.facebook.com/ChristopherLBennettAuthor.

COLONY SPONSORS

A. Parsons
Allyn Gibson
Amy Laurens
Andrew Corvin
Andrew Glazier
Andrew Timson
Andy Hunter
Anonymous
Ashli Tingle
Barb and Carl Kesner
beardedzilla
Bradij
Brenda Cooper
Brendan Lonehawk
Brian D Lambert
Brian Griffin
C. Frost
C.A. Rowland
Caleb Monroe
Carol Gyzander
Carol Jones
Carol Mammano
Charname
Chelsea Provencher
Cheri Kannarr
Chris Matthews
Christopher D. Abbott
Christopher J. Burke
Christopher J. Ford
Christopher Thompson
Chuck Wilson
Cody Steinman
Craig "Stevo" Stephenson

Dale A. Russell
Daniel Lin
Danielle Ackley-McPhail
Danny Chamberlin
David Holden
Dawfydd Kelly
Diánna Martin
Dominic
Donald J. Bingle
Dr Douglas Vaughan
Dr. Karen
Eli Berg-Maas
Eli Mellen
Emily Weed Baisch
Eron Wyngarde
Evan Ladouceur
Frankie B
Gary Vandegrift
Gavin
GraceAnne DeCandido
Håkon Gaut
Hiram G Wells
Howard J. Bampton
Ian Harvey
Idran
Isaac 'Will It Work' Dansicker
J Paulus
J. B. Burbidge
Jakub Narębski
James Flux
James Goetsch
Jaq Greenspon
Jeff Metzner

Jeff Singer
Jennifer L. Pierce
Jeremy Bottroff
Johanna Rothman
John Green
John Idlor
Joseph Charpak
Josh Vidmar
Josh Ward
Judith Waidlich
Keith R.A. DeCandido
Keith West, Future Potentate of the Solar System
Kelly Pierce
Kerry aka Trouble
Kierin Fox
Kyle Franklin
Lark Cunningham
Larry
Leon W. Fairley
Lewis Phillips
Lisa Hawkridge
Lisa Kruse
Lorraine J. Anderson
MaGnUs
Malcolm Eckel
Margaret M. St. John
Maria T
Mark Beaulieu
Mary Catelynn Cunningham
mdtommyd
me@edmondkoo.com
Michael Brooker
Michael Doyle
Mike M.
Ms. Dyane Stillman
Nathan Turner
Norman Jaffe
Pam DeLuca
Patrick Foster
Paul van Oven
Peter D Engebos
Phillip Thorne
PJ Kimbell
Pulse Publishing
Ralph M.Seibel
Richard P Clark
Richard Todd
RKBookman
Robert C Flipse
Robert Claney
Robert M. Sutton
Samara N. Lipman
Scott Crick
Scott DeRuby
Scott Mantooth
Scott Schaper
Serge Broom
Shane "Asharon" Sylvia
Sharon Abdel-Malek
Shervyn
Sheryl R. Hayes
Stacy Butcher
Stephanie Souders
Stephen Ballentine
Stephen Lesnik
Steven Callen
Stoney
The Amazing Maurice
The Creative Fund
Thierry Millié
Tim DuBois
Tom B.
ToniAnn Marini
Tony Hernandez
V Hartman DiSanto
Vince Kindfuller
Wayne Garmil
William C. Tracy
Zeb Berryman